Cuthbert of Farne

A Novel of
Northumbria's Warrior Saint

— Katharine Tiernan —

Sacristy
Press

Sacristy Press
PO Box 612, Durham, DH1 9HT

www.sacristy.co.uk

First published in 2019 by Sacristy Press, Durham

Sacristy Limited, registered in England & Wales, number 7565667

British Library Cataloguing-in-Publication Data
A catalogue record for the book is available from the British Library

Paperback ISBN 978-1-78959-009-8
Hardback ISBN 978-1-78959-013-5

It is in itself a ready path to virtue to know what he was.

Preface, Anonymous Life of Cuthbert

Cast of Characters

The Northumbrian Royal Family: the Idings

Oswy   King of Northumbria

Enfleda   Queen of Northumbria, daughter of former King Edwin

Oswy's child from his first marriage to Reinmeillt, a British princess:
- Connal

Oswy's children from his second marriage to Enfleda (above):
- Edfrith, later king, m. (i) Audrey; (ii) Ermina
- Aelfled, later Abbess of Whitby
- Edith
- Aylwin

Oswy's child from a liaison in his youth:
- Aldfrid

The Deiran Royal Family

King Selwin   Vassal of King Oswy and cousin to Queen Enfleda

✝HE MERCIAN ROYAL FAMILY

King Penda

Penda's children:

- Cynburh (f) m. Connal of Northumbria (above)
- Wulfhere
- Athelred m. Edith of Northumbria (above)

CHURCH LEADERS

Aidan	Bishop of Lindisfarne
Eata	Abbot of Melrose and Lindisfarne, subsequently bishop
Boisil	Prior of Melrose
Cuthbert	Soldier, monk, hermit and bishop
Wilfrid	Priest and bishop
Hild	Abbess of Whitby
Aelfled	Second Abbess of Whitby
Colman	Bishop of Lindisfarne

O✝HER CHARAC✝ERS

Kenswith	Foster-mother to Cuthbert
Gartnait	King of the Picts
Aniel	Daughter of Gartnait

ΠΟΤΕS ΟΠ ΤΗΕ ΠΑΜΕS

Anglo-Saxon names are made up of two parts, a prefix and a suffix. Cuthbert, for example, is *cuth* = famous and *bert* = bright. When naming a child, parents often used part of the mother or father's name for the child. Thus Cuthbert might become Herebert or Cuthlac. The resulting similarity of the names can cause confusion! Among the main characters there are two particularly confusing similarities:

- King Oswy of Northumbria and King Oswine of Deira
- Alfrid and Aldfrid, half-brothers and sons of Oswy

To aid the reader, I have made the following changes:

- King Oswine of Deira becomes King Selwin of Deira
- Alfrid, eldest son of Oswy from his first marriage, becomes Connal, a Celtic name honouring his British mother

I apologise to historians of the period for taking this liberty.

I have also used contemporary versions or contractions of names that appear particularly challenging to the modern eye. Thus:

- Aethelthryth becomes Audrey (a medieval corruption of the name)
- Osryth becomes Edith
- Aelfwine becomes Aylwin
- Eorminburga becomes Ermina

Northumbria in the Seventh Century AD

The kingdom of Northumbria was one of the seven Anglo-Saxon kingdoms in the early medieval period. On the east, it stretched from the Humber in the south to the Firth of Forth in the north. To the west, it extended as far as Carlisle, but elsewhere was an overlord to British kingdoms and tribal territories.

The kingdom was divided into two provinces, Bernicia and Deira. Bernicia extended from the Forth to the Tyne, while Deira extended from the Tyne to the Humber. During the period of the novel, Deira was regarded as a sub-kingdom owing allegiance to the over-king of Bernicia.

Northumbria had borders with Mercia and Wales to the south, southern Pictland and Dalriata to the north. Mercia was the most powerful of these kingdoms and vied with Northumbria for dominance.

I have generally used contemporary versions of Anglo-Saxon place names, with two exceptions:

- Ad Gefrin—now known as Yeavering, a corruption of the Anglo-Saxon. It is a farmstead near Wooler, where the site of the palace can still be seen.
- Muickross—now known as St Andrews.

Contents

PROLOGUE

CHAPTER 1

LEADER VALLEY

634 AD

A month after she had lost her own, they brought the infant to her, because she still had milk in her breasts. When Kenswith saw him, she knew he would be her consolation. He was as blithe as her own babe had been, strong and lusty with a howl to bring the roof down. When she put him to her breast, he suckled her dry. She bent over and kissed him, her heart full of joy.

"He is Cuthbert," his father told her. "Famous, for he is my eldest son and will be a great warrior. And bright, after his mother." His voice faltered. She had been a beauty, Kenswith knew. "My man will bring you everything you need for him. Just tell him what you want. Come up to the hall with him sometimes." He stared at his son, lying content and warm against her breast. He squeezed the baby's tiny hand and put it to his lips. "You'll soon grow strong, eh, little fellow?" He turned away, stooped down under her low door and swung himself up onto his horse. He was gone, and the babe was hers.

It was the same year that Father Aidan came from Iona to bring Christ's word to the kingdom. When he came to Melrose, she had walked all the way there to hear him preach, with Cuthbert strapped to her back. The bishop smiled when he saw the bright-faced child peeping over her shoulder. He put his hand on Cuthbert's head and blessed him.

He wasn't the only infant there. She was standing close to a young woman, well-dressed, with a servant with her who was carrying her baby. He was screaming, arms flailing, trying to escape her grip. The young woman turned towards them and caught sight of Cuthbert. She cried out at once, "How like he is to mine!"

When the preaching and the prayers were done, they set the two infants down on the grass and sat together. The two fair-haired infants stared at one another, and Kenswith saw the mother was right, they were like as two peas. She laughed to see them clutching up daisies and stuffing them into their mouths. "His name is Wilfrid," said his mother. When she spoke, Kenswith saw that she had none of the strength and brightness of her son. She was very thin, and her face was pale as whey. It was more than the fatigue a babe brought, and besides, she had a servant with her.

"I have a wasting sickness," she said, seeing Kenswith's eyes on her. "I came to see if the new priest could heal me. But the journey has worn me out." She leaned towards Kenswith so the servant wouldn't hear her. "I won't see my son grow to manhood," she said. "God will take me soon. But at least I have the priest's blessing."

There was a sudden sharp gust of wind and a downpour of summer hail. The babies started to wail. Kenswith jumped up at once and caught up Cuthbert in her arms. Everyone was running for the shelter of the trees and there was confusion for a few minutes. When she looked around, there was no sign of her new friends. The woman, her babe and her servant had disappeared.

PART 1

THE HOUSE OF IDING

643–50 AD

"Lord, see what evil Penda does!"

Bishop Aidan, from Bede, Ecclesiastical
History of the English People, *III, 16*

CHAPTER 2

RECULVER

643 AD

At last, the wind had gone round, a raw-fresh spring wind sending dry seaweed skittering across the shingle. It was a south-westerly, blowing scales of cloud across the grey dawn sky, pierced by the first streamers of radiance from the heavenly kingdom above. They would sail on the ebb tide.

"It is God's will that you should return," Paulinus had assured her. "You will be a beacon in their darkness." But his bones ached too much for him to ride down to the shore this morning with her other well-wishers. So Enfleda had sat by his bed last night holding his hand, while he gave his farewell blessing, his bony knuckles sticking out above her small soft hand. He smelled of musty poultices and pain.

"Dear child," he said, "*amica mea.*" When the pain was bad, he forgot English altogether and spoke to her in his native Latin. "You came here as a fugitive. Now you are leaving as a princess. As a bride." He clasped her hand tightly, and tears stood in his eyes. "Such is the greatness and mercy of God." Enfleda had bent down and kissed him, her fresh lips on his withered cheek. She knew she would never see him again.

Now the riding party clattered down the old road to Reculver, the king in front with his bodyguard, swords and spears glinting, Enfleda and her mother, the king's aunt, following behind with their attendants. The king was in a mellow humour. It was a good match. A useful match, like pieces on a game board unexpectedly fitting together. Of course, there was gossip, about an Irish princess rumoured to be Oswy's concubine, who had given him a son. The king had decided not to discuss the matter with Oswy. The man was a widower now, and he needed a wife. That was enough. It was easy to see he was pleased with Enfleda. She had turned into a pretty little thing; enough of the Frank from her mother's side to give her full lips and dark eyes. And Oswy hadn't let the religious side of things get in the way. The girl could have her own household, her own Roman priest. Oswy had seen too many battles to stand on principle. He was a survivor. Unlike his brother.

They reached the old Roman fort that stood above the shore, the walls crumbling now under the battering of salt winds. They would take shelter here till the ships were ready. Attendants unpacked the saddle bags and brought wine to the riders. Enfleda felt the alcohol warm in her belly. She kicked her horse forward to the shore.

The ships were riding at anchor, the wind tugging at their furled brown sails. Pale lines of surf coiled round the bows. As the tide started to recede the men were loading two of the ships. There were chests and bales bound with leather straps containing the embroidered hangings that were her wedding gift from the king, fine silk and linen for her gowns, a silver cross chased with gold with matching chalice and paten for her priest. All her household goods. She had become a weighty person. The third ship was for her reeve, Kenneth, the master-to-be of her household, with the house carls he had chosen. The last ship would carry her with her women. The sailors had rigged up a canopy for them behind the rowlocks, and laid rugs and furs on the benches.

"You see?" her mother said, bringing her mare up beside her. "They'll take care of you. You'll be there in two days. Or three. It won't be like last time."

The two women stared down at the ships, at the men already hanging forward over the oars, rubbing grease into their bare arms and shoulders, calling jokes across to their neighbours that set off roars of laughter. The voyage held no fears for them. Enfleda could hardly remember the last sea journey. She was only a child at the time. But sometimes at night she would dream of a dark ship adrift on the waves, climbing a swell that seemed endless till it dropped sickeningly into a fearful deep. She would see a great wave surging towards them, looming higher and higher above the ship. As it started to fall, she would waken with her heart racing and mouth dry with fear.

She felt a shadow of the nightmare as she stared at the ship. "Dear Lord," she prayed, "bring us to safety. And let me not be sick." What if she arrived at Bamburgh like a puking child? What if Oswy saw her like that? "Dear Lord. Not sick." She resolved that she would say prayers all the way.

"Yes," she replied to her mother. "I suppose so." She didn't talk to her mother about the dream. Or, indeed, about Oswy.

"Oswy!" her mother complained, whenever he was mentioned. "I could have found you a good husband in East Anglia or Wessex. A godly man of the right sort. This Oswy is nothing but a mercenary, he never expected to be king. And he's too old for you."

But Enfleda thought of Oswy all the time, how he looked at her at their first meeting, looked at her so directly that she had to drop her gaze, and then look at him again. He was slim and straight, his hair streaked with grey but his eyes bright and his whole being full of such strength it made her giddy. He wore gold round his neck and arms. She felt faint in his presence and stammered over her greetings. He smiled at her, took her hands and drew her close to him. "Princess Enfleda." He bowed over her hands with just a glance at her breasts. "I am come to be your suitor."

Everyone told her how it was God's will for her, King Edwin's daughter, the last of his line, to marry into the new Northumbrian royal house. The Idings. It meant nothing to her. All she could think about was Oswy. Being his wife was what she most longed for, and she feared it too. She was afraid of Northumbria. It didn't feel like her home. Kent felt like home; Kent, and her mother.

"Come with me!" she had begged her mother. But she wouldn't.

"I will never return, never. Edwin was the greatest king they ever had, and I was his queen. How could I endure to live in a hall full of strangers, to live as a nithing?"

"If you loved me, you would. I'll have my own household. There'll be friends."

"Not my friends. My friends are here. Or maybe I will go to Frankia."

Below her on the beach one of the cargo ships lifted and lurched on the shingle as the tide ebbed. The lading was finished and the captain sent word to the king. Servants moved forward to help the two women dismount from their horses. Enfleda looked at the cold waves snapping at the ships, ready to swallow them up. She stumbled close to her mother, then clung to her, burying her head in her soft cloak as if she were a child again. She started to cry. Her women gathered round, stroking her hair and fussing with her gown.

The king was impatient to go hunting and grew bored with the little drama. He strode across, sending the women scuttling to the side.

"Come on, little cousin. Courage!" He took hold of her and gave her a little shake. "No more tears! You must be a queen now!"

She lifted her wet face to him. He embraced her, so tightly the silver studs of his tunic dug uncomfortably into her shoulders, and kissed her farewell. Then he looked round.

"Where's your priest? Has he no blessings for us?"

So Romanus must stand on the shore blessing the ships and praying for their safe voyage, while her people scrambled on board and Enfleda herself was lifted in as carefully as a treasure. She felt the ship rock and sway beneath her, tightening the shore rope. At last, when they were all boarded, the king shouted to Romanus, "Enough!", and the priest had to stumble quickly down over the shingle, losing his footing in the water so that his robes were half-soaked. A little murmur of laughter ran through the ship, and suddenly Enfleda wanted to laugh too. She looked at her women, and as the men heaved the ship out onto the water they broke into giggles like foolish children, covering their mouths to try and stop themselves. By the time they recovered the ships were well afloat. The oarsmen picked up pace and the sailors let the sail slip loose. As the wind took it, the ship leapt forward on bright waves that glittered and sparkled in the sunlight. Her heart lifted in spite of herself. Already the figures on the shore seemed faraway. In a moment she would always remember, she cast off her childhood and became a woman. Soon she would be a queen.

CHAPTER 3

THE FORTRESS ON THE ROCK

650 AD

She thought of it now, as the east wind blew hard against her and made her tug her cloak more snugly about her. At her favourite vantage point, where the seaward cliffs of the great rock were too lofty to need fortification, you could stand and look directly out to sea. On the sand below sailors were bringing a ship into shore. For a moment it reminded her of her Kentish ship, grounding on those same sands at the end of her voyage north. It had been just such an April morning, with lowering cloud blowing off the sea and an icy wind. How fearful a shore it had seemed then! Was it seven years ago, or eight? She was an eight-year queen, she decided. She could hardly remember anymore the girl she had been when she left Kent. Little more than a child, she thought, full of silly dreams and fears. She paused a little longer, watching the men hauling the ship up the beach, pulling sacks out of the hold and running them ashore. It was familiar now, but then she had been filled with dread. Nothing her mother said had prepared her for Bamburgh. When she was lifted out of the ship onto the pale sand she and her women had huddled together, staring up at the dark fortress that was to be their home. It sat on top of sheer rock, ringed with a massive wooden palisade pierced only by black arrow slits. There was no sign of dwellings, only the walls and the great cliffs looming over the restless waves of the North Sea. The raw chill of the morning had added to the desolation of the place.

"A wizard must have built it," one of her women said, eyes round. "It's a dragon's lair," said another. What would they find inside? Would they ever come out again? She had been trembling by the time they were taken up the steep causeway at the far end of the fortress, through the heavy gates of wood and steel. Shadowy figures in the gatehouse peered down at them.

She would never love Bamburgh. But she had grown used to it. In those first months Oswy had been so attentive, so tender that it had calmed her fears. He had a bower hall built within the fortress enclosure for her and her household. There was even a small chapel where she could say Mass according to the Roman rite. She had hung the tapestries her uncle had given her on the walls and set up a gallery where she and her women could stitch and spin, where they could sing together and laugh, away from the hard-faced warriors who filled Oswy's hall. There were always a score or more around him, the land-hungry fighting men who formed the royal bodyguard. When they were not fighting or hunting, they lounged around the hall, playing dice and drinking, shouting lewd jokes and harassing the hall servants. They were respectful towards her, but she was never at ease with them. In the king's hall she did her duties as his queen; welcoming guests and bearing the mead cup at feasts, sitting with him in council, organising the running of the household.

But the bower hall was her home. It was like a little piece of Kent. When Oswy visited, she saw him become softer for a while. He liked to hear music, and her women would play the harp and sing for him. When their son was born, he showered her with gifts—beautiful necklaces and rings of gold and pearls and garnet, perfumes from Frankia. But he never stayed for long, even with little Edfrith. He would return to his warriors, and his face would grow hard and watchful.

He was often away, holding court at the other royal estates, or riding with his men against some incursion of the Mercians. It was always the Mercians. Their king, Penda, had fought as a youth in the fateful battle where King Edwin, her father, had been killed. Now, fifteen years later,

Penda was still hungry for Northumbrian land and riches. When she thought of Penda, she was glad to be at Bamburgh. The massive timbers of the palisade no longer seemed forbidding. They were like protective arms about her.

So she stood this April morning, queen of all Northumbria, looking out at the sea and thinking about destiny. The sun broke through the clouds and sent shafts of silver light across the waves. A few miles out to sea, the dark rocks of the Farne Islands loomed out of the waves. They were haunted by demons and no-one lived on them. But they did on nearby Lindisfarne. She could see its low outline on the horizon. It was not a proper island—at low tide you could ride across the sands and save yourself the trouble of a boat journey. Bishop Aidan had chosen it for his monastery. Perhaps it made him feel at home, after Iona.

Bishop Aidan was coming to see her, she remembered. It might be today. She thought about the request she had for him, and felt uneasy, wondering if it was foolishness on her part. She turned away and went back to the bower hall.

When Aidan arrived, she had Edfrith with her. They were playing Prisoners' Base, and Edfrith was the guard, on his riding horse stick that Kenneth had made for his fifth birthday. It had two handles near the top of the stick and a snorting horse's head carved from horn at its end. Edfrith was galloping furiously down the hall in pursuit of his nurse, Ella, who was still at liberty. His mother, securely imprisoned behind him, cried out to Ella to be released. Edfrith yelled at Ella, curly fair hair flopping over his face, and waved his wooden sword at her. "No, no!" he shouted. "I shall have you! Here I come!"—but a too-vigorous wave of the sword overbalanced him. He lost his grip on his mount, and it slid ignominiously between his legs. Tripping over it he landed hard on his bottom, with a face of such dismay that both women broke into laughter. "Stop it!" he shouted at them, "stop it!", and suddenly he was close to tears. His mother caught him up in her arms and covered his face with kisses.

"Even the bravest horsemen take a tumble sometimes. See, you have caught us both now!" Then she looked up and saw that the bishop was waiting at the door with an attendant. At once she put him down and straightened her gown.

"Look, Edfrith, Father Aidan is here! Say good day to him." But Edfrith clung to her legs and refused to look round. She picked him up and held him for the bishop to see. "I'm afraid he has just taken a tumble." She kissed him and handed him to Ella. "We'll play again later. Now I must talk to Father Aidan", and Ella bore him off screaming with rage at the sudden end to his game.

She turned back to the bishop, summoning her dignity. "Good day, Father. I'm sorry he hasn't better manners."

"He is growing into a fine boy."

"Thank God." She looked at Aidan, in his undyed woollen habit, his beads tucked into his belt. He made no concession to the court: he dressed the same for kings or churls. The curling hair on either side of his tonsure was silver-white, his face lined and weathered like a field man. He stood without deference, waiting to find out what her summons might mean. She felt suddenly shy. She had never spoken to him on her own before. Romanus was her confessor. She wished, sometimes, it was someone else.

"Father Aidan," she began, and then broke off. "Will you sit, Father?" He was so tall; it made her feel awkward, looking up at him like a supplicant. She sat on her chair and retrieved her dignity. He smiled at her, amused, and settled himself on a bench.

"The king said I might speak with you," she began. "About a young man who came to court last week." Aidan nodded, listening. "He wanted to enter the king's service."

It was the custom for young noblemen to join the king's household for military service. They all wanted the same thing: to become part of the king's bodyguard, gain renown as a famous warrior, and be rewarded with land.

"But he was young."

"Too young, perhaps?"

"Yes." But it was not that. How could she explain what she needed to ask of the bishop? She sat back for a moment, trying to gather her thoughts.

She and Oswy had been holding court in the king's hall. They sat on their royal chairs with high seats and cold stone sides. Oswy was dressed in a long robe trimmed with otter, a gold chain round his neck. She had worn her favourite blue gown threaded with silver, and a gold circlet on her head. The men of his household stood behind, legs apart, hands resting on the swords hanging from their belts. It had been a long morning, the usual petitioners, and then one of the king's old kinsmen, who spoke so slowly that Enfleda squirmed with boredom. She marvelled at Oswy's patience with him. She distracted herself by looking at the walls of the hall and deciding how they should be re-painted. She imagined patterns of scarlet and ochre, and dark blue above the pillars. The distant sound of the waves breaking on the beach below the fortress lulled her into a daydream. Her mind drifted away.

When her attention returned, she saw that the kinsman was gone. In his place stood a young man—hardly more than a boy, with downy hair on his lip but cheeks still smooth, and fair as an angel. For a moment she thought she was still dreaming. Then she heard her husband speaking to him, and she was jolted back into the world.

"How old are you?" asked Oswy.

"Fourteen years, Lord."

"Has your father sent you?" A pause. "No, Lord. But I am ready to serve. I have trained since I was a child."

Enfleda stared at him. He was on the brink of manhood, but there was still an innocence about him that reminded her of Edfrith. His fair hair was like a bright halo round his head. She thought of Oswy, sitting beside her. She could see, sometimes, that original nature in him, the light that was still there somewhere, but which had been coarsened, brutalised, by the years of warfare and blood-lust. Suddenly she couldn't bear it, couldn't bear the thought of the light going out in this boy who looked like an angel. She leant forward.

"Why have you left your home? Are you so keen to be a warrior?"

Oswy swivelled round on his seat, staring at his wife, surprised by her intervention.

"It's not my home any longer."

"Not your home? Is your father still living?"

"He lives."

"Have you any brothers?"

"Only a step-brother. He is older than me, and my step-mother has persuaded my father to give him our land."

"Ah." She saw his lips tighten like a sulky child. "Isn't there enough for you both?"

"It is wrong. Our family has held the land for generations. I couldn't agree to it."

He was stubborn, she understood. Stubborn and self-willed, but it only amused her. She had a step-son too. She turned back to Oswy, speaking in an undertone. "He is too young. Why not send him with your kinsman Godfrey to Lindisfarne? He has asked for a companion to help him."

"To Lindisfarne? The boy wants to be a warrior."

"He's too young. He's a child still." She leaned forward and took his hand. Her gown dipped forward, revealing the smooth curve between her breasts. She was eager now, her small face turned up like a flower towards him. He would visit her later, he decided, losing interest in the youth.

"Let him be educated first," she continued. "I'll sponsor him, and Godfrey will be pleased." The king turned back to the boy.

"Wait upon the queen. Go and speak to her reeve." He nodded to one of his men, the youth bowed and the audience was over.

✛

Now she had to seek Father Aidan's help. How could she say, he is too fine to be a warrior?

"He is bright and quick-witted. He has been baptised, but he wants to know more, to learn."

"Does he want to be a servant of God?"

The question took her by surprise, but she answered at once, "Yes! Yes, he does!" Enfleda felt sure she was truthful, though she had never asked him. She hurried on, "The king has a kinsman, Godfrey, who wants to retire to Lindisfarne. He needs a companion."

"I can arrange it. But I must see the boy first. What is his name?"

"Wilfrid, Father." Impulsively she took his hand. "I'm so grateful to you."

CHAPTER 4

EVERYTHING BURNING

650 AD

At first Wilfrid was often in her mind, and she would send to Bishop Aidan for news of his progress. But when summer came, and with it the court's move to the king's palace at Ad Gefrin, she forgot all about him.

It was her favourite time of year. She loved to get away from the close confines of Bamburgh into the space and freedom of the hill country at Ad Gefrin. The fortress was a turmoil of packing and preparation. For the hall servants with all the carts and chests, it was a long journey; they would start at dawn and camp overnight. But on horseback, she and Oswy and the royal household could ride out there in a day. When their cavalcade clattered down the causeway and away through the village below the fortress, her spirits lifted. In summer, the Northumbrian countryside lost its winter bleakness and seemed to pour all its energy into a wonderful outburst of greenness and growth. The ash and oak trees were in full leaf, and the dainty greenery of the birch trees lifted in the wind like flags waving before them. Green barley and beans grew tall in the fields beside the trackway and smooth-skinned cows grazed the pastures with their calves beside them. She felt the same sensuous pulse of growth beating in her blood. She wanted to feel her belly swell, wanted to hold a babe against her breasts again. She thought of the long summer nights at Ad Gefrin and hoped that the old magic of the place would work its charm.

For Ad Gefrin still belonged to the old gods. It had been a sacred place for the First People; and you could still see the stone circles where they worshipped the sun and moon and the traces of their fortress on the hill. When the Saxon kings came, they took the valley from them and made it theirs. They built a royal palace on the raised ground above the river where the First People had held their rites and ceremonies. Paulinus told her she had been baptised at Ad Gefrin when she was a babe in arms, down in the river Glen with all the other converts. She tried to imagine it, but the valley never seemed Christian to her. When the moonlight cast pale shadows from the stones the spirits felt close enough to touch. No wonder the people had drifted back to the old ways. At solstice time, they lit midnight fires and danced till sunrise, as their pagan ancestors had done, and there were many children born in spring.

When they rode into the valley, they found it busy with hay-making. Men and women worked together in the flowery grass, in a constant rhythm of bending and cutting, leaving long lines of grass behind them for the sun to dry. Peewits startled from their nests by the hay-makers cried and swooped among them, dipping half to the ground before angling away. The reeve rode out from the palace to greet them, and soon the air was full of talk and laughter. Servants came to help her from her horse, bringing cups of mead and ale for the travellers. The summer had begun.

Her father's palace had been burned out by Cadwallon of Wales. No trace of it remained; in any case, she was too young then to remember it. The new palace that stood in its place was awesome in its size and magnificence. Massive carved beams flanked the entrance, and inside the space was light and lofty, with painted walls and tapestry hangings, and casements that could stand open on summer mornings. There was a long gallery where she and her women did their needlework and sang together while the men went out on hunting parties. Outside, there was a great meeting hall, built with high steps like one half of a Roman amphitheatre, where Oswy held council. Scores, hundreds of men could talk together out there, their voices clear for all to hear. His thegns and vassals brought their tribute and the pens filled up with cattle. In the evenings there was feasting and music, praises were sung and stories told. Then she and Oswy would sit with their household on the dais at the far end of the hall, looking down on the company. Sitting there, at the high table, with the weight of her gold circlet pressing on her brow and Oswy solid and smiling beside her, she felt herself complete. They were king and queen, and the kingdom turned on their union. When it was time for ceremony, she would take the mead cup and give it first to Oswy, and then carry it to their guests, the strong sweet liquor a fiery draught of fellowship. She knew he liked to watch her as she moved between the men. When she returned he drained the cup and kissed her.

At night she and Oswy lay together, their bodies smooth and warm in the summer air. He came to her night after night, and she gave herself to him with abandon. She was certain that he loved her, certain that she would conceive. This one would hold, a love-child of the summer with the strength of the sun in him.

One midsummer morning they rode together down to the river. The water was bright in the sunlight. She wandered along the banks while Edfrith paddled in the shallows with Ella. Upstream the river plunged over a broad rock and fell into a deep pool shadowed by trees. Oswy and his men were swimming. She could see Oswy's body gleaming like amber in the peat-brown water, see him diving under the fall of water from the rock, sluicing the water through his hair. Two of his men splashed and wrestled behind him. In the shallows, Edfrith screamed, "A fish! I saw a fish!" One of the servants beckoned him to lie on his belly on the bank, to watch for the dark outline of the trout and slide a hand softly under its belly. He lay agog, and she felt a sudden intensity of love for her son. She stood still, watching him.

The wind blew her hair across her face. As she pushed it away, a smudge of wood smoke reached her nostrils. She hardly noticed, and then wondered at it, since there were no huts close by. Perhaps the woodsmen were burning charcoal. The smell grew stronger, more acrid. It wasn't a hearth fire. She looked back to the palace. There was a line of dark smoke above it, higher than any hearth fire. A first ripple of fear went through her belly. Then she saw two horsemen galloping down the track towards them. She started to scream. By the time the men drew close, Oswy was out of the water pulling his clothes over his wet skin. The men swung down from the saddles, sweating and urgent.

"Mercians, Lord. Penda's men. We had no warning."

"How many?"

"We don't know. Many. A hundred at least."

Oswy picked up a rock and hurled it into the pool. "God burn them with hellfire!" He grabbed one of the messengers and shook him. "Where were my spies? Where were the watch?" He pushed the man away, shouting curses. Already the other swimmers were transformed into warriors, buckling on sword belts. He bellowed at them, "What are you standing there for, like a bunch of women! Get on your cursed horses! Bring my horse, fools!"

Edfrith had scrambled out of the river and stood with his mouth open, still wet from the water, staring at his father, at the warriors. They had turned into a war band. About to spur his horse, Oswy wheeled round and shouted at the servants, "Take the queen and Edfrith to Bamburgh. Tell them to make ready. They'll be at Bamburgh next."

As Enfleda stared after him, the image of his body leaned low over his black stallion's neck burned itself into her mind. He was gone. Gone. In front of Ad Gefrin the smoke rose higher, and there were flames now, leaping through the smoke. She heard a woman shrieking so loudly that the sound seemed to fill the valley, and from a long way off she saw it was herself. She felt herself lifted onto a horse and held by the man sitting behind her, and a new panic assailed her. "Edfrith!" she screamed, trying to hurl herself from the horse. The man held her tightly. "He is safe, Lady. Look—he is there." And she saw him, held pillion like herself, and the horses gathered pace till the motion jolted the screams from her and she lay forward and wept into the mane. Time had revolved upon them; the burning hall was Edwin's, she was her mother, and soon she would be a widow too, a fugitive queen with a fatherless son. The dark wave of her nightmares loomed above her till there was nothing but blackness.

A day after their return to Bamburgh she lost the child she was carrying. As she lay on cloths wet with blood, exhausted beyond grief, she knew that God must be angered with them. Why else would He let their enemies surprise them? Had she turned pagan at Ad Gefrin? She swore to Him she would be faithful. She would give alms. She would try harder to bring the kingdom to the true Christian faith. When she was well, she would confess to Romanus and do penance. Not yet. The pain in her belly was too great. And she did not know the worst yet. Oswy had not returned.

"He is a great warrior, Lady," her women told her. "Don't be afraid. He will be back very soon."

But the fort was holding its breath, waiting. The men reinforced the palisade, stacked spears high, and filled the store rooms with provisions. They talked in low voices about Penda the Mercian.

At last, three days after the attack, the men returned. Lying by the casement, she heard the shouting and din of their arrival through the north gate. Her maidservant, Gudrun, ran down to the courtyard. She returned breathless.

"He's back, mistress! The men are back!", and all the pain was swallowed up in relief that he lived, that life could go on. The two women held each other, crying and laughing. "Thank God!" Enfleda said, again and again. He had punished her enough.

It was the custom, in her condition, to be seen only by women. She didn't mind. She didn't want him to see her in the aching sickness of the aftermath. She heard him once or twice, shouting orders. Her household was the only still point in the tumult. The women told her that Penda and his army were camped below the castle. They were tearing down huts in the village; fuel for a great fire. All through the day, the Mercians dragged wood over to the rock, piling it up outside the gatehouse at the north of the fort.

"They are going to fire it so they can get through the gates to attack us," Gudrun told her. A new fear gripped them.

"They'll never get in. Even if they do, our warriors will hold them back." But neither of them believed it. They lay awake at night, waiting for men mad with victory and blood lust to break down their doors.

Early next morning Enfleda smelled smoke again, saw pale clouds of it drifting down the hall. This time she clamped her will tight as steel around her throat, so that no cry would escape, no sign of weakness. She had her women dress her and put the gold circlet on her head. She was the queen. This time she would not waver. For Edfrith's sake. When Nurse brought him, she smiled as she caught him close to her, so he wouldn't see her fear. He pulled back from her arms and stared at her, uncertain.

"Daddy will fight the bad men and drive them all away," she told him, kissing his head. "Come! We'll go to the big hall and play."

"Why is it smoky?"

"There are fires outside. That's all. See if Nurse can catch you if you run to the hall!"

As he ran ahead of her, he stumbled into his father. Oswy loomed out of the smoke in full battle gear; chain mail vest over his leather tunic and helmet in hand, with six of his household warriors behind him. Edfrith at once burst into tears and ran to his nurse.

"Stop that," said Oswy, cuffing his head. "Show courage. God knows we need it." He looked up and saw Enfleda. "My dear." He took her hands, but his face showed no tenderness. He was war-wrought, deadly. "These men will stay with you and the boy, and your household. They will defend you with their last breath."

Wraiths of smoke blew between them. She found a breath and called up the last shreds of her courage. "God go with you, my Lord."

He nodded. It was impossible to know if he were pleased. He turned, and in seconds was lost again in the eye-stinging fog of smoke. The warriors took them, not to the hall, but to the church at the southern end of the fortress. The smoke had not yet penetrated and the air was clearer. Enfleda went forward to the altar and sank to her knees.

Although the castle rock was sheer to the south and west, with the sea to the east, it was vulnerable to the north, where the crag sloped away, allowing access to the fortress. It was defended by a double-beamed palisade, massive gates and an inner gatehouse, but if the fire grew hot enough, the timbers would burn out. Penda's army numbered hundreds. Oswy had had no time to raise an army; he had only his household warriors to hold them back. The men hurled spears down on the invaders, but the smoke was too thick to take clear aim.

The fire was well alight, and the flames started to pierce the cracks between the timbers. The Mercians threw on leafy branches and the smoke became choking thick. It rose in sudden violent plumes bursting upwards at frightening speed. Men wrapped wet cloths round their faces, but their eyes smarted so they could barely see. Flames leapt unpredictably out of the dark clouds of smoke. Buckets of water were brought at a run from the fortress well, but even as they doused one flame another two burst out. The heat and smoke grew ever fiercer and more suffocating. Outside, downwind from the furnace, the Mercians used long poles to shove the burning wood closer and closer to the main gates and to the great palisade on either side.

In the midst of the attack some—a few—men heard another sound, above the roar and crackle of the fire. They heard a psalm, they said, whose words pierced the air. They heard it distinctly. It was scarcely possible; although the wind was blowing from the north-east, Lindisfarne was ten miles up the coast. But they were certain they heard the sacred words and knew that Aidan and his monks were praying for their deliverance. The same wind that carried the sound blew the flames towards the gatehouse at the north of the castle. The timbers of the gates started to scorch, but still the echo of the psalm was audible. Then the sound disappeared. For a moment the men fell into deeper despair. "We thought the holy men had given up!" they would say, telling the tale round a winter hearth in years to come. "Then we understood."

As they stood high up on the fortress rock, looking down on the gatehouse, they saw that the wind had gone round. It had shifted south easterly. It blew downwind of the fort now, sending smoke billowing towards the Mercian warriors. Soon they were forced to retreat as the fire burned towards them. The Northumbrian warriors, no longer smoke stifled, hurled spears after them, and under the cover of their attack men ran through the side gate to beat out the flames and push the burning wood into the dunes below. The wind blew strongly, and within the hour the smoke started to clear from the fort. It was over. The attack had failed.

In the church, Enfleda and her women heard the shouts and whooping of the warriors. At first they took it to be the start of the attack, and moved closer together. Enfleda could feel only the hammer-hard beating of her heart. She was certain her death was approaching. They heard footsteps outside running towards the church. A man burst inside.

"They are defeated, my lady! God has sent us a miracle."

There was a moment of unbelief, then screams and tears from the women, and cries, dear God, thank God! His nurse seized Edfrith and hugged him. He, understanding only that joy had returned, ran to his mother and tugged at her sleeve. But she stared at him unseeing. Her limbs had started to shake, and her body would no longer hold her upright. Her women hurried to help her, but she sank sideways from the altar to the ground and lay there unmoving.

"She is still suffering from shock," the physician said, kindly, looking down at her, and then turning to her women. "That, and the loss of blood when she lost the baby. Keep on with the bone broths to nourish the blood. It'll strengthen her. Have you finished the herbs? Good. I'll send some more up."

She lay very still in her bed, listening to his voice without heeding him. How long had she been lying here, she wondered. When he had gone, she told them to open the casement. The cold air blew across her face. She sniffed cautiously. It was wonderfully fresh. She felt the sensation of the breath on her lip, in her nostrils, felt the cold current of air entering her body. She breathed again, and again, and allowed the air deep inside her. How good it felt. She opened her mouth wide to gulp it in, but it was too much and the dizziness returned. In the long nights while she had lain here, she dreamed often that she stood again in a dark hall filling up with smoke. In her dream she would stop herself from breathing, hold her mouth shut and force the smoke from her nostrils till blackness rose up and took her. Then she would wake suddenly, gasping for breath like one drowning and her body shaking. But this, this sweet air, was like streams of clear water through her body.

"I want to go out," she said, and at once the women were shaking their heads, "Oh no, my lady! Not out there! You must rest." But she persisted.

"Carry me then. I want to go outside. Out of the fortress."

In the end they made a litter for her. She was grown so thin it hardly needed the four servants to carry her. Gudrun and another of her women attended her, Nurse brought Edfrith, and two men of Oswy's household escorted the little procession. As they carried her past the blackened gates, she felt the breeze blowing from the sea and tasted its salty seaweed tang. Edfrith shouted with delight at their release, and ran headlong down the causeway, Nurse in pursuit. Below them, soundless surf fringed the beach. Long rays of sunlight pierced through the clouds onto the wet sand, making it gleam and glitter. A line of white seabirds flew low across the water. The loveliness of it made her heart lift, and for a moment all seemed as it always had been.

Then they turned down hill, and she saw it, saw the ruin, saw the burning and the blackness. It was ruined, the village, the land; all ruined. Blackened sticks and beams had been shoved away into the dunes, and grey ash still thickened over the causeway. There was mud everywhere, churned up and stinking. Where huts with their backyards and pig sties had stood, where weaving sheds and workshops and grain stores had been, there was nothing. Blackened stumps of house posts remained, or part of a hut where the side had been ripped off and carried up to the fortress to feed the fire. Utensils lay tumbled in the ruins. The outline of a hearth could be seen half buried in ashes. A dog sniffed at a dead piglet in a broken pen. Beyond the village, the field strips once filled with ripening barley and wheat were trampled mud and stalks. The noise and clatter of the village was gone. There was only silence.

Her body was cold as ice. She wanted to weep, but her tears were frozen. Edfrith ran back to her in the litter.

"Mamma! Why have all the huts burned down?" His face was staring up at hers, fearful and pale. She summoned speech to her lips for his sake.

"It was our enemies. They are bad, wicked men, and God will strike them down. May they be accursed for ever." She held his hand, but her body was trembling and her hand would not still. Her women looked to one another.

"My lady—we should return now."

"Where are the people?" she asked, ignoring them. One of Oswy's men leaned towards her. "They're hiding. If they got away in time. They're afraid the Mercians will return."

A wave of fear leapt up in her. "Will they return?"

"No, Lady. Penda's army is large, and there's nothing left here for them to eat, nor for miles around. He's returning to Mercia. He'll be pleased enough with the plunder they take on the way home."

In her mind's eye she saw Penda and his army sowing a black swathe of malice and destruction through the kingdom. She saw her people fleeing in terror before them and felt their despair.

"What will they do—the villagers, what will they do?"

The thegn shrugged. "There'll be a hard winter ahead."

A few days later Oswy came to see her. They spoke little at first, as if too much had happened for words.

"Are you well, my Lord?" she asked at last, though it might have been his enquiry. He looked utterly weary, his face old and grey. He looked at her. She was still lovely, he thought, pale and weak as she was. He bent over and kissed her lips. She clung to him. "Why did he attack us?"

"Penda?" He straightened up, still holding her hands in his. "He's ambitious. And he's a heathen. He thinks Northumbria will ally with the Christian kingdoms in the south and surround Mercia. Would to God we could." He frowned.

"When Penda attacked Ad Gefrin, he got past my spies. Do you know how?" She felt his grip tighten. "It was Selwin. Your cousin, king of Deira. I gave him the kingship and he is my sworn vassal. Somehow he forgot all that and gave the Mercians safe passage through Deira."

She stared at him, bewildered.

"Maybe you don't know Deira so well. Dere Street, the Roman road, runs directly past York and up the east of the Pennines, so Penda wasn't troubled by having to cross the hills. And for good measure, Selwin sent a band of his own men along with the Mercians. We know that because we captured two of them."

He paused. "Clearly, Selwin thought I was finished. Did he send men to help me? No. He thought, Penda is going to be my overlord, and I'll make sure of his favour."

"No, Oswy. It can't be. He is my cousin. You and he have always been close."

"Not close enough."

"Send word to him. Talk to him. Find out what the truth is."

He ignored her. "It's too late for campaigning now, and I have to treat with Penda. But when the deal is done I shall raise the fyrd and go after him."

"He is my kinsman, Oswy."

"He swore fealty. He broke his oath. He's the one who's broken ties." With one of his sudden bursts of temper, he dropped down beside her. "Do you want to beg on your knees for a living at some foreign court?" he shouted. "Do you want Edfrith to be a pitiful supplicant like I was? Do you?"

She dropped her head, tears starting from her eyes.

"For God's sake, Enfleda!"

Her shoulders shook with sobs. He continued to hold her for a while without moving. At last, his anger spent, he softened his grip on her arm, and drew her towards him. She was so young still. So innocent. Still capable of tears.

As autumn brought the first frosts, Oswy sent messengers to the Mercian court. They offered Oswy's eldest son Connal, from his first marriage, as a husband for Penda's daughter Cynburh. It would be an alliance that might seal a lasting peace between the kingdoms. He wouldn't even insist on the girl's conversion.

He was grim-faced through the autumn days, spending his days in council or training with his warriors. Enfleda stayed within her household, slowly recovering her strength. She meant to keep her oath to God, to make Him see that she had repented of any unfaithfulness and that she was truly grateful for their deliverance. Romanus was surprised at her zeal. She attended divine service daily with her household and summoned him to give her teachings on scripture. But her attention wandered. How she missed Paulinus! He liked to tell her stories, full of drama and Latin phrases. His Christ was God's warrior, fearless and merciful. Romanus was a scholar who was only interested in doctrine.

In December Oswy's kinsman Godfrey arrived from Lindisfarne to join them for the Christmas feast. He brought his young companion with him. When she saw them in the king's hall, she felt a lift in her spirits—not at the white-haired old man, but at the sight of the handsome youth at his side. Wilfrid, she remembered. She would send for him. Find out how he liked his life on Lindisfarne.

When he arrived in her hall, there was a little flurry among her women. He was taller now, more assured. He was starting to grow a beard, as fair as his hair and neatly trimmed. His face was losing its boyish fullness, and his strong regular features were more apparent. He had not taken a novice's habit; his tunic was of fine linen and he wore a silver chain. When Enfleda greeted him, he moved forward bright-faced to kneel in front of her, bowing low with his hand to his heart.

"Lady Enfleda! I'm so glad to be here, to thank you for your great kindness to me." He took her hand to kiss her royal ring. His eyes met hers. She remembered that morning in the great hall, when he had seemed like a vision to her.

"I thank God that through you I have been brought close to Him."

She faltered for a moment, thrown off balance by his intensity. "Please stand! Do you study with the novices?"

"Yes."

Romanus interrupted at once. "What rites do they teach you?" Wilfrid shifted his attention to Romanus. "The Ionan tradition. But I am eager to learn from you of the Roman rites, Father. Have you visited Rome?"

Delighted with the question, Romanus embarked on a discourse about his experiences of Rome and of its superiority in matters of religion. What a bore, thought Enfleda, embarrassed. No stories or descriptions. Just discourses on doctrine. But when she looked at Wilfrid he appeared to be hanging on Romanus' every word. Can he really be interested? Or is he just courteous? Irritated, she interrupted.

"Let me hear about you, Wilfrid! How is Lord Godfrey?"

"Forgive me, Lady Enfleda. We don't have anyone at Lindisfarne versed in the Roman tradition, and Father Romanus is so knowledgeable."

His boyish zeal amused her, but her soul was unsettled. Why didn't she desire God with such passion? "Thou shalt love the Lord thy God," she thought. But fear was what she felt. Not love. Perhaps Wilfrid could change that.

After the visit was over, she found that Romanus was full of Wilfrid, his intelligence, his openness. He begged her to arrange regular visits so that he could instruct the youth. Then Enfleda had an idea. If Wilfrid could be instructed in the Catholic faith and ordained, she would appoint him as her chaplain. Romanus could be sent back to Kent. She gave her assent.

✛

When the Christmas feast was over, Oswy came to her household to see her privately. Her household people withdrew. They stood alone together under the embroidered hangings given her by her uncle of Kent.

"We have good news," he said, embracing her with a kiss. "We're ready to sign the treaty with Penda, and God willing it will hold." He paused. "But he's made another condition. I wanted to tell you first." She stared at him, wondering.

"Once they are married, princess Cynburh will come to Northumbria, to live with Connal. So the Mercian people want one of ours in Mercia."

"Who else is there?"

"They have asked for Edfrith as a hostage."

She felt blackness open in front of her.

"No", she said. "No."

"It's not for ever. A year or two, till things have settled down and the marriage is established. He can take his nurse, and two of the brothers from Lindisfarne to teach him. He'll have some of our household with him."

"No!" she repeated. "He's too young. He's only six, Oswy."

Oswy shrugged.

"I was younger than that when I went into exile. I had no-one to take care of me, no nurse, no household."

"But they're pagans! How can you trust them? How could you give him up to them?"

"If there is to be peace, we have no choice."

"Don't I have a choice?"

"Enfleda. You must understand. It is agreed."

She understood then that she had been a fool to think that Oswy loved her. His heart had closed long ago. All he cared for was power, was his kingship, and he would sacrifice whatever he had to in its name. His son. Herself, if it came to that. She turned from him and wept alone.

PART 2
CUTHBERT

651–63 AD

He loved games and pranks, and as was natural at his age, loved to play with the other children. He was naturally agile and quick-witted and usually won the game. He would often still be fresh when the others were tired, and would look round in triumph, as though the game were in his hands, and ask who was willing to continue. He used to boast that he had beaten all those of his own age and many who were older at wrestling, jumping, running and every other exercise. For "when he was a child, he understood as a child," but when a man, "he put away childish things".

Bede: Life of Cuthbert *ch.1*

CHAPTER 5

Leader Valley

651 AD

His sword bit down with a sudden flash of sunlight and clashed blade on blade before leaping back. Half a man's height of razor-sharp steel, ridged at the centre from the point of the blade to the hilt, it formed a deadly extension of his arm and shoulder. It moved with him, the impact singing through his body, every sinew taut, ready for the next blow. He wore a plain padded jacket for protection, and although a sharp wind blew down the valley, the collar and cuffs were soaked dark with sweat. For all the strength of his sword arm there was a lightness about him, a vivacity that made him look as if he were dancing more than fighting. His opponent was as powerful and dangerous as he, but more dogged and watchful, waiting for advantage. He feinted a blow; for a second Cuthbert was deceived and slipped right, and then had to pull back to parry with his shield. The force of the blow knocked the breath from him, but he was still there, a half smile on his lips, lunging forward to meet the blade hard and straight.

His recovery won a cheer or two from the onlookers. Half a dozen young men stood around the hard earth of the practice ground, drinking ale and shouting comments. Cuthbert heard them with some part of his attention, but his focus didn't waver. He meant to win. Yesterday Roderic had outwitted him, but today he would not. He struck again and again, in a ringing clangour of assault, but neither of them was able to gain advantage. At last they both drew back, gasping for breath. There was a moment of hiatus; Cuthbert recovered first, and with a sudden skip and charge he was on the other, hitting shield to shield with such force that his opponent stumbled and fell backward. The sword jumped from his hand. Cuthbert stamped his foot on his chest to pin him down. A long moment held, both men sweating and panting. The defeated man pushed the foot off and rolled sideways.

"You win. That's enough."

"Another."

"Enough. I need a break."

Roderic leaned sideways and pulled his bag towards him, found a bottle and drank. Then he pulled out a little pot and started rubbing grease into his elbow. Cuthbert feinted his sword around Roderic's body, right, left, right, the light shining on his friend's hair, taunting him with each thrust. Roderic ducked forward under the blade and grabbed his tormentor's thighs with such force that he was toppled sideways onto the ground. His forehead hit a stone and blood started out over his left eye, half-blinding him.

"Go and clean yourself. It'll be all over you." But Cuthbert staggered up, onto his feet again, stubborn, impatient. Roderic rolled over, turning his back. "For God's sake. You'll have all the fighting you want soon enough."

Another pair of youths picked up their weapons and took the ground. Cuthbert shrugged, laid down his sword and shield and walked off over the water meadows. The Leader flowed between low banks, running shallow over rocks and stones before the channel narrowed, forcing the dark water in a sudden moiling rush into the deep pool below. Here Cuthbert stripped off his jacket and waded into the water, feeling the sharp chill on his thighs. He ducked down, soaking his whole body and washing the blood from his face. The stone had cut deep into his brow and blood still flowed from the wound. He pulled moss from the stones on the bank to staunch it. He was aware of the pain but took no notice of it. Although he was glad of victory, he was elated still more by his own strength. He felt the power in his body. It was ready for war. It would endure.

When the morning's session was done, he and the other men unhitched their horses, buckled on swords and shields and mounted, making mock charges and parries at each other. They were all excited, like young stallions the reins could barely check, fight-ready and spoiling for war. They taunted and teased each other, picking quarrels and roaring with wild laughter at any joke. A couple were gesiths, experienced warriors, and they made the most of their status with the younger men, boasting and swaggering. They turned their horses up the valley towards the thegn's hall, where the warriors were gathering.

But Cuthbert turned his mare, Mayda, aside. Roderic swung round on his saddle. "Not coming?"

"I've got a visit to make."

"You can eat first!" Cuthbert shook his head. "Not sneaking off, are you? We leave tomorrow."

"I know. I'll be here."

Roderic shrugged and spurred his horse after his comrades.

In the morning the fyrd would gather at the old Roman fort at Melrose, war bands like his from all over the district, called up for the king's campaign in Deira. His first campaign, his first taste of battle. He was wild with it all, wild with his own strength and ambition. But first he had a visit to make. He set Mayda on a spanking trot down Dere Street, her hooves ringing on the cobbles of the Roman road half buried under turf. As they neared the valley foot, he turned her down a track towards the Leader. She waded in, dropping her head for gulps of water and shaking the drops from her muzzle. Once on the other side she headed for the track leading back up the valley, back to his father's hall.

"No! No, not today!" He leaned forward and fondled her ears as he tugged the rein away. And not for many a day, he thought, urging her in the other direction. Would he ride again up the valley? Would she?

Their track wound upwards round the side of the hill. The slope was covered with rough grass and bracken, and gorse just coming into flower. He caught a whiff of its buttery smell as he passed, and saw the bees on it already, hungry for spring nectar. Soon they would be driving the sheep and young lambs up onto the hills for summer pasture. He felt the lurch in the saddle as the mare's fore-quarters strained against the steepness of the track. He leaned forward to help her, slackening the reins. As they gained height, the winding line of the Tweed came into view below them. The river coiled like a silver serpent in the gorge below, between the thickly wooded banks that rose up steeply from the river. It was a favourite spot for circling birds of prey, and he had lain here often as a boy, watching their slow hover and sudden plunge. On an impulse he pulled Mayda up and let her crop the grass while he looked again across the valley.

As always, two kites were circling on the updraft. The air was bright and clear. Opposite him, the long flank of the south Eildon sloped down towards the green semi-island formed by the curve of the river. A movement there caught his eye. He could see two men, tiny in the distance. Brown clothes. Not fighting men. It would be the monks, he realised. He had heard that the king had given Bishop Aidan the land for a monastery. He looked again. He saw the land was no longer forested as it had been in his childhood. Much of it had been cleared, and he could see huts, a hall, a church. There was a line of some sort across the neck of the peninsula-island. Probably they had made a wall, or a ditch of some sort. To cut themselves off. Suddenly curious, he wondered what it would feel like to be behind the monks' wall. Cut off from the world. No going to war. No women. The strangeness of it stirred him. To be a man, and yet not to fight for your king. Yet the king was pleased enough to give them land. Perhaps they did battle for him in the heavenly kingdom.

He shook himself out of his musings, and tugged Mayda's head out of the grass. It was none of his business anyway.

He rode on till they reached a fold in the hillside, where water gushed out from a spring into a little stream lined with a low scrub of alder and birch. Mayda picked her way across, and the hamlet came into view. It was tucked into the south side of the hill some way below the summit, sheltered by the hills behind from the north and east winds. The huts were clustered on two areas of level ground, one above the other, with their fields stretching away down the slope.

As he rode closer, he could see women sitting outside the huts working their querns. There was a sound of hammering from a workshop, and down in the fields, a man bellowing at a stubborn ox. A group of children armed with sticks ran helter-skelter down the slope, shouting war cries. Everything was as it always was.

He dismounted and led the mare behind him along the winding track between the huts. When he reached Kenswith's, he hooked the bridle over the door post. He knocked on the door—pushed it open—but though the fire was still red in the hearth, she wasn't there. The weaving shed perhaps, and yes, he found her there, absorbed as her hands shuttled to and fro over the broad stripes of the cloth, till she sensed his presence and looked up. She gave a little cry of joy and left off her task, limping towards him. She seemed to have grown smaller. Her head barely reached his shoulder now, and he hugged her carefully, holding back his strength so as not to crush her. She drew back to look up at him and had to stand tiptoe to kiss him. He half-lifted her up so she could reach him. She scolded him for his long hair to hide her joy.

"Come into the house. There's fresh curd, and the hearth's warm."

"Are you lame, mother?"

"The knee swells. When it's damp, I can hardly move. I'm not young anymore."

It was true. Her hair, dark from the side of her British mother, was turning white, and her pale skin had lost its smoothness. He took her arm, and she leaned against him as they walked over to the hut. Swifts screeched through the air, flying up into their nests in the thatch and away with hardly a pause. Kenswith pushed open the door. In the smell of smoke and bread and drying herbs he was a child again. His father's hall was where he belonged as a man, but his foster mother's hut was still home.

He sat on the bench, at the table where he'd eaten every day of his childhood. Kenswith leaned over and tugged at the leather string round his neck.

"What's this?"

"My step-mother gave it to me." He lifted it over his head and handed it to her. She pushed the amulet away.

"Why do you wear it?" He shrugged. "It won't help you."

"You must give me your blessing then."

"Not for war. Not for this war."

"Don't fear for me, mother." He leaned over to tease her. "Who do you think is stronger than me?"

"No. You shouldn't go."

"Not go? Do you want me to be a battle-shirker?"

She sat silent for a moment. Perhaps she was starting to lose her wits, he thought.

She spoke again. "Do you know what people are saying? Bishop Aidan has refused his blessing. He has told the king so."

Bishop Aidan. They'd heard the same story at his father's hall, but his father had scoffed at it. "Kings don't need bishops to tell them what to do," he had said. "Deira owes allegiance to the king, and Selwin betrayed him. He broke his oath. This hall supports the king." He had put his arm round his warrior son's shoulder and taken him to the stables to choose his horse.

Kenswith persisted. "Selwin of Deira is well loved by his people. By Bishop Aidan too. He's never raised his hand against the king. Think what you're doing."

"I can't tell the king how to act, mother. I have to serve him. It's my sworn duty."

"You're sworn to serve God."

He stared at her in surprise. Suddenly irritated, he pushed aside the table and got up. "Don't try and stop me."

He swiped the amulet away from her and went over to the door. He looked out, feeling his heart beating uncomfortably in his chest. He had come for a blessing, not an argument. From the gatepost, Mayda whickered at him, hoping for barley. He went over to her, unhitched the saddle bag and pulled out a handful of feed. Her soft mouth nuzzled his hand as she ate.

"Sworn to God!" How could she say that? He had been baptised, true, but he was a child then, and it had been Kenswith's doing, not his. He couldn't even remember what he had sworn. Yes, she had taught him prayers and scripture. He could remember all that. It was part of his life in the village, and he accepted it. But when he came to manhood and went to live in his father's hall, he had put it aside. His father had no interest in religion. The king was a Christian, so he had been baptised, but that was the end of it. His step-mother was pagan still and prayed to the old gods.

The mare nudged him for more. He pulled out another handful and fed her, rubbing his hand in her mane. It was Kenswith's way to talk like that, he told himself. Why should it trouble him? He was seventeen years old now; a man. Not a child. Not a nursling clinging to his mother's gown.

He shook off his annoyance and went back inside. She was bent over the fire, warming some old bread for him. He leaned down to kiss her head. She took his hand and held it to her cheek. "No more about God," he said.

She said nothing but set a bowl of curd on the table with the warmed bread, and suddenly he realised that he was famished. He pulled the bench up to the table and tore at the food. When he'd finished the curd, she toasted hard cheese on the embers for him and filled his cup with ale. They sat together, eating cheese and talking about her neighbours and the spring planting, and the five goats she kept in the field behind the hut.

When it grew dusk, he went out and walked Mayda to the spring at the side of the hill to water her and let her graze on the new grass. The spring water tumbled down the hillside in a thin clear stream. He stared down the hill. Up in the valley, in the thegn's great hall, his comrades would be drinking and singing and listening to tales of great warriors of long ago.

Getting ready for war. He should have stayed with them all. Coming here had unsettled him. His home-coming was not as he'd imagined it. He'd thought Kenswith would be proud of him. The truth was, he wanted to go into battle with her blessing. He believed that her Christ-blessing would protect him.

He took down his sword from the saddle straps, drew it out of the scabbard and took a whetstone from his pocket. The stone ran along the steel with a regular rasping hiss and return, hiss and return, sharpening the blade more and more finely. He stood there till night fell and stars brightened in the sky like sparks from fine steel.

When he returned to the hut, the door stood open. He paused before he went in, looking inside. The hearth fire burned low, and Kenswith had set a tallow candle on the table. She sat beside it, eyes half shut, her fingers moving round the beads on her lap. The candle-light took the wrinkles and blotches from her face. She seemed ageless, enduring, a spirit carved in pale wood. Was she a seer? In the valley she was known as a holy woman, he knew, and people came to her for counsel. Where had her words come from? What had she seen? In spite of himself he muttered a prayer against ill omen. Entering the hut, he went to her, dropping to his knees beside her and taking her hand from her beads.

"Give me your blessing."

She sighed and put her hand on his thick fair hair.

CHAPTER 6

DERE STREET

651 AD

Dere Street stretched north all the way up the Leader Valley, past his father's hall and beyond into Pictland. Now, for the first time he tasted its length southwards. It seemed that however far they rode, it was still the Street. It unrolled before them, past Melrose, past the Eildons and the Roman camp till the familiar was lost altogether; but the Street went on, beside rivers never seen before, past farms and settlements and woodland, over desolate moors and upland till on the third day of the march they came to the great wall of the Romans. Cuthbert could see that they liked everything to be straight. The wall was as unwavering as the road, pouring itself over the landscape in a single line with no regard for what stood in its way. It astonished him. He thought of Kenswith's village, of the track that wound round the contours of the hill. Of the huts, each one different because of the shape of the tree whose wood had made its frame. The Roman builders had worked in a different way. Square forts. Straight roads. It didn't matter whose lands they passed over or what the terrain.

The Street didn't falter when they reached the Tyne but continued over a great stone bridge broad enough for four men to ride abreast, with perfectly spaced arches dividing the water. How had they built it? How, with the waters of the river deep about them? He started to believe that the Street was unstoppable and endless, or that it would be consummated only when it reached Rome itself.

His companions had no interest in such questions. For now, for them, the Street had only one purpose. It was the road that was leading them to war. It was carrying them into Deira to wreak King Oswy's vengeance on his treacherous vassal. They didn't march in legions like the Romans. There were no camps and forts waiting for them with barracks and warm ale. In the Saxon army, pack horses carried provision for the warriors and tents for the king and his commanders. The warriors carried their shields and weapons, their helmets and mail. At night they slept rough, with a blanket wrapped round them.

On the fifth day of the march they woke to a bright dawn, but the skies soon clouded and a sharp shower doused the last embers of the camp fires. After he and his company had broken camp, Brand shouted for them.

"We'll reach Catterick by nightfall," he told them. "Anyone been there? No? A walled fort, close to the river crossing. It'll be our base. Once we get there, the scouts will find out what the Deirans are up to."

Brand's face was weatherworn, like tanned leather. He was their commander, a veteran who seemed devoid of fear. "Not long now!" he exhorted them. "Start sharpening your axes! They're going to get a lesson they won't forget in a hurry!"

The war band gave a ragged cheer, but Cuthbert could find only half his voice. He had started to think, soon I will kill a man. He imagined his sword piercing skin and guts and bone, and dancing out red with blood. He had killed deer, slaughtered cattle; he knew well enough what killing felt like. But he had not killed a man.

He pulled himself up into the saddle and gave Mayda a pat. The mare had settled into the rhythm of the long days of the march without protest. He wished he could be like her. Unresisting. Unquestioning. A gust of rain spattered across his face. The day was overcast, and now the clouds were darkening. Another storm. The weather had turned humid a couple of days back, and thunder rumbled along the hills in the afternoons. Yesterday a sudden cloudburst and lightning had sent horses bolting sideways off the road, knocking men sprawling and sending provisions flying. There was an uneasy, edgy sense in the air; men fingered their secret amulets and muttered invocations to the old gods for protection.

Sensing an absence at his side, he swung round in the saddle. Roderic's horse had suffered a kick to the hind leg in the confusion yesterday and had been stiff and sore this morning. Now Cuthbert saw he was off the horse, bending over the leg. He turned and rode back.

"Look at that." Cuthbert got off and squatted down beside his friend. The horse was standing on three legs, resting the left hind leg. Around the fetlock the wound from the kick had started to fester and swell. When Roderic touched the leg, he was shaken by a violent spasm, and Thunder threw up his head in protest. "All right, old fellow. All right." He rubbed his ears.

"You can't ride him like that."

"Tell Brand, will you?"

Cuthbert remounted and cantered up the line till he was alongside Brand. The commander listened, nodded. "Find another. There are plenty of farms down here—you'll have to take what you can find. Go together and watch out. Catch up with us tonight at Catterick."

They left the Street on the first track they found, Roderic leading Thunder and Cuthbert riding beside him. The din of the army started to grow faint. For the first time in days, they could hear birdsong in the trees. The track was leafy and overgrown but there were recent cart-tracks and cattle prints. It would certainly lead to a hamlet of some sort. They went on in the heat of the day. The track seemed endless, and without the energy of the company moving them forward, weariness from the long march took hold of them. At last the track took a sharp bend round an old tree, and they found themselves in front of a farmstead. Its owner was bent over a wattle fence half a hide away, mending a hole in his pig run. When he saw the two warriors he straightened up quickly and reached for his knife.

"Good day!" Cuthbert called out. "We've a lame horse here." The man tightened his grip on his knife, eyes shifting sideways. "We can leave him and take one on loan. Can you help us?"

At home, in the valley, any farmer would have helped them out, made a poultice for the swollen leg, lent them a ride. But this was Deira, and they were warriors. The man's face showed only fear. He started to run, back towards the hamlet to raise the alarm. Cuthbert kicked his horse forward quickly, came up behind him and leapt off onto him, bringing him to the ground before he could reach his farm. They struggled together on the ground. Cuthbert got hold of his left arm, twisting it hard behind his back. He held him close while they both gasped for breath.

"We won't hurt you. Or your family. We need a horse." The man's face was close to his, livid and sweating. He was an older man, like a score of neighbours he loved and respected. How could he do this to him? He let go of the arm lock and let the man get up, though he kept his grip tight. "I'm sorry. Please. Just a horse."

He held him while Roderic went to search the sheds. The man's face and neck were running with sweat. He was shaking with the shock of the sudden violence, muttering curses as he gasped for breath. At last Roderic came back with a short-legged pony.

"It's all he's got." He shrugged and handed over Thunder's bridle to the farmer. "Look after him. He's worth twenty of this one."

They rode away down the track. Neither spoke. When they reached the Street, it was empty and silent, only hoof prints and dung to show where the army had passed. Roderic kicked the pony into a trot beside Cuthbert.

"He's a donkey."

"Yep."

"We had to do it. Anyway, it's a good deal for him."

"Yep."

"Poor old Thunder."

As they trotted down the empty road Cuthbert tried to push away his unease. This was war. War was another country, where all the rules were different. If he were to be a warrior, he would have to learn to live there.

CHAPTER 7

A BETRAYAL

651 AD

Sometimes Oswy envied the Romans, with their professional soldiers and their long straight roads, their fortresses with barracks and grain stores. They had a military machine far greater than anything a Saxon king could muster. But it didn't make any difference in the end. They still lost, lost everything they had fought for and went back to Rome with their tails between their legs. What mattered was the will, the fighting will. Oswy felt his like iron against his backbone. It was as big an army as he'd ever put in the field. He was certain they would outnumber Selwin. They would crush him.

He knew that by the time they'd got the army through the ford over the Swale the Deiran spies would have tallied up his numbers, counted his horses, reckoned up his companies. Selwin would be deciding his strategy, or his commanders would be. Selwin was a battle-shirker, a nithing who had never stood in a shield wall. Oswy's position was strong. The river would prevent any surprise attack from the north and enough of the fort remained to give some protection. They had the road from the south covered. He sent out his scouting parties and waited.

Two days after their arrival at Catterick visitors arrived at the fort. A Deiran thegn with a small company of retainers was taken within the walls of the old fort to where the king and his company were camped. Within the hour, the news had spread through the army.

The king's tent was large enough for his war council—his general Ethelwin, his first son Connal and his commanders; hardened warriors all save for Connal, who was still untried. The thegn was brought into the tent; a distinguished man dressed in fine linen with silver studs and buckles on his belts. Wine was brought and the men drank together, watchful and waiting. At last Oswy nodded to the man to speak.

"My name is Hunwald of Faresdun."

"Are you sent by my vassal Selwin?"

"No, Lord."

"Are you his thegn?"

Hunwald didn't reply.

His silence was immediately understood. He meant to betray his lord. The air in the tent was very still.

"Don't hold back, thegn Hunwald. If you choose to help us you'll be rewarded."

Still Hunwald hesitated. Oswy signed to the servants to bring more wine. Hunwald gulped down a cupful. "I would prefer to speak with you alone, Lord."

Oswy nodded to his chiefs to leave. Only Connal and the general remained. "Now, thegn Hunwald. Where have you left Selwin and his army?"

"Selwin's spies have told him your numbers. He's decided to withdraw. He's sent his men home."

"God damn him! Where is he?"

"His men were camped near my estate." Another pause. "He has taken refuge at my hall."

Oswy smacked his fist down on his knee with a shout of glee. He jumped up and embraced Hunwald. "Good man! Good! You'll have gold for this. How far is it?"

"Half a day's ride to the north-west."

"We'll have him! We'll smoke the fox out of his den! Thegn Hunwald, you have acted like a bold and honest man, and you'll have your reward. We must borrow your men to take us to your hall. You'll be our guest here."

He would hold Hunwald hostage against the truth of his information. It could be a decoy, a bluff. But in his heart he was certain it was true. His scouts had found no trace of an army.

By the time the guards had been called to escort Hunwald away, Oswy's mind was made up. Ethelwin, his commander, was a tough man, long since hardened to blood. When he heard Oswy's orders, he didn't flinch or question. But when Oswy rose to leave the tent Connal pulled at his father's arm. "You can't, father. It's dishonourable. He's the queen's kinsman."

"He's broken his oath."

"Why don't you exile him?"

"Exile? To stir up trouble in Kent or Frankia? Are you mad?"

"It's a sin."

"Would you rather lose fifty men in the shield wall?"

Connal stared back at his father, dark-faced and defiant. "It's a sin", he repeated.

Oswy struck him across the head, sending the youth staggering across the tent. "Don't question what I do."

CHAPTER 8

Dividing the Spoils

651 AD

When dwelling in camp with the army, in the face of the enemy and having only meagre rations, yet he lived abundantly and with Divine aid.
Anonymous Life, I, vii

He sat round the fire with the others, holding a piece of stale bread on a stick to the embers and watching it blacken at the edges. They had been in Catterick for days now, and supplies were running low. Foraging parties had to stay close; no-one knew when the call to arms would come. The camp was full of rumours. The older warriors said there would be no battle now that the Deirans had scuttled back to their dens. But the young ones were still on edge. Still waiting. They would start a game of dice and break off if a horseman rode into camp; was there news? They were all bad-tempered. Blood lust had curdled into spats and arguments—over food, over dice, over what was going to happen. They talked endlessly.

"We'll go after them. Wherever they are."

"Maybe we'll ride to York. There'd be rich pickings there."

"Not if Selwin's surrendered."

"What difference does it make? They've got to be taught a lesson."

"Yes!" Roderic joined in. "It's not over. Even if he's surrendered. The king wouldn't march us down here and send us home empty-handed. We'll teach them a lesson they won't forget."

Cuthbert laughed aloud at his fiery friend whose nag could barely break a trot swearing vengeance on the Deirans. He rolled over and punched Roderic. Annoyed, Roderic swung his fist into Cuthbert's gut and winded him. Cuthbert tumbled backwards, still laughing.

After two days of waiting, the camp was suddenly shaken with a commotion of shouting, horns blowing, men yelling and cheering. Men leapt up, grabbing at swords and axes. Then they saw it was Ethelwin and the king's household warriors riding into the lines, whooping and shouting battle cries. In their midst a rider was leading a horse with a man's body strapped across it. The man had been beheaded, and his tunic was covered in blood. Another man rode behind. Holding the reins in one hand he held up the man's head in the other, his fingers knotted through the long fair hair.

"Selwin of Deira!" he yelled. "Death to traitors!" He shouted it again and again as the war band made its way up and down the camp, displaying Selwin's body and head so that every man would see it. The men stood agape, trying to take in what they saw. No-one found his tongue to respond to the shouts of the warriors. As the head was carried past, Cuthbert saw the unshaven pallor of the face, the eyes still wide open and staring, the lips parted as if to cry out against his assassins. They had sliced cleanly through the neck but clots of blood still hung from the cut veins. The brutality of it made Cuthbert retch suddenly, and he had to turn away to spit. When he looked back, it had already been carried up the line.

In spite of the clamour of the victory ride, unease possessed the men. To kill a king in battle was honourable, a glorious victory—but Selwin had been defenceless. Put to death like a common criminal. Surely it was a sin. God would bring down vengeance on his killers.

Oswy didn't let them pause to think about it. As soon as the body had been displayed and Selwin's head rammed onto a stake outside the fort, he gave orders for the whole army to be rallied in front of it.

"Selwin of Deira was a traitor and a coward!" he roared. "God has given him into our hands! He has paid for his treachery and let those who followed him pay! They'll have no hiding place before us! We'll wait for them no longer—we ride today! We will search out the last of his followers and empty their coffers!"

Cuthbert heard not a word of Oswy's rant. Try as he would, he couldn't stop looking at the head staring down from the post. Flies darkened round the eyes but there was still colour in the cheeks and lips, as if he lived. Cuthbert had seen sickness and old age before, had seen death. But not like this. How could a king come to this? It felt blasphemous. For a moment Selwin's head seemed like Christ's hanging forward on the cross. It was horrible to him. He thought suddenly of the Roman soldiers drawing lots for Christ's garments. He was part of it. Revulsion overwhelmed him.

When Oswy was finished and marching orders given, the camp sprang into an uproar of preparation, men dousing fires, grabbing possessions and filling bags. Cuthbert saw it in a kind of dream. At last he pulled his gaze away and walked unsteadily back to their camp.

"Where've you been?" Roderic yelled at him. "We're leaving!" Cuthbert unhitched Mayda, saddled up and strapped on his bags, sword and shield. Minutes later the company was riding down the road.

They were heading towards York, Roderic told him. Cuthbert listened to his friend, watching his face. He had known him since their boyhood, knew his nature. How could he take this?

"Are you going?"

"What d'you mean, am I going?"

"Selwin was murdered."

"He could've been killed in battle, if he hadn't shirked it."

"Roderic. It's . . . "

"Don't you Roderic me. I can see what's happening as well as you can." He kicked the short-legged pony forward, away from his friend.

✛

The weather was dry now and settled, and the countryside had all the mellow loveliness of summer. They rode past fields ready for harvesting and farmsteads, but no smoke came from the hearths. The hamlets were strangely quiet and still. Everyone had fled from the approaching army. This is what we bring, thought Cuthbert. Fear. This is what war is. He thought of his own valley and imagined a war band riding through the familiar tracks and fields, firing the huts and driving off the cattle. Thought of Kenswith standing at her loom. He was filled with deep emotion. She had told him, warned him. She had been right.

When the night camp was made, his companions sat round the fire, drinking and singing, roaring songs into the night. Cuthbert had no heart for it. His mind was in turmoil. Was this what all his dreams had come to? He had seen himself fighting for a great cause, for the king's honour and his own. He had wanted to prove himself a man, to win glory for his strength and courage. Instead, he found himself complicit in the murder of a king. The campaign had turned into a raiding party.

At last Cuthbert went to find his commander. Brand stood on the edge of the camp, looking down the road. In the dusk it was visible only as a line of deeper darkness than the countryside around it, disappearing into the night. He turned to see Cuthbert's face behind him, pale in the darkness.

"What do you want?"

"I want to leave."

"What do you mean?"

"Leave. Go home." Brand leaned towards him, trying to make out his expression in the darkness. "You're on a campaign. You don't go home."

"What we're doing . . . it's not right." There was silence. Brand would despise him, he knew. He braced himself for shouts and curses, but when the commander spoke his voice was kindly. "It's your first campaign. You're seeing things you don't like, and maybe none of us like. But you don't quit."

Cuthbert was silent.

"Think about it. If you go home, your father will be shamed because of you. Your honour will be lost. You'll be empty-handed when everyone else has plunder to spare."

"I don't want plunder."

"If you were killed in battle, your family would grieve for you but they would be proud. Your death would give them honour. Desertion gives them nothing but shame."

"I'm not afraid, Brand. It's not that."

"Aren't you?" he said, taunting him now. Silence. "Sleep on it. Talk to me in the morning."

When he returned to camp, the other men were already rolled up in their blankets near the fire, snoring. He hunched down, staring at the hot embers. This was how men fought. They closed their hearts. Even Roderic. Cuthbert repeated the blessing Kenswith had said over him to himself: "Lord Jesus Christ, have mercy on me."

By the time the embers had faded into the darkness of the night, his mind was made up. He picked his way over the sleeping men and made his way to the lines where the horses were tethered. Mayda knew him and whickered softly. He buried his face in her neck. Animals were always truthful. Always themselves. He felt for the harness and saddled her up. "We're going home, Mayda."

He rode through the night, back up the Street. Now the decision was made, his mind was empty. He thought of nothing, aware only of the night air on his cheek and the noises of the countryside, owls calling and a fox yowling for its mate. He felt Mayda's steady movement beneath him, felt her moving forward strongly as if she was of the same mind as he. After the days of waiting at Catterick the mare was well rested and needed only short halts the next day. A fever possessed Cuthbert to shake the dust of Deira from his feet, to be gone. But by the evening he knew they had to rest. He turned off up a track beside a stream and dismounted. He knelt by Mayda, both of them drinking together. He saw a shepherd's hut close by, where men slept at lambing time, with only a door and a stable lean-to beside it. He peered inside. There was hay piled up on a bench at the back. He started to pull some down for the horse. As he tugged, a bundle fell out of the hay. He picked it up, unwrapped the cloth and pulled out bread. He'd eaten nothing for two days, and it seemed like a miracle. A gift from God. He gave Mayda the hay and sat beside her eating his bread. Then he wrapped himself in his blanket and slept on the floor till dawn was long past.

When he got home, nothing was as he'd expected. He walked into his father's hall with Brand's words still in his ears, braced for a torrent of recrimination and rebuke. But his father embraced him almost absent-mindedly.

"We've heard the news. The messenger came from Bamburgh yesterday. Shocking. You've returned early? Best you did. It could only bring shame on you." He leaned forward. "The queen is threatening to return to Kent. Selwin was her kinsman, you know. They say she loved him as a brother." He shook his head. "Shocking. A shocking thing. She is distraught. And Aidan. When Bishop Aidan heard the news he was heart-struck with grief. They think he won't recover. He's a dying man."

Cuthbert was bewildered. There were no reproaches, no questions, no demands for plunder. The servants greeted him with lowered eyes, as if everyone understood a crime had been committed. No-one asked him about it. No-one blamed him, but a shadow had fallen between him and the household. He felt like a stranger. The familiar work, the jokes, the meals together, all seemed distant to him.

He hung up his shield on the beam in the hall beside his father's. He had the servants bring him a length of cloth to wrap his sword against rusting and stowed it in his chest. The bright steel was still virgin. After he had put it away, he missed its weight against his thigh. When he woke in the morning, he reached out with his hand to find it. He felt as if he had lost part of himself. A dozen times he went to take it from the chest again, then stopped. What was the point? He was a battle shirker. He didn't want to fight. He wasn't worth his sword. All that he had strived for, since his boyhood, had come to nothing. He tried to urge himself on, to remind himself it was only one campaign, and one different to all others. But his fighting will was lost.

After a few days he saddled up Mayda and rode out, up into the hills at the end of the valley. The shepherds had started moving the flocks down from the summer pastures and extra hands were welcome. Being out in the hills brought him relief. The heather-covered uplands smelled of honey and though the early mornings brought a tang of autumnal cold, the air was still summer-mild. The summits of the hills stretched away beyond the valley into an endless indigo distance, immense and indifferent. At night he slept with the shepherds on the hillside.

On the last night of August he sat up late after his companions had fallen asleep. It was a still night and a slight shaving of a new moon hung pale-gold between the hills. The sheep had settled, and a profound silence possessed the valley. Far away the stars lit the vast darkness of the skies. As he watched, a sudden silent trail of light rushed through the darkness and was extinguished. A few minutes later, another followed. The August star-bursts, he realised. The souls of the saints entering eternity, Kenswith had said. For a long while nothing moved. Then suddenly there was another, a star of dazzling brightness piercing the silent darkness, leaving a glittering wake that seemed to hang in the sky. A great saint, he thought. A starry soul. His father had told him that Aidan was close to death. Was his the soul that shone so bright?

The skies grew still, and he reached for his blanket. As he settled himself down for sleep, a memory came to him. He remembered how he had stood on the hill above the Tweed before he left for war, looking down at the monastery. Aidan's monastery. If Aidan were not close to death, or dead, he would have gone to see him, he thought suddenly. Would have asked him, what he should do, now that everything he had lived for seemed to have come to nothing.

Perhaps he should ask one of Aidan's monks. Tomorrow, he thought, I will ride down to the monastery. When he heard the thought in himself he was surprised. His heart lightened. He would do it. He turned over and went to sleep.

Towards the evening of the following day he found himself in front of the earth wall he had seen from the hillside. There was an iron-studded timber gate set in it, too high for him to see over. He sat on Mayda, uncertain what he should do, letting his spear rest on the ground. A shutter slid back to reveal an aperture in the gate. He saw two eyes looking at him. A few moments later the door was pulled slowly open. Two servants stood at one side, and a monk came towards him. He put a hand on Mayda's flank and looked up. He was not a young man, Cuthbert saw. His head was tonsured, and the strip of hair remaining was white. But his face was full of warmth and friendliness.

"God be with you!" he said. "My name is Boisil. Welcome to Melrose." His accent sounded Irish. Perhaps he had come from Iona with Aidan.

"I'm the prior here. Do you know, I just happened to be passing the gate, when one of the servants called out to me that we had a visitor. Look, our brother here will take your horse." He waited while Cuthbert dismounted and Mayda was led away. "We'll go over to the guest-house and see if they've got some food for you. A drink too, I should think, it's a warm afternoon for riding. Look, here we are now, the brothers will take care of you, and when you're ready we'll show you round. Show you what we get up to here."

He gave Cuthbert's arm a little pat and was gone. Cuthbert looked after him. It wasn't what he had imagined. The guest-house stood outside the monastery; he hadn't even got inside. Boisil had gone away before he could talk to him. But he was thirsty, and hungry too. He would have something to eat before he tried again.

The guest-house, he learned from the young monk who brought his ale, was for lay people. Only the monks and novices were allowed within the enclosure. Cuthbert looked at the monk. He was hardly older than himself, but he wasn't weather-tanned and ebullient like Cuthbert's friends. His face was pale and there was a gravity about him that Cuthbert found disconcerting. This wasn't who he wanted to talk to.

"Can I talk to the prior?" he asked. The young monk nodded.

But when Boisil came and found him he was tongue-tied. How could he explain what he wanted when he hardly knew himself?

"My foster mother told me I was sworn to God."

Why had he said that? It wasn't what he had meant to say. But Boisil didn't seem surprised.

"And you want to find out what that means."

Cuthbert stared at him, dumb.

"Why don't you join us for a few days? Come along to the offices, see how you get on."

"But I don't know the words."

"No, no, but you can listen! You'll pick it up. The abbot will be back in a day or two, he'll have a talk with you."

He stayed on in the guest-house. At dawn every morning a novice opened the monastery gate for him and he went to the small church in the middle of the enclosure. He stood with the monks and listened to the offices, to the constant recitation of psalms and prayers and scriptures. They started to fill his mind. Sometimes the writer of the psalms seemed like the voice of his own soul, crying out to God, a man like himself who fought and lost and knew anguish and despair. The words were a solace to him. At night they moved in and out of his dreams.

During the day he helped with the work around the place, hewing timber into planks for a new hut and digging over the vegetable plots that had been harvested. The monks worked too, but they seemed to be always starting and stopping to go to another service.

At the end of the week the abbot returned. Cuthbert watched him as he took his place at the front of the church. He was called Eata, he learned from the young monk at the guest-house. Eata was about ten years older than himself, Cuthbert decided. And English. He was a straight-backed, well-built man, strong enough to have been a warrior and stood in the shield wall. What had made him turn away from that life? Why was he a monk?

A few days later the abbot came and found him in the guest-house.

"How are you finding the monastery?" he asked, and they talked together for a while. Abbot Eata was pleasant but without Boisil's ready warmth. He was more detached. Watchful. Cuthbert felt himself observed.

"You were on the campaign in Deira?" Eata asked. Cuthbert nodded.

"My father gave me to the church when I was a boy", Eata told him. "I used to spend all day wishing I could be a warrior instead of singing psalms. I wanted to be a great hero and have men sing tales of my battles." He laughed. "It's not so simple, is it?"

Cuthbert flushed. Did Eata think he was a child? But the abbot spoke on.

"I'm grateful for it now. To have been under Aidan's care. Father Aidan was a great man. A saint. Worldly things—riches, honour, position— meant nothing to him. He was free. Utterly free." He paused, and Cuthbert saw that tears stood in his eyes.

"He is with Christ now. We buried him at his church in Bamburgh, as he wanted. Close to the people." There was a long silence. Eata turned to Cuthbert and put his hand on Cuthbert's shoulder. "Boisil told me that you arrived here the day after Aidan's soul entered heaven." He paused. "He thinks Father Aidan sent you." He smiled at Cuthbert, his hand still on his shoulder. Then he turned and walked away before Cuthbert could ask any more.

The day after his conversation with Eata, Cuthbert was suddenly angry. What does he mean, Aidan sent me? How could that be? Why should he, Cuthbert, give up possession and position because Aidan chose to? Eata was wrong if he thought he had come to the monastery with the intention of giving up his old life. He would leave in the morning.

But next morning he found that actually he didn't want to leave. Not yet. He passed through the monastery gate and went to matins.

He went on thinking about Eata's words. What would it mean, giving up the world? As his anger faded, he found the idea no longer dismayed him. What did he care about possessing things? On the campaign the idea of plunder had disgusted him. He had never wanted to fight for gain. He wanted to fight for honour. Could he win a different honour here, where a man's heart did not have to turn to stone?

He thought of Kenswith too. He had set his face against her counsel once. Should he not heed her now? But what would his father say? His friends? He reminded himself of all he would lose. But he could think only of freedom, the freedom Eata said that Aidan possessed. More than anything, he wanted that. Freedom from his own confusion and doubt and unhappiness. Beyond the turmoil of thoughts in his mind, he felt himself starting to be borne along by a current too strong to resist. It half-frightened him, yet he felt a constant undertow of excitement too.

A week later, at his own request, he stood in the abbot's room. This time Eata spoke to him more formally.

"Do you want to serve God with us here?"

The question made his heart beat wildly. Under the abbot's gaze he searched in himself for his answer.

"Yes."

"This life is not for all men. Stay with us for a few more weeks. If you feel certain, then you'll start as a novice for a year, before you take any vows."

He smiled, and Cuthbert felt his kindness. He saw that the abbot would not fail him. Eata held out his hands to Cuthbert.

"May God make it easy for you."

EXPIATION: THE FOUNDING
OF GILLING ABBEY

*At the place where King Oswine [Selwin] had been killed, Gilling,
his kinswoman Queen Enfleda in expiation for his unjust death,
petitioned King Oswy to grant God's servant Trumhere, who was
also a near relation of the king, land on which to build a monastery.
In this way prayer could be offered for the eternal salvation of both
kings, slayer and slain alike.*

Bede: **Ecclesiastical History,** *Ch. 24*

CHAPTER 9

THE NOVICE

651 AD

*For the good that I would I do not: but the
evil which I would not, that I do.*

Romans 7:19

Life in the monastery was a new world to him. Everything was strange. The services started before dawn and were repeated again and again. He no sooner got involved in work than the bell was ringing again, he must down tools and stand through another hour, trying to learn the unfamiliar words of the liturgy, stumbling through the prayers and responses, listening to yet more scripture. He started to learn the psalms, the songs of devotion that were to become his most intimate thought patterns. He was taught prayers to say, constantly calling on Christ to have mercy on him. There was no room to think about his old life, which nevertheless visited him in strange vivid fragments of memory, of riding down the road to Catterick, or shouting uproariously, full of mead, at his father's feasts. There was no mead here, or wine. They drank small ale or water. He learned to fast and learned the loosening of the physical world that hunger brought.

At this time, while the life was still strange, ordinary moments became unpredictably luminous for him. The dawn stumble across the cold-dewed grass to the church or the silver arc of a salmon leaping from the Tweed, the faces of his brothers or a phrase in a psalm, would suddenly seem imbued with radiance. There was a different movement of life here, an interior pulse that moved through the monastery, the new life of Christ that had overflowed from the mother house at Lindisfarne out here to the hills. All of them, the monks, the novices, the lay servants, felt its movement even in the ordinary tensions of daily life. He found himself in a brotherhood, as close as warriors but fighting to a different end.

Nevertheless, the unfamiliar inactivity of the routine made him restless. He longed for wildness, for swordplay, to go hunting all day in the forest. He missed the girls looking up from their stitching as he passed. He longed for the gold rings he used to wear on his strong brown arms. He experienced the longings as a condition of his new life, to be endured, and it did not occur to him to doubt his vocation. But the conflict in himself bewildered him. How could he want it, and yet not want it? He watched the abbot. He was alert, kindly, always vigilant. He attended all the offices and worked alongside his brothers, encouraging and counselling, but it seemed to cost him no effort. He was at ease. It was like watching a master swordsman, who could make his weapon move like fire, weightless, slicing through a silken thread. Now he, Cuthbert, was like the clumsiest boy, unable to hold a weapon without dropping it. He was a novice, stripped of his familiar powers. He tried to subdue himself, taking on the heaviest tasks, ploughing, lifting timber for building, working till he was exhausted.

"Just give up," Eata urged him. "Let God direct you."

He learned that Eata had been one of twelve boys chosen by Aidan to be trained as English monks, so that they could take Christ's words to the people in their own tongue. The boys had grown up learning the scriptures by heart, so used to the religious life that it seemed as normal as breathing to them. No wonder it seemed so easy for Eata. He spoke three languages; English, Irish-Gaelic and Latin and could read and write in Latin and English. He was the first of the twelve to become an abbot, entrusted by Aidan with the foundation of a new monastery.

Cuthbert felt an immeasurable distance stretching between them. It seemed impossible that he would ever have such mastery. The other novices felt the distance too, he saw, and they were good-humoured together, tolerant of each other's failings in the face of their stumbling progress in their new world. He shared a hut with two other novices. One, Tondhere, was hardly more than a boy, brought to the monastery by his father to be educated. Garth was a few years older, a rough working man who had found himself called to the monastic life. He had entered the monastery a few months earlier and was struggling with the constant round of offices.

"It's not for me. I want to be here, but that's not for me. I want to be outside. Doing something. Not all that chanting."

He would become a lay brother when his year's novitiate was done, he told Cuthbert. His special loathing was reserved for Latin. He would sit in Latin classes, clumsily holding the stylus in his big hand, grumbling at Prior Boisil.

"Why, Father?" he would complain. "We can learn the prayers by heart, like we do now. Why Latin? Why writing"?

Boisil's old face would wrinkle into smiles. "Do you think Christ's religion is just for you? What about the Franks? The Jutes? The Irish? We must have one tongue. Latin is for everyone. Christians learn Latin."

They would all sigh and scrape away at their slates, groaning at the strange words to tease Boisil. He had left Iona with Aidan to bring Christ's word to Northumbria. He still struggled with English and used Gaelic words when he couldn't find English ones. The novices respected the abbot wholeheartedly, but they loved their prior. He was a holy man, given over to the other world, and full of affection. When he read the gospels in church his face was luminous with joy. He could be heard singing psalms to himself at every hour of the day. He was a healer, and the sick came to him from great distances.

After a time, the abbot gave orders for Cuthbert to help Boisil during the afternoon work period. Instead of physical labour, he had to help with his patients. He saw all the complaints—the skin eruptions, the bilious attacks, the palsies, people possessed by evil spirits. He had not known there was so much suffering in the world. He watched Boisil, learned to make up infusions and poultices, held damaged limbs straight for binding, dug out beds for the physic garden, planted and gathered.

"God has given us plants for healing, so we use them," Boisil told him. "But not herbs alone. The healer is He who made the herbs."

He would call Cuthbert to stand with him as he listened to a patient, asked questions, felt pulses.

"Now you."

At first Cuthbert was at a loss. He would talk again to the patient, or say a prayer with them, but knew it had no effect. He watched Boisil more closely. The old man would put a hand on a shoulder, on a head, and stand quite still. It was impossible to say what he was doing, but a change would come about in the patient.

"Just do it," he encouraged him. Cuthbert tried. Did he feel for a moment a fleeting connection between himself and the patient? He could hardly say.

At other times Boisil recited from scripture, a story of one of Christ's miracles. Cuthbert had to learn it, repeat it till he was word perfect. "You will be a healer," Boisil told him. Cuthbert shook his head.

As the months and seasons of the novitiate passed, he settled into the rhythm of monastic life. The words of the psalms and intercessions came to his lips without thought. He woke from sleep in the darkness of the night and knew he must rise. He sat with his brothers at table, day after day, eating his bread and beans in silence while the scriptures were read. In the fields, the long rhythm of the farming work, threshing and winnowing, ploughing and sowing, formed a more ancient counterpoint to the Rule. He learned to do women's work, making cheese, baking bread. He saw that his brothers were finding ways of accommodating themselves to their new life. Tondhere loved to sit and whittle away at a stick and spent his work time carving and working wood. Garth had been given the task of overseeing the vegetable garden and took pride in his rows of leeks and cabbages. They had given themselves up to serve God, but as they settled, Cuthbert saw that they were finding an identity within the monastic life that gave them ease.

He knew no such ease. He was at war with himself. He had discovered a renegade in his soul, who had little regard for the monastic life and still hungered for honour, wealth and riot. The renegade could remove himself from the chanting of the office altogether, in a daydream of old friends and hunting days. He could spend a fast day docile and silent, only to assail the novice all night with reproaches for weakening his body and destroying his strength. He would seethe with restlessness and boredom during the long silent meals, wanting to leap onto the table. He dreamed of women with laughing eyes and yearned to hold them close. The renegade was a shape-shifter, letting Cuthbert imagine he was defeated, before slipping out in new forms.

He was hungry for penance, but Abbot Eata listened to his confessions without judgement or surprise. "It's not intentional sin," Eata said. "You don't have these thoughts deliberately. Christ himself suffered temptation from the devil." He leaned towards him. "Be patient. You can't change yourself overnight. Ask for grace."

Although he was strong enough to excel at any task, the work did not engage him. The intensity of his nature that, in his worldly life, had made him constantly strive for perfection as a warrior and swordsman, now drove his spiritual life. He wanted more. He wanted perfection of himself. When the monastery was fasting, he would start his fast sooner and prolong it. He would rise in the night before the offices and spend hours in solitary vigil. He pushed himself to work harder and longer at every task.

As the novitiate went on and the brothers became familiar with each other's failings, they would sometimes squabble with each other over a bad-tempered comment or a task shirked. Cuthbert took no part in the arguments. He felt no judgement towards his brothers. His own inner transgressions seemed far worse to him. Nevertheless, a distance started to open between him and his brothers, hardly noticed. At last Abbot Eata spoke to him.

"Your brothers are finding you exhausting. They feel you are trying to be more righteous than them."

He stared at the abbot. "Trying to be more righteous?" The accusation was astonishing to him.

"Yes. You fast for longer, work for longer. They resent it. They feel they are doing their best, but you always go one further."

"It's only for myself I do it."

"Yes. But your brothers are as important as yourself. This is the novitiate. You must all move together. Do what is required of you. That is what obedience means."

He was cut to the quick by the injustice of it. There was a pause. "Yes, Father."

"Good." As Cuthbert turned to go, Eata said, "Your striving is a God-given gift. You are blessed in it. But we must also love our neighbour as ourselves."

He was plunged into a new bewilderment. Did loving his neighbour mean sharing their sins? After the conversation with Eata he was filled with resentment of his brothers and their gossiping and criticising. Not love. He watched Boisil at his infirmary, saw his tenderness as he listened to a sick child or bound a poultice on a wheezing chest. His love was palpable. For sure, Boisil loved his neighbour. It was as natural to him as his breath. Why did he find it such a struggle? He had spent his life with friends, family, neighbours; had been loved and accepted. Now he found himself an outsider.

"You should find someone else to work with you," he told Boisil at last. "I'm no good with people."

Boisil laughed. "What has put that into your head?"

"It's true. Nobody likes me."

Boisil came over to him. "My dear son," he said. He paused for a moment. "Who is this 'nobody'?"

"The other novices. They think . . . the abbot says, they think . . . "

"Why do you worry what they think? It doesn't matter what they think. Look more deeply." He waited. "You know that Christ forgave even his tormenters. He saw they had no understanding of Him, so He pitied them. Perhaps your brothers don't understand you."

"Why? I hide nothing." But as he spoke, he knew he did. He hid the renegade so well his brothers didn't suspect its existence.

"Look deeply," said Boisil again. "Try and understand how they feel. Then your anger will go."

Taking Cuthbert's arm, Boisil took him over to a cupboard at the back of the room. "Come and see what an old woman brought for me today." He pulled out a round dish. In it was a honeycomb, full of heather-rich dark honey. "Smell that."

Cuthbert smelled the fragrant flowery sweetness of it, like the hills on an August day. In spite of the turmoil within himself, he smiled. "Mmm."

"Here—sit down. I want to try it."

They sat together on the bench. Boisil took the knife from his belt, cut out a chunk of comb and picked it up on the end of the knife. Gold syrupy strands dripped from it. "Quick," said Boisil, holding the knife towards him. Cuthbert opened his mouth and took the honeycomb, licking his tongue round his lips. The intense sweetness filled his mouth. Boisil cut a piece for himself, and they sat together sucking the last drops of sweetness from the comb, till there was only the fine wax of it left to roll round on the tongue. Sitting there, beside Boisil, sucking honeycomb, Cuthbert felt suddenly light-hearted.

"Out of the eater came forth meat; out of the strong came forth sweetness," quoted Boisil. Cuthbert stared at him. "It's a riddle. Samson's riddle. None of the Philistines could guess it. No, no"—he saw Cuthbert's brow creasing with concentration—"don't try and solve it now. Just keep it in your mind."

Eata and Boisil were conspiring against him, he decided. A few weeks after his conversation with Boisil he was made responsible for the guest-house, where he had stayed when he first came to the monastery. It was a small hall that stood outside the monastic compound in a pleasant sheltered area. There was a hearth in the centre where the guests' meals were cooked, a couple of tables, and sleeping benches round the sides. It was as plain as the monks' own cells, except for the fire. Guests had warm nights.

Until he started his new duty, Cuthbert had hardly been aware of the guests who came to stay at the monastery. He noticed when visiting monks joined them for the offices, but other guests were not invited within the monastic precinct. Now he knew of every arrival. One of the lay brothers would come and get him. He had to leave whatever he was doing at once, brush down his habit and compose himself, before passing through the gate into the outer world. The monastery had many guests, he discovered. Sometimes other monks would come to visit, from Lindisfarne or Tynemouth or even faraway Iona. More often it was lay people. Men came wanting land, to ask if the brothers had a hide or two to spare in exchange for a tithing of barley. Others came for counsel from Eata or Boisil, about troubles in their family or disputes over an inheritance. Sometimes a straggle-eyed madman would turn up, begging the holy men to cast out his devils. Travellers came, interested only in a bed for the night. The monastery offered hospitality to all of them.

Boisil taught him what to do. His first duty when welcoming guests, he learned, was to wash their feet. Cuthbert was shocked. "We follow Christ's example," Boisil explained to him. "He washed the feet of his disciples, he who was their teacher and the Son of God. How much more should we show humility before the least of our guests. We do as He did."

Boisil took him to the guest-house and showed him where the jug and bowl were kept. "Now—the water. You must warm the water. The servants will make sure stones are kept in the hearth for you. Two hot stones are enough to warm it. So—the water is in the jug, you have a bowl for their feet. Then you need the towel, round your waist, like this. Good. Practice on me."

Boisil sat down on the bench, his feet stuck out in front of him. Cuthbert wanted to laugh. What foolishness this was. But Christ himself had done it, he reminded himself. Awkwardly he took hold of Boisil's boot. It was worn leather, muddy underneath.

"What if I get my hands muddy on the boot?"

"Ease it off at the heel. Don't worry, it'll wash off as you do the foot."

Once the boot was off, he took hold of Boisil's foot. It was white and hairy round the toes. He lifted it into the basin and poured water over it. He looked up at Boisil. "What now?"

"Swill the water round over the foot and rub off any dirt, between the toes as well. Hold the foot carefully. As if it were a treasure you were cleaning. Good. Now the towel."

Cuthbert felt for the towel round his waist and laid it over his knee. He lifted the foot out and water splashed over Boisil's legs.

"Gently."

He dried the foot and tried to shove it back into the boot. It was surprisingly difficult to put someone else's boot on.

"Our Lord's disciples had sandals. Easier than boots."

He turned to the next foot. At last it was done. He straightened up in relief. "Good," said Boisil. "You're ready."

He started to get to know people by their feet. Tough brown feet that went unshod, calloused feet, feet swollen with arthritis, soft feet, stinking feet. He washed them all. Sometimes he was revolted. But other times he felt an unexpected affection for the foot lying vulnerable in his lap.

Sometimes the visitors would tell him their troubles as he pulled off their boots and poured warm water over their toes. Their fears. Their failings. He had no idea how to help them. He kept washing and listened. At night he found himself thinking about all he had heard. He started to say prayers for his visitors. During the day he was in and out of the kitchen for fresh bread, for ale, for milk for a child.

"Good!" said Boisil. "You're becoming a guest-master."

CHAPTER 10

A LETTER

653 AD

From Honorius, by God's grace Archbishop of Canterbury and servant of the servants of God in all the provinces and kingdoms of this country, to her royal majesty Enfleda, queen of Bernicia and Deira in the kingdom of Northumbria, greetings in Christ.

Your majesty commended to us your servant Wilfrid, who is desirous of visiting the holy places of Rome and seeing for himself the rites and customs of Pope Martin, in accordance with your majesty's desire to guide your people to the true religion of the successors of St Peter.

Wilfrid has been graciously received by your cousin of Kent, King Arcenbryht, and has been residing in our monastery at Rochester where the Abbot has instructed him further in the beliefs and practices of the Roman Church, which until now he has tasted only from the holy discourse of your majesty. For while the monastery at Lindisfarne, where he has drunk with joy the first draughts of God's wisdom, has like a beacon spread the light of Christ's word to the people of your kingdom, yet it still clings to certain erroneous traditions and practices expounded by the Irish, such as the dating of Easter according to false calculations.

That noble thegn and ardent seeker of knowledge, Biscop Baducing, intends shortly to travel to Rome and has agreed to allow Wilfrid to accompany him. We could not recommend a wiser guide or more trustworthy companion for his pilgrimage. Therefore, most gracious queen, with gratitude and thanksgiving for the gifts you have most generously made on Brother Wilfrid's behalf to permit the undertaking of his journey, we may assure you that they will be most fruitfully expended.

May God preserve your majesties in peace and harmony, and bring prosperity to all your people,

In Christ,
Honorius, Archbishop of Canterbury

CHAPTER 11

THE HERESY OF ANGELS

661 AD

The edge of the blade cut cleanly into the turf, turning up long pale roots of couch grass with spear-like shoots and small bright cups of celandine. The stems left a milky trail on his hands as he shook the earth off the clod. He tossed it onto the pile at the side, then straightened, lifted back the spade and drove it in again. The regular line of dark earth lengthened behind him. A robin hopped close to the spade, darting at the fat worms squirming in the clods. Although the wind was still bitter, there was a cold vigour about the day. The sap was rising and he felt spring in his blood. Their second winter at Ripon was nearly over. Spring came sooner here, in the lowlands of Deira.

He thought of the long winters at Melrose, of the river covered in green ice, the long icicles hanging down from the cliffs by the river, the snow-covered slope of south Eildon. When Eata had invited him to go with him to Ripon, he had talked about *peregrinatio*, about being willing to give up home and all familiar things for Christ. But the only thing that troubled Cuthbert was leaving Boisil. Through all his time at Melrose Boisil had been a father to him. He had wept when they said goodbye. It might be years before he returned to Melrose, and Boisil was an old man. But Boisil only smiled.

"Don't think you're getting away from me," he teased. "I shall know what you're up to."

He had been eight years at Melrose and a monk for seven of them. Melrose had held him in the first years of his vocation, in all his struggle and restlessness. It had given him a deep foundation to build on. But still he wanted more; wanted to push himself harder, further. The new mission, helping to build a new monastery, taking Christ's word where it had not been known before, filled him with inspiration and eagerness. When they came to Ripon, he had done the work of two men, clearing the land and helping build the first cells and buildings. With God's grace, nothing was too much for him. Once the guest-house was completed, he became its first master, welcoming their new guests and visitors through its doors.

Absorbed in his work, he didn't notice the first cry. Garth shouted louder. He straightened, shading his eyes, and saw his brother standing outside the monastery, pointing to the river. Cuthbert turned and looked along the path to the Skell. A party of horsemen were fording the river. It was running fast after the spring rain and the horses were picking their way across slowly, the water halfway up their hocks. It was too far to see who they might be; in any case, they were not expecting guests. He tried to count. Four, maybe five. He leant down, pulled a handful of grass and wiped down his spade, then waved to show Garth he was coming.

By the time the visitors were dismounted and the horses led away, he had the guest-house ready. As the men entered he clasped their hands and spoke the blessing. Standing in the doorway they blocked the light so he couldn't see their faces clearly. But even in the shadow he could see the colours of the cloth they were wearing, the glint of silver buckles on their belts. He gestured for them to sit on the benches and knelt before the first man to help him pull off his boots. He felt a small moment of surprise. He hadn't seen such boots before. They were made of a dark, stiff leather that didn't look like cowhide, and the surface was stamped with intricate patterns of silver. In spite of their recent soaking in the river, they showed no signs of mud or dirt. Cuthbert recalled his attention to his task, cupped the heel of the left boot in his hand and eased it off. It slid off its owner's foot with no resistance; it was a perfect fit. Involuntarily, the guest-master looked up.

He found himself looking at a man of his own age, who was observing him keenly. The visitor's eyes were quick and bright, like an eagle waiting to pounce. Neither spoke. Cuthbert dropped his gaze, reproving his thought, but he couldn't drive the impression away. He removed the other boot and stocking and started to wash the visitor's feet. When he had dried them and was picking up the stockings to put them back on, the guest leant down, and taking them from him, did it himself. Cuthbert saw that his fair hair was cut short but nevertheless curled round the nape of his neck. He moved on to the next man. None of them spoke. By the time he had finished the bell was sounding for Terce. He sent a servant to fetch ale and excused himself. He felt oddly relieved to pull the door of the guest-house shut behind him.

As at Melrose, the guest-house stood outside the inner buildings of the monastery. To reach the church, Cuthbert walked across to the monastery gate, set in an earth bank several feet high which surrounded the monastic compound. The soil was still raw on the banks; it was hardly a year since they had dug them. When they'd arrived from Melrose, their first task had been to complete their cells, simple huts that were quickly built. Next was a hall where they could meet and eat together. Then they had started work on the church. It stood in the centre of the compound; a long building of daub and wattle like the cells, but with oak roof trusses that reached high above the simple walls. The task had been beyond the brothers. They had recruited skilled carpenters to choose timber for the beams and set the frame and worked with them. The building grew into a fine hall, with clear straight lines and a timber cobbled roof. They had a wood carver decorate the two huge uprights at the doorway with figures of Christ and the seven Archangels; Gabriel, Michael, Raphael, Azrael, Salafiel, Uriel and Rumiel. Now, when they sang the offices, they often felt the wings of the angels stirring the air, carrying their praise to God. It was their temple, their holy place, and although they were accustomed now to worship there, their joy in it had not diminished. Cuthbert hastened inside for the office.

After Terce several of the brothers lingered outside the church with the guest-master.

"There are five. A royal alderman, with three men from his household. Then another; a cleric of some Roman order."

"I know him," said one of the brothers, Bertram. They all stared at him.

"From Lindisfarne. He's called Wilfrid. He thought himself too good for Lindisfarne."

Gossip. Malicious gossip. But the abbot was still inside the church, and they all waited for more.

"He was a favourite of the queen's. Her Kentish priest filled his head with talk of Rome. The queen was so taken with him she arranged for him to travel there, so he could learn all the Roman ways. He must have been there for years."

Rome. Cuthbert imagined caparisoned horses clattering down paved streets and the Tiber flowing dark between palaces. This Wilfrid had been there. Had lived there.

"The alderman is from the court. The prince must have sent them."

"They'll want meat."

"Not in Lent." Abbot Eata overheard them as he left the church. He sensed the disturbance.

"This is a monastery, not a mead hall. Let them have what they need of our supper, brother Cuthbert, and plenty of bread. If they've come from York, they'll stay the night. A fire must be lit. Is there fresh linen?"

He gave orders; paused, checked that everything had been remembered. No more discussion. They would do what was necessary and let God take care of what this visit might portend.

Cuthbert stood at the side as the brothers' food was served to the guests. He watched the men at the table. The alderman and his household were absorbed in eating and drinking, tearing at the bread and scooping up the pottage with suppressed contempt. Cuthbert salivated involuntarily, and for a moment the imagined savour of the herbs and beans filled his mouth. At once he called on God to chastise his weakness. He would extend his fast as a penance. Swallowing the rebellious saliva, he returned his attention to his guests. He saw that the priest, Wilfrid, held himself aloof from the company. He used a knife to cut his bread, then held the bread between thumb and fingers and dipped carefully into his bowl, avoiding any drips on his clothing. He ate sparingly, looking round for a finger bowl when he was done. Finding none, he took a piece of linen from his tunic and wiped his hands. He wore a russet-coloured woollen tunic, with a linen shirt beneath, and a fur-lined dark blue cloak over, clasped at the shoulder with a heavy silver buckle. It seemed the warmth of the fire was not enough for him. He paid no attention to the growing rowdiness of his companions. Cuthbert wondered if he was a cold man. Or haughty? He was certainly a young man. His own age, near enough.

When the meal was cleared away, Wilfrid beckoned the guest-master over.

"I took the opportunity before we ate to inspect the church, brother."

Cuthbert waited.

"I noticed the carving at the entrance."

"It was done by Master Tondhere, one of the brothers. He is a fine carver."

"Was the subject matter his choice"?

"Our Lord in glory? Or the Archangels?"

"Is the abbot aware—are you aware—that the Roman Church does not permit reference to angels whose names are not found in the canonical books of the Bible?"

He paused, his intense gaze on the guest-master.

"Michael, Gabriel and Raphael. These are the only Archangels recognised by the Holy See."

Cuthbert laughed out loud.

"The only ones recognised?" It made him laugh again. "Maybe there are things the Holy See is blind to."

The strong features of Wilfrid's face stood out in the firelight. They showed no flicker of amusement.

"Superstition, brother. Worshipping angels. There is no sanction for it in Holy Scripture."

He turned away. "I will sleep now."

The next morning after Matins Cuthbert went to the guest-house with a servant to redd up the hearth and set out bread and curds for their breakfast. It delayed him, and he was late going to the hall for Chapter. But when he entered he saw at once it was not to be Chapter as usual. Brothers were bringing extra benches over, everyone was shuffling round to make room, someone was sweeping the floor. No-one spoke, but he felt the unease in the air. What could these visitors want? Chapter was not for outsiders. Some special permission must have been given. The abbot sat as usual in his chair of office at the end of the room, calm and watchful. Like the other monks he wore a plain habit of undyed wool. He and the brothers made a line of pale brown against the whitewashed walls. There was a deep silence in the hall as the visitors entered, like bright birds from a far country blown ashore by ill weather, dressed in red and green and purple with light glinting from their silver clasps and rings. The abbot gestured to the benches, but they ignored him and remained standing close together. The alderman fumbled beneath his cloak as if ruffling his plumage. At last he pulled out a parchment.

"We are sent by Connal, Prince of Deira, to his monastery at Ripon." He glared round the room for emphasis. Then he unrolled the parchment and read aloud.

> *Connal, Prince of Deira, sends greetings to the brothers at the monastery at Ripon, which land and living was given for the glory of God. Whereas the monastery was founded in the former traditions of the Church in this kingdom, after careful consideration and searching of his conscience, the prince now makes known to you that it is his earnest wish and desire that the usages and practices of his monastery at Ripon be made conformable with the true Catholic Church of Rome, and no longer hold to certain heretical forms and*

> *beliefs concerning the calculation of Easter and Christ's resurrection. To that end he has commanded his beloved priest and counsellor Wilfrid to take up the abbacy of the monastery at Ripon in order that he may convert its practices and lead the brethren to truth. He commands that thenceforth the monastery of Ripon be governed by Wilfrid, and that Eata, first Abbot of Ripon, resign his place accordingly.*

He had got it out. He glanced at Eata. The air was still with shock. Dust motes drifted in the light coming through the casement. Outside, a blackbird sang a spring air from the top of the church. The alderman pressed on.

> *The prince orders and commands that from henceforth the brothers follow the practices and rites of the Holy Catholic Church. They must take instruction from Abbot Wilfrid and make themselves conformable to his will in all matters concerning the monastery, and make the true religion of Christ known throughout the kingdom. This is our order and command sealed this 10th day of Lent in the year of our Lord 660.*

The silence lengthened. At last, Abbot Eata rose.

"My Lord, I am completely amazed. I am at a loss to know in what way our practices can have caused offence to Prince Connal. May I remind you and the prince that I was appointed abbot of the monastery at Ripon by Bishop Finan of Lindisfarne, who was in turn directed by King Oswy. I am astonished that the prince should now propose to set aside an appointment authorised directly by his father."

The alderman looked at his feet.

"Ah . . . the prince . . . that is . . . "

Wilfrid stepped forward. He addressed Eata directly.

"Perhaps concern for your position is a stumbling block, Eata. But what is important about the prince's message goes far beyond concerns for personal position or aggrandisement."

A sigh of indrawn breath came from the benches. A few of the monks half rose from their seats. Wilfrid heard it and turned to face them.

"Brothers, the prince has concern for the good of his subjects. The Gospel was brought to this kingdom by men raised in traditions long separated from Rome. Falsehoods and errors in our understanding have crept in. They need to be corrected in the true light of the Church of Rome, which was appointed by Christ himself."

In spite of his effrontery, there was something compelling about him. He had undeniable presence; his voice was eloquent and assured, and he gestured with his arms and hands as he spoke. Like a Frank.

"Prince Connal desires this monastery to be a light to all the kingdom. I will establish here the monastic tradition of Saint Benedict approved by the Pope. Any of you who wish to remain will have the joy of serving God according to truth."

The sighs turned into hostile muttering. Wilfrid ignored it.

"The prince will endow a more suitable church to the glory of God, a basilica of stone and glass in the Roman style . . . ."

Fearing an outburst from the brothers, Abbot Eata interrupted him.

"Father Wilfrid, it is past time for the office. I will return afterwards to confer with you further."

He bowed, then turned to the monks.

"Brothers."

They rose as one and pressed in closely as they left the hall, as if to form a shield around him.

After they had said the office together, Eata spoke directly to the brothers before they left the church.

"What we have heard this morning has shocked us all. I can't say yet what will happen. A storm has come suddenly upon us, and we must hold strongly to our faith as Christ has taught us. Don't let your hearts be troubled, and don't let anger take hold of you. Remember that nothing can separate us from the love of Christ."

No-one moved or spoke.

"Work!" he chided them. "Carry on with your tasks as normal."

They filed out in silence. As Cuthbert was leaving, Eata drew him aside. They went back into the church.

"We must send word to Lindisfarne," Cuthbert said. "The prince has gone mad."

Eata sat down on a bench, his face white.

"No. Not mad, but wilful. This Wilfrid—this business with the Roman Church—it's a way to oppose his father."

"The king? Why?"

"Connal is young. He wants to set his own stamp on Deira. And clearly Wilfrid is very persuasive."

"He can't oppose an appointment the bishop himself has made. The land was given to the Church."

"We'll see. The bishop won't want conflict with the prince. It could cause more trouble between Connal and the king."

Cuthbert thought suddenly of the Deiran campaign, of the youth Connal was then, like himself on his first campaign. He remembered him riding behind his father like a dark shadow—black-haired, moody, no smile on his face.

"We'll see what the bishop chooses to do, but for now, we've got no choice. It is not our place to oppose this." He looked up at Cuthbert.

"I've got to go. There's no doubt about that. But the rest of the brothers can make their own choice. You can make your own choice."

He saw the shock on Cuthbert's face and smiled.

"Don't worry. It's a lesson, about the ways of the world. Go back to the guest-house. Find out what they mean to do. I don't think our pottage will tempt them to stay."

There was no sign of the alderman and his companions when he reached the guest-house. Wilfrid sat alone at the table reading. When he saw Cuthbert, he rose at once, closing his book.

"I would like to know your intentions, guest-master."

For a moment, Cuthbert recognised his own intensity in him.

"Intentions?"

"I want you to stay. You're young. I can see you have a strong spirit."

Cuthbert was silent.

"Were you a warrior?"

"Yes."

"A nobleman?"

He shrugged.

"No—it's important. The Church needs people of power and influence. How else can we build Christ's Church on earth? The Church must be strong. Must be powerful."

He leant forward, looking directly into Cuthbert's eyes, as if searching for his soul.

"You are guest-master now, brother. If you stay in Ripon, I will make you my prior. We'll travel to Rome together. I'll show you the magnificence of the true Church."

Cuthbert was astonished. A sudden image of riding through Italian fields under a hot sun possessed him. He saw the distant skyline of the Holy City rising before his eyes with high towers and domes shining with gold.

He shook the vision from his head. A sudden anger flared in its place.

"Why are you doing this? Why don't you found a new monastery instead of taking this one? Isn't there enough space in Deira for you?"

"No man puts new wine into old bottles; else the new wine will burst the bottles, and be spilled, and the bottles shall perish," Wilfrid quoted. "The old ways have got to go, go altogether. Deira is a backwater. Believe me. It has to change. Of course Abbot Eata is a good man—a holy man even—but he is set in his ways. He'll never accept change. But you—you're young still. We are of an age. You have your vocation ahead of you. You can't let old allegiances get in the way."

He leant forward again and clasped Cuthbert's hands in his, gripping them for emphasis as he spoke.

"I didn't expect this either, you know. When Prince Connal sent for me, I was at the court of the West Saxons. I had no thought of returning to Northumbria. But when I met Prince Connal, I understood what God meant for us. It was as if I could see into his heart and he into mine. Our souls are twined together like David and Jonathan, and he has sent me out to do battle, as David did against the Philistines, for Christ's true Church."

Cuthbert was too amazed to respond. He tried to withdraw his hands, but Wilfrid clasped them tightly.

"You are a warrior too. Join us, brother."

There was a moment like slack water, the equal and opposite forces held still between them. Then the tide turned within him, and his heart was suddenly eased. He took his hands from Wilfrid.

"No."

A long pause. Wilfrid shrugged and turned away. He drew his book out again and started to read.

"May we know how long you and your companions plan to stay?"

"They have left already. I will stay."

CHAPTER 12

IN A TIME OF SICKNESS

661 AD

Wilfrid had shown no emotion when they left. Not a single monk remained to serve him as abbot. Did he say the Mass alone with the angels in their church? Would he send to Frankia for his monks? Or would he, like Aidan, train up his own English boys as servants of God? Cuthbert pushed away the thoughts. He recited psalms and sang hymns with his brothers as they retreated. But it was a wretched journey. It rained, day after day. They tramped onwards through the mud with sodden habits and wet boots, heads bowed against the weather. There was nothing to distract them from bitter thoughts. At night they looked for shelter in the farmsteads and settlements along the way, eager for a warm hearth to dry out their clothes.

"You can come in if you please," a farmer said to Cuthbert one night. "But you'll not want to stop." He looked into the hut. Lying on blankets on the far side of the hearth was a child. In the firelight Cuthbert could see the red sweating face and limp body, his mother leaning over him to bathe his limbs in cold water.

"He's taken the sickness," his father said. "God knows if he'll last the night."

Cuthbert and his companion muttered condolences and drew back into the night. "Is it the plague?" his companion asked.

"Perhaps. I don't know."

But as they travelled further north, they found every settlement struck with the sickness and saw the same fever. As they drew close to Melrose, they passed a small group following a cart to the cemetery. Cuthbert felt a premonition of death. Whether his or another, he could not tell. In the dread that entered him, all thoughts of Ripon, of Wilfrid, were gone.

Within days of entering the gates of the monastery the infection started. A deathly chill spread through his body, through his very bones. It felt as though rigor mortis had already begun. In the evening of the same day, it turned to fever. His body burned and sweat ran from him copiously, soaking his clothes. He could no longer stand upright, and his brothers laid him on a straw pallet beside other plague-struck men in the infirmary. Terrible hallucinations afflicted him; he saw his father's hall burning, and the clothes of all the people inside flaming with an unquenchable fire. The flames burst through the sides of the infirmary so that he too was set alight, feeling his head and body scalding. He cried aloud for water, but no matter how much they poured on him, he could feel no coolness. It was like a torment of hell. Suppurating boils erupted in his groin, behind his knees and in his armpits. At last the fever reached its crisis, its fiercest onslaught when it seemed impossible he could endure the suffering and live. But slowly, slowly it abated. When he returned to himself, he saw the scarring from the boils on his body, the vestiges of the sickness that had swept through him. All his strength had gone; he was utterly weak. He saw the anxious face of one of his brothers peering down at him, and he tried to speak.

"We are all praying for you," his brother said. A shock passed through him. He knew their faith had saved him. "Help me up," he said. He staggered to his feet and leaning on his brother, went outside into the daylight, into the precious living world, alive. Weak as he was, he felt he had been reborn.

"Where is Boisil?" he asked when he could move again. No-one replied. "Has he taken the sickness?"

He found Boisil lying, not in the infirmary, but in his hut. When he saw him, Boisil stretched out his arms to embrace him.

"What strength God has given you!"

"But you, Father . . . "

"Now you have survived, it will never trouble you again."

"You'll recover too, as I have."

Boisil shook his head. "Don't fear. I'm ready."

"Not yet."

"A few more days. Sit with me."

As the wild cherries on the riverbank blossomed, he sat at Boisil's side in his hut, the casement open to the spring air. Boisil suffered bout after bout of fever, each one leaving him weaker than before. He had intervals of lucidity and had Cuthbert read to him from a commentary on St John, a passage at a time. He could scarcely speak, but Cuthbert knew he was still teaching him. By the seventh day his body was almost wasted away. Only a little life still flickered in his eyes, till with a sudden flash of light he half sat up and tried to speak.

"I want to tell you of what you will become . . . " The words fluttered and fell away into silence. When he fell back, Cuthbert wiped his forehead for the last time and closed his eyes.

He laid Boisil's body in the stern of the boat, straightening the shroud and propping his head against the side planks. Turning back onto the bench he picked up the oars and nodded to the waiting men to push him out onto the stream. Eata stood with the watching men—brothers, servants, lay people, anyone well enough to come and make their farewells. Cuthbert leaned into the oars and started to pull downstream. He was still weak, but the dark current of the river soon bore them away. It would hardly take an hour.

As he rounded the bend in the river, he saw the flat haugh ahead and started to pull the boat across the current to land. The boat drifted for a few moments before grounding in the shallows. He shipped the oars, stepped out and pulled the boat up. He stood for a moment, letting the pain lessen in his groin. The sickness had left him with a hard swelling as a reminder of his suffering. Of God's mercy in sparing him. He leaned into the stern, sliding Boisil's body onto his arms and lifting him out. The body felt as light as a child's. He carried it across the haugh to the rough steps cut in the bank, up to a small cell built of wattle and daub and roofed with reeds. Boisil's retreat cell. It was where he wanted to be laid to rest. Where he had been alone with God. Cuthbert laid the body down on the grass beside the church and straightened up to get his breath.

He looked down at the river flowing beneath him. The willow trees on the banks were coming into leaf. Ducks and coots worked in and out of the roots reaching down into the water. An eagle hung in the air above, watching for salmon running. In the freshness of the morning it was hard to believe there had been so much death. So much loss. He glanced at the shrouded body, half expecting Boisil to speak, to exclaim with delight at the loveliness of the day. God willing his joy was perfect now.

Cuthbert dug out a deep grave beside the hut. He was weak still and had to rest often. When it was done, he laid Boisil in it and said the prayers for the dead. Later, when the plague was past, he would return with others and lay a proper gravestone over it. For now, he marked out the grave with river stones, making a low wall around it, and set a larger stone as a headstone. When all was done, he was exhausted. He lay down on the floor of the cell and fell asleep.

When he woke next day, the sun was already high in the sky and he was famished. He walked over to the burn that ran down into the river, dipped in the bread he had brought and devoured it. He drank deeply and splashed water over his head. He felt Boisil's presence close and strong. It would be a place of healing, he thought. People would come here. They would wash in the waters of the burn and lay their sickness and their sorrow before the saint. He had loved them all his life. How would he not still love them in death?

Eata had been unscathed by the sickness, but many had suffered. It would take time for the monastery to recover. They had buried seven of their brothers as well as Boisil, and many of the lay families who farmed the monastery land had suffered as badly. Land lay unsown, and children had to do the work of men. A hard year lay ahead. Eata made Cuthbert prior in Boisil's place. There was much to be done in the monastery, but his first task had to be further afield.

"No-one is coming to the monastery now," Eata said. "The plague has made them doubt God. People are turning back to the old ways. You must go out to them."

Cuthbert set out on preaching journeys in the surrounding country, as Boisil had done before him. Uncertain at first, what he saw in the valleys and hillsides soon drove him on. The servants dreaded being asked to accompany him. He would travel to the most remote villages, where there was hardly a crust to eat and only flea-ridden straw to sleep on. He didn't care. Pity filled him at the suffering and pain he saw. For the first time he started to teach and counsel and found that it came easily to him. He started to be spoken of, and when he arrived in a hamlet, folk came out to greet him, and called their families. He was gentle with them and didn't rebuke them for the amulets and totems that he saw. He told them stories of the miracles Christ had performed and of how he himself had been saved from death by the faith of his brothers. If their faith wasn't strong enough to work miracles, they could be certain that Christ was with them in all their suffering. Had Christ as a man not known the terrible anguish of death on the cross? Had he not known how it felt to be alone and abandoned by everyone? He would be with them, whatever happened. His love would never fail them. He blessed the children that were brought to him, prayed over the sick in Christ's name, listened to the grieving. He felt Boisil constantly at his side.

He felt another presence too, on the long journeys through the valleys. In spite of himself, he thought of Wilfrid. The thought always aroused the same emotions. There was a still-lingering aftershock from their expulsion from Ripon, of the anger and bitterness it had brought about in him. But beyond that was a kind of fascination. Wilfrid's certainty, his intensity, found an echo in his own soul. What if he had accepted Wilfrid's invitation? What if he were riding with him now, not along these rain-streaming valleys but through the streets of the imperial city? What might he have seen, what might he have known? As soon as he discovered such thoughts in himself, he would shake them off and say a prayer. He had seen Wilfrid to be arrogant and humourless, he reminded himself. And ruthless in his actions. How could he be drawn to such a man?

They heard little of what was happening at Ripon. Empty as it was, the plague had not touched it. It seemed a few monks had been brought in, and builders from overseas. No doubt they would have taken down the carvings of the angels long ago. At least, he thought, the monastery continued. Christ's teaching would be witnessed. What else mattered?

CHAPTER 13

ANIEL

663 AD

Two years after the start of his preaching journeys, a messenger came with a request from one of the Pictish kingdoms of the north, the Niduari. He savoured the strange supple sound of the word. Sometimes Pictish people used to come down into the Leader Valley to trade, painted men on tough little ponies with bales of patterned cloth. But he had never been to the land of the Picts. The prior at Lindisfarne had declined the invitation; no-one could be spared. Who would want to travel on winter seas? And miss the Christmas feast? But Cuthbert felt an immediate impulse to accept. The Niduari were newly converted to Christianity, and they wanted a preacher to teach them the prayers and rituals suitable to the season.

"I'll go," he told Eata.

"Yes," said Eata. "But you might have trouble finding anyone to go with you."

A month later he was at Cramond with two reluctant servants as his companions. Their ships were tied up at the old Roman jetty, waiting for the tide to turn and carry them down the firth, out into the open sea. He had stood on the top of Soutra often enough as a boy, staring down at the wide blue waters of the firth. But he had never come close to the rocking restless swell, had never sailed out on the ocean. Although the wind was bitter and his face nipped with cold, he felt exhilarated. New lands. New people. He prayed God to bless them in it.

Gartnait mac Dungail's fortress at Muickross stood on sloping land above the shore where they beached their ships. High stone walls wide enough for a man to walk on surrounded it; not cut and mortared stone, like the walls the Romans left behind, but round black stones fitted close together. The settlement was enclosed within. Like the walls, the windowless huts were made of stone with overhanging thatch and low doors. But Gartnait's hall was built of wood, with a high entrance flanked with massive door posts carved with pagan patterns and symbols and painted with bright red and ochre. Inside, the hearth fires burned aromatic wood and herbs that filled the air with smoky fragrance. Cuthbert found himself bewildered, with the strange Pictish tongue spoken all around him. The men had blue patterns cut into their skin and face and dark hair and beards. Pictland was another country.

Each day, he was summoned from the guest-house to preach to the king and his court. Gartnait sat on his royal chair with his queen beside him and their daughter, while his household stood around him. His translator, Talorcan, was a dark Pictish man, as small as Cuthbert was tall, who spoke English with a lilting accent. He was agile-witted, quick to grasp the sense of Cuthbert's teaching so that they could work together, not sentence by sentence, but in longer passages, the translator adding a joke or reference for his audience. Together they seemed to delight their auditors. As Talorcan translated, Cuthbert was able to watch them. The king's daughter sat close to her mother, her mouth slightly open with concentration as she listened. He noticed that she watched him, too, as he spoke. One day, after they had finished, Garnait beckoned him over. He pointed at his daughter. "Aniel!" he prompted.

"I speak English," she said. Everyone laughed and clapped. Cuthbert found himself suddenly tongue-tied.

"Shall you teach me?" she said. He saw she was looking directly at him. Her eyes were grey-green, fearless as a cat. He bowed. No Saxon woman would accost him so directly, in public. But who knew how they did things here?

At first Aniel came to see him in the guest-house where he and his companions were staying. She wouldn't sit with them but walked up and down the room with him.

"Tell story," she would say.

He spoke slowly, as simply as he was able. She walked beside him, eyes downcast as she concentrated, then turning her face up with puzzlement when she couldn't grasp the meaning. When he looked down at her, he saw the perfect smoothness of her white skin, furrowed only on her forehead. When she smiled, he saw the small sharp teeth beneath her rosy lips. She wore soft gowns of green and blue trimmed with fur and finely wrought silver bands around her neck. Sometimes when they walked, he would feel her hair against his hand. Her head was unveiled in the Pictish fashion, and although it was braided through with silver cords, her gold-red hair hung loose.

As the days passed, he could see that she drank in all that he taught her, and still wanted more. When he spoke to Garnait and the court, he watched her expression, rapt with concentration. He knew that her soul was open to God, and he loved her for it.

A fortnight after his arrival, Aniel came to find him late in the afternoon. He and his companions were saying Compline. She waited by the door, silent, till he came to her. She took his hand and pulled him to the door, laughing and pointing.

"Look! What is word?"

"Snow!"

"Come!"

He took his cloak from the peg and went with her. To the east, the clouds were iron grey and light snow was falling from them. The last rays of sunlight still glowed in the west, lighting up the pale snowflakes against the dark sky behind. Already the ground was turning white. He walked beside her to the gatehouse and out onto the track that led down to the sea. When they reached the shore they stood together, watching the snow fall on the shifting water. There was no sound but the rhythmic slapping of waves on the shore and a gull wailing far out to sea. The snow fell silently. He found himself in a state of intense awareness, as if a vision had taken hold of him. He was at one with the mystery of the world, with the falling snow, the sea, the cold air in his nostrils. And Aniel. He looked at her face turned up towards him, at her eyes as green as the sea. Brushing the snow from her forehead, he leaned down and gently kissed her; a holy kiss to sanctify the vision.

Next morning she was not in the hall for his preaching. He felt a shock of disappointment. The light seemed to have gone from the room. Afterwards, as he and his companions were leaving, a maidservant came with a message. She had little English, but Cuthbert understood that her mistress was sick and had asked for him to attend on her. He nodded and followed the woman to the bower house. She led him to the back of the hall, to a private chamber, and showed him inside. Aniel was lying on a couch beneath a coverlet, her eyes closed, her red-gold hair like a shower of meteorites on the pillow behind her. A rush of tenderness filled him, to see her in sickness. The woman withdrew and closed the door.

He knelt beside the couch. She opened her eyes and smiled at him.

"Cuthbert!"

She took his hand and held it to her cheek. It was warm, but she did not feel feverish, he thought. Then she sat up. As she did, the coverlet slid away and he saw that she was naked. His hand slipped down to her breast, and she leaned towards him, lips open for a kiss. For a moment bliss overwhelmed him. He felt the softness of her breast, saw her red lips close to his. A shattering instant later his reason returned to him. He, a monk sworn to chastity and obedience, had betrayed his vows and was on the brink of mortal sin. He must tear himself away before he was utterly lost. With a terrible effort of will, he pulled himself away from her, staggered to his feet and with a single backward look pulled open the door and went out.

He stumbled back to the guest-hall in turmoil. No-one was there. He fell to his knees and found that he was sobbing. How could he have been so blind? Why had he let her speak with him alone? What madness had possessed him? But even as he reproached himself, he could hardly control himself from turning back, from running into her arms and losing himself in her. He heard men at the door. He pulled himself up, seized a pitcher of water and poured it over his face. His companions entered, staring at him. He turned away from them and busied himself with his bag.

In the days that followed he found that although he felt immeasurably distant from himself, he was able to sit and stand and say the offices. He was even able to preach as if all was normal. But at night nothing could contain his torment. He was sleepless, hour after hour. Suddenly lust was let loose in him like an inferno ravaging his innards. All the years of discipline and obedience were turned to ashes in the flames, and he was a burning torment of desire. His longing for her tortured him till he was ready to throw his vocation to the winds, to stay for ever in her arms, to marry her. Did she not suffer also? Was he not cruel to deny her? The sin was not hers. She had been raised a pagan, she knew no better. She had sought God through him, and would he now reject her?

One night when he could endure no more he left his sleeping companions and walked down to the midnight shore. It was bitterly cold. His breath froze in the air. He stripped off all his clothes and walked naked into the sea. The shock of the icy water emptied his mind of thought. He could feel nothing but the physical pain of his body and was grateful. He stood in the lapping waves till all sensation was deadened. Half-frozen, he stumbled from the water. His hands were too numb to pull his clothes on over his wet skin. He could feel himself starting to lose consciousness. With a final struggle he tugged the habit over his head and stumbled back up the track. He fell onto his bed and slept at last.

"We'll leave as soon as the Christmas feast is over," he told his companions. "As soon as we have a north wind."

It was unbearable to be here, to see her every day, to avoid her eyes. They must leave. He could not trust himself to withstand her. He wanted to get back to Melrose, to Eata and sanity, to put this madness behind him for ever. But even as he resolved it, the thought that he would never see her again brought a fit of weeping he could not stem.

Once started, his confession spilt out of him like milk boiling out of a pan, in a wild torrent of words till nothing was left. He was empty. Hollow. Eata leaned forward, kind and calm. He questioned, clarified. Then he was silent, considering. "Your penance is to give her up. In your thoughts. In your heart."

As he spoke, Cuthbert knew he had not. Doubted even that he could. "Isn't it possible to love God through her?"

"Through a woman?" Eata looked at him in surprise. "In worldly life men take women in marriage, and there's no wrongdoing in it. God made Eve as a wife to Adam and put love for her in his heart. But your heart is for Christ alone. That's your vocation. Not through anyone else. Through Christ alone."

Tears started from Cuthbert's eyes. These days he wept like a child. He was as weak as a child. All his strength was gone.

"Pray constantly. Let the Rule hold you. Whatever trials we suffer, the Rule is there, and it will sustain you. You must continue with all your duties as prior and help and counsel your brothers. But you are not to leave the monastery again till the devil has quit you."

Aniel, a devil? How could that be? An angel, rather. But he was a drowning man, clutching at scraps of reason. He could only cling to the Rule. Cling to Eata.

He bore his penance through the dark days of the winter, through the Lenten fast and the first stirrings of spring at Easter-tide. He schooled his thoughts till he reached a sort of calm and kept all his waking moments busy. Time passed. The first crops went into the soil, and the birds sang all day in the briars. The fields beyond the monastery were noisy with lambs bleating for their dams, and the milk from new pasture was sweet and rich. All his life, spring had brought an upwelling of joy and eagerness in him. But he found himself dead to it. He saw the tender yellow of the primroses in the hedge, smelled the April wind full of green scents and showers, untouched. Only sometimes in his dreams he gazed at the heavens and saw a cloud of red-gold hair spread out across the night sky like a shower of meteorites, dazzling for a moment in their brightness before they turned to ashes.

PART 3

A Black Shield
across the Sun

660–65 AD

CHAPTER 14

THE STORY OF ME

660 AD

The Princess Aelfled wore a brown homespun tunic like everyone else in the minster, hitched up with a belt, so she didn't trip over it, but round her neck was a necklace of amber delicately interlaced with gold. Her mother had given it to her for her seventh birthday, Abbess Hild had given permission, and Aelfled had worn it every day since. The gold gave a pale sheen of light to her throat, a little halo of nobility. Otherwise she could have been taken for any village child, with hazel-blue eyes set in a regular-featured open face, sturdy limbs and curly fair hair tugged back into a pair of pigtails.

In church she had to sit as silent as the nuns. Through the tedium of services that went on for hours, she had to sit close to Abbess Hild herself. If she fidgeted or talked to her nurse, the abbess would reach over and slap her. The abbess was not unkind at other times, but she would have no disturbance in the church, and because she was kin, she had the right to slap Aelfled. No-one else did. When she ran over to the novices in the middle of their washing and tugged at them to come and play with her, they had to leave their tasks and pretend to run after her. They played tig and hopscotch and blind man's buff on the flat ground between their huts, and she always won. When gusts of icy rain blew over the exposed headland, she would take refuge in a weaving hut, snuggled down in the piles of wool, and have the weaver tell her tales.

But only Nurse knew her favourite tale, and after her mother had been to visit, she made Nurse tell it again and again. She would curl up in Nurse's comfortable lap, finger her amber necklace, and say, "Tell the story. Tell the story of me." Nurse would shift a little on the bench to get her legs comfortable beneath the child's body, and the story would begin.

"This is a famous story of our kingdom," Nurse would begin, "and of Oswy its king." She paused to let the child settle. "When King Oswy had ruled for many years, he sent his priests to bring the light of Christ to other Saxon kingdoms. Penda the Heathen, King of Mercia, saw what he did and grew jealous. He envied King Oswy and the devil filled his heart with malice. 'I will bring death and destruction on their heads,' he said, 'I will destroy their Christian god and make their kingdom subject to me and my kin.'

"Penda raised a mighty army. First he conquered the kingdom of the East Angles, and then he sent word to the Middle Angles, the South Saxons, to Kent and to the West Saxons, saying, 'Send your warriors to join me, or I will invade your kingdom too. I will burn your barns and take your gold.' The rulers of all the kingdoms trembled with fear and sent men to join the great army of Penda. And the people of Wales, pagans like Penda, sent their warriors too for a share of the plunder.

"When King Oswy learned of Penda's malice, he sent to every corner of his lands for warriors to defend his kingdom. But for every warrior he commanded, Penda had three. Oswy knew he could not defeat him in battle. He left his fortress of Bamburgh, with Enfleda his queen and his family . . . "

Here Aelfled wriggled and nudged her. Nurse looked down and smiled before continuing,

" . . . and all his faithful warriors. He journeyed to the farthest reach of his kingdom, where the Forth flows down a long inlet to the sea, to a fortress far from his enemies.

"Then Penda's army came into the kingdom with fire and the sword. He carried off slaves and cattle, destroyed farms and villages, till King Oswy surrendered to him to save his people from destruction. He had to give him all the treasure of the kingdom and do homage to the evil king. Then Penda was satisfied. 'The gods of my ancestors have given me a great victory!' he cried. 'I have ground the Christians beneath my heel and ended their dominion.'

"All the people of Northumbria lamented and cried out, 'God has forsaken us!' But God heard their cries. He put it into King Oswy's mind to pursue the army of Penda as they marched home for the winter. Oswy put his faith in God the Redeemer and led his warriors out from their fortress in the north. They followed the pagans till the army came to ford the river that divides Northumbria from their kingdom of Mercia. Then God stretched forth His hand and sent a great storm of wind and rain. When they tried to cross the river at a place called Winwaed, a flood swept down upon them. Many were carried away in the waters, and those that remained were unable to move. Then King Oswy cried aloud to heaven and made a vow to God. 'You have delivered my enemies into my hand,' he cried. 'If I should prove victorious in this battle, I will give you my dearest possession for ever!'"

Aelfled took her thumb out of her mouth to give a little cry.

"Then King Oswy, his son Connal and all his warriors fell upon the pagans and slaughtered them where they stood. King Penda was killed in the midst of the treasure he had stolen, and many of the treacherous princes and nobles beside him. In the very hour of his defeat God raised up King Oswy and gave his enemies into his hand.

"Then King Oswy knew that he must fulfil the promise he had made to God, and tears filled his eyes in the midst of his rejoicings. He returned home to his fortress at Bamburgh, and his wife, Queen Enfleda, came to greet him.

"'Enfleda my wife,' he said, 'we have won a great victory at Winwaed.'

"She clapped her hands with joy. Then he continued:

"'Before the battle I swore to God that I would give Him my dearest possession for ever if he brought about victory for me and my people. He has answered my prayer, and now I must make good my promise.'

"'What possession is this?' asked the queen. 'What is it that you hold so dear?'

"'It is our little daughter.'"

"At that the queen broke into weeping, crying and pleading with her husband to let her keep her only daughter, who was an infant and whom she too loved above all else.

"'Dry your tears,' the king told her. 'I will give her to God, to the minster of your kinswoman Hild at Whitby. She will serve God and help bring us to salvation.'

"So the queen gave her consent, and when the spring came, the little princess was set upon the seas and brought to the minster, where now she lives! And what is her name?"

"Her name is Princess Aelfled!" squealed the little girl, jumping up and hugging her Nurse.

And Nurse bent down and kissed her.

Aelfled knew that once she had lived in a palace with her queen-mother and king-father. It was in Nurse's story. But she couldn't remember living anywhere but the minster at Whitby. It stood on a grassy headland overlooking the bay. If you climbed down the steep cliff path from the minster, you came to the river and the sandy shore where ships were beached. Once upon a time, Nurse told her, the Roman people from far away had brought their galley ships ashore there and had built a light-house on the cliffs to guide them safe to harbour. That was why British people still called Whitby Streoneshalch. It meant the bay of the light-house. Aelfled's king-father had given the land at Whitby for the minster and had made cousin Hild the Abbess. It wasn't just for nuns. There were monks at Whitby too. Their huts and living hall were in a separate enclosure, but everybody prayed in the same church. It was a good idea, Aelfled thought. She liked listening to the men's deep voices when they sang together. The monks were nice to her too. Sometimes they gave her little presents—a spinning top, or a little carved doll.

Sometimes it was freezing cold, and it was always windy. Cousin Hild wanted the minster to be close to the sea, like Lindisfarne. It was nice to look out at the sea, but Aelfled preferred the hall where her king-father and queen-mother stayed when they came to Whitby. It was a little way up the river valley, sheltered by the hillside from the winds that scoured the headland. It was bigger than any of the minster buildings, with a gallery along one side for the queen and her women. The walls were painted different colours and there were woven hangings to keep out the draughts. It was always full of people when king-father and queen-mother came— local thegns come to wait on them, servants running in and out with big jugs of ale and mead for visitors, women spinning and chatting. When Aelfled visited, she and Nurse climbed up into the gallery to sit with her mother. From there they could watch all the goings-on in the hall below. The servants brought her honey cakes. She loved the first moment of biting into the soft warm crust, feeling the sweetness filling her mouth. As soon as she had finished, she pressed the next one into Nurse's mouth. Then she would scramble up to sit in her mother's lap. She loved the softness of her gown, the fine linens and silk that she wore. Her mother would press her tight and stroke her hair and call her precious darling. She smelled different to Nurse. Nurse was warm and sweaty, but her mother had a cool, bitter-sweet smell of perfume and oil.

One visit she found that her mother's belly was grown very large, and there wasn't room for her. "You will have a little brother soon," her mother told her. "Or a little sister." "Is she in your belly?" Aelfled asked, and her mother nodded. "Just like you were, once upon a time."

It would be better if it was a sister, she thought. She already had a brother. He was called Edfrith. He was 15, eight years older than her, and tall and lanky. He tried to teach her to play jacks, but she couldn't pick up the knuckle bones quickly enough to please him. He had been a hostage

of Penda the Heathen. "Are you a heathen?" she asked him. He got cross
and pushed her away.

Now he was going to get married. To a princess called Audrey from
the kingdom of East Anglia. Princess Audrey was quite old. Not as old as
mother, but as old as Nurse, and a lot older than Edfrith. She had a thin,
red face and a long nose. But she was very nice. She called Aelfled "little
sister" and wanted to know all about Aelfled's life in the convent. "Oh!"
she sighed, "I wish I could join you!" Aelfled had heard the novices talking
about her. "She'd sooner be a nun than a bride," they said. "Poor thing."

Aelfled hoped Edfrith and Audrey would get married at Whitby and
have a great feast. She and Nurse could eat all they wanted and drink
mead. But mother said no, it was going to be at Bamburgh, and the bishop
from Lindisfarne would marry them. "When you are older you can come
and visit Bamburgh," her mother said, to comfort her. "But you are too
young now."

Aelfled liked her mother. She was always affectionate and generous
with her presents. Sometimes she held Aelfled so tight she could hardly
breathe, but Aelfled didn't cry out, because she knew that it was hard for
her mother not to have her for her own. But it was difficult to believe
that she had ever been king-father's dearest possession. He sat on his
throne at the end of the hall with his warriors around him, his face hard
and unsmiling. He took no notice of her, even when she wore her amber
necklace. Perhaps he was still thinking of all the wicked things Penda the
Heathen had done and the battles he had had to fight. She imagined him
at the Winwaed with the great waters of the flooded river rushing past,
standing with one foot on Penda's body waving his sword triumphantly.
Perhaps he would notice her more when she got bigger.

CHAPTER 15

THE EASTER FEAST

664 AD

It was a morning of early March, unusually mild. The casements in the queen's hall had been set open and a spring giddiness filled the air. The women were singing, trying out a new round. They hadn't got the tune yet, and sudden discords set everyone laughing. The queen laughed with them. Enfleda had just turned 38, but everyone agreed she was still in her prime, still beautiful. True, she had filled out and her gowns hung wider, but her plump cheeks were smooth, with a rosy bloom on her white skin. The dark years of the Mercian wars were behind her. Although she had thought the loss of Aelfled would break her heart, it seemed the sacrifice had pleased God. He had given her another daughter, Edith, and a second son, Aylwin, when she had thought her child-bearing days were past. Aylwin was the apple of her eye, the most beautiful of all her children, and sweet-tempered as a saint. And Edfrith had been returned to her after the victory at Winwaed, from his exile as hostage in Mercia. Returned in body at least, though he'd felt like a stranger.

When he came home, he was changed. He'd been away five years. The headstrong curly-headed little boy, as quick to break into laughter as tears, had become a quiet, withdrawn youth. He had grown to twice the height and was awkward with his mother. He seemed hardly to remember her. She had hugged him, kissed him, ruffled his hair and told him how handsome he'd become, till at last he smiled uncertainly at her and she could see her son again. But the closeness between them was gone. Before he went to Mercia, his soul was open to her; she knew his joys and sorrows, and what he wondered about the world. Now he had learned to hide his feelings. Even with her, he was wary.

"Tell me," she said. "Tell me what it was like. Did you play with the Mercian boys?"

"No."

"No? Did you have no-one to play with?"

He looked at her. "I wasn't supposed to. I did play with Wulfhere though. And some of the others."

"Is he nice?"

"He's all right. For a heathen." He paused, and then in a rush, "He let me ride his pony. Will father give me a pony now?"

He wanted to be with the men, to start his training, become a warrior. I have lost him, she thought. If things had been different, she might have spent more time with him, tried harder to talk to him, but her belly was quickening with child, and her life was taken up with her new family. With the new babes to care for, there'd been no time to spend with Edfrith.

And then Oswy had married him to the East Anglian girl, because he needed to strengthen his alliances in the south. Edfrith was only 15 at the time, and Princess Audrey 24, widowed already and looking twice her age. She was devout and dressed so plainly you might have taken her for a servant. Yet Edfrith suddenly became happier. He spent hours closeted up with her, and he was always at her side. He even attended Mass with her. It wasn't sex, Enfleda was sure of that. It had been three years since the marriage, and there was still no pregnancy. The rumour in the hall was that she had pleaded with him not to lie with her, because she wanted to be pure for Christ. There was nothing about her to lust after, in any case. She had no flesh on her at all, and she did nothing to make herself attractive. It was something else. The way she listened to him and praised everything he did. She was like an elder sister. Or a mother. Was that what he wanted? The mother she should have been?

He was a man now, in any case; part of Oswy's household, one of his young warriors. He sat in council with his father and drank with the men. Whether he visited slave girls in the village was no concern of hers.

One of her women tugged at her sleeve and pointed. She saw her reeve waiting down in the hall. Ah yes. This business of the Easter feast. Her heart sank a little. She would have to go and discuss it with him.

Her household used the Catholic method of calculating Easter, and sometimes it meant that they were celebrating Easter on a different Sunday to the king, who had been raised in the Irish tradition. It was always awkward, if one household was still fasting for Lent while a feast was going on in the other hall. But it was accepted. Bishop Aidan had never objected to it. Suddenly it had become controversial. Because of Connal. Her step-son.

This year was one of those where it would be Palm Sunday for the rest of Northumbria, but Easter Day for her household. Audrey came from East Anglia and had been raised in the Roman tradition. So she would want to celebrate with the queen's household, which meant Edfrith as well. It would displease Oswy. But that was nothing to the upset over Connal.

Oswy had come roaring into her hall, shouting at her servants and hardly able to be civil. "Why have you invited Connal? Why have you taken it on yourself to invite my son to your Easter feast?"

"I haven't invited him."

"Don't lie to me!"

"Oswy!" She had stood up from her work and nodded to her women to leave with her. She wasn't going to be shouted at in front of them all. There was a flurry of distaffs rewinding and cloth being folded up. Oswy stood in her way, banging his fist on the table.

"He has told me so! He has sent word that he will attend the Easter feast according to the Roman calendar."

"Ah." She understood, and her heart sank. Why should she be pulled into this?

"Are you trying to side with him?"

"I didn't ask him, Oswy. I swear it."

"But he has sent word."

"I will forbid him if it's your wish."

He stared at her. Her step-son Connal, she understood, had found a new way to provoke his father. His new Catholic faith. At once her annoyance with Oswy left her, and she felt only pity for him. As much as Oswy could love anyone, he loved Connal. In jealous moments she thought, perhaps it was because he had loved Reinmeillt his mother, and Connal looked like her. He was nothing like her fair-haired children. There was a fey quality about him, with his pale British skin and brooding, coal-dark eyes.

She remembered seeing Oswy and Connal ride together into the fortress when they returned victorious from the Winwaed, Penda slain and his army routed. Oswy could talk of nothing but his son's courage and bravery, how they had fought shoulder to shoulder against the Mercians, what a fine warrior his son had become. He made him Prince of Deira. But Connal still held aloof from them. He refused to be part of Oswy's new family. He resented her, Enfleda felt; resented her and her sons who might contest his birthright.

Now, by the strangest twist of fate, Wilfrid was at his court. Not at hers, for all she had sponsored him, had paid for his journey to Rome. Wilfrid had become Connal's favourite, his bosom companion, and it was Wilfrid who had taught him to adopt the Roman rite. A few months after Wilfrid's arrival, Connal had visited his father at Bamburgh. For the first time she could remember, Connal looked animated and joyful.

"Father," he said. "I'm going to change my life. I want to give myself up to God. I ask your permission to travel to Rome."

"To Rome?"

"I want to visit the shrine of Saint Peter and receive instruction from the holy fathers of the Church."

Well, Enfleda thought. Why not?

"Where has this come from?"

"I have discussed it with my chaplain. Father Wilfrid. The queen sponsored him, he has been to Rome. He'll be my companion."

Enfleda had looked at Oswy, expecting an outburst. But he was quiet, careful.

"Connal. Many men are called to serve God and can leave everything behind. It is praise-worthy. But you are a warrior and a ruler. You are called to rule and defend your kingdom."

"I will return."

"It's a long journey, and it's dangerous. You could be killed. I made you Prince of Deira to govern at my side. My wishes haven't changed."

"The reeve can govern in my absence."

"In your absence? Are you blind? Our enemies won't wait quietly for you to return in two years' time. There'll be no kingdom of Deira waiting for you when you get back."

"But I will go."

"You will not."

The two of them fought and raged, but Oswy would not yield.

Now Connal had found a different mission. He and Wilfrid would convert Northumbria to Catholicism and root out the Irish heresies. Already he had made Wilfrid abbot of the new monastery at Ripon. Lindisfarne had petitioned Oswy to reinstate Abbot Eata, but Oswy refused.

"I have made him Prince of Deira. Let him rule as he wishes," he said.

Now Connal was challenging the court directly. He would ignore his father's invitation to his Easter feast, which he had attended every year of his life. He would attend the queen's feast instead. With Wilfrid at his side, no doubt. After the Winwaed he had repudiated Cynburh, his Mercian wife, and had vowed not to marry again. Wilfrid seemed to have taken her place.

It disturbed Enfleda that Wilfrid had been drawn in, that he had become part of Connal's contest with his father. Through Wilfrid he had found a cause. But she knew it hid a deeper, older cause that Wilfrid might be blind to: Connal's belief that her children would dispossess him. Oswy never talked of the succession, never let slip his intentions by a hint or a murmur. He was still watching Edfrith. But she had a certainty in her heart that he would make Edfrith king of Northumbria. Then Connal, although he were king of Deira, would be Edfrith's vassal, as he was Oswy's. He would not endure it. He could not contain his high spirit, his burning will to be high king and lord of all. Why did Oswy not see it? Why had he not let Connal go to Rome, let him find some other outlet for his nature? Now it was cloaked in religion, in his passionate attachment to Wilfrid. But the fire that burned beneath had only found new fuel.

Enfleda dismissed her women and talked to Oswy alone. He loved his son, and it was easier to blame her than face the truth. But he listened.

"I could go down to Kent, and then there'd be no feast," she said. But they both knew it was a folly, with the seas still cold and rough in March. The rage drained out of Oswy. He wouldn't intervene. Let Connal do as he pleased.

"But," he added, "I won't have this happen again. The bishops will have to sort this out. There must be one date. One date that everyone can agree on."

And now her reeve was here to be told. He would not be happy. Her Easter feast was usually a modest affair, for herself and her household. She liked the intimacy of it. It was the only time they held a celebration like that, just themselves, all together. With all the visitors, it would take on a different character. She stood up and gathered her cloak around her shoulders before going down into the hall.

"Prince Connal and his retinue will join the household for the celebration of Easter according to the Roman rites. Prince Edfrith and Princess Audrey will also join us."

"But my lady . . . "

"I know. It'll be difficult."

"Surely it will give offence to the king."

"It will . . . " And suddenly she felt, she could not bear it, could not bear all the gossip it would cause. Everyone would be upset and at odds. Let Connal stay in Deira.

"I will talk to the king again," she said.

CHAPTER 16

The Eye of God

May-day 664 AD

Aelfled knew her king-father had ordered there was to be a great gathering of the Church in June. Everyone was talking about it. Her king-father and queen-mother would be coming to Whitby for it, and preparations had started already. But today she was going a-maying. She and Nurse had risen early and slipped out of the minster before anyone could give them tasks to do.

They would pick flowers for May-day garlands for the church. They took bags and baskets with them out to the fields beyond the minster. Sometimes a May-day morning could be wet and cold, with a stinging wind blowing out of the bay, so that it was hard to believe that spring had really come. This morning, though, was perfect. There was scarcely a breeze, the sky was blue and the blackbirds were singing in the hawthorn at the field margins. The meadow was covered in cowslips. The flower stalks rose up from tight rosettes of wrinkled leaves, with clusters of bright yellow blossoms hanging from each stalk. Aelfled loved to pull the flowers out of the pale baggy calyx that held them and stuff them into her mouth. They were sweet and soft, with a slight pungent smell. She and Nurse wandered from clump to clump, picking handfuls of stems into their baskets till they were full. The sleek-bellied cows raised their heads from cropping the new grass to stare at them, and their calves skittered off across the field, tails in the air. Although it was still early, they could feel the warmth of the sun on their faces. After the long cold of the winter, it felt like a caress. Nurse started to sing, an old song about Freya and her flowers of the spring. Aelfled put cowslips in her hair and did a dance through the green grass. Was there ever a lovelier morning?

When they had filled their baskets to the brim they turned back towards the minster. As they walked they felt the sunlight become less warm, less strong, though they could still see their shadows distinctly. The sky in front of them became a deeper blue, without the brightness it had had earlier. Aelfled stopped and stared up at the sky, wondering if it was going to cloud over. But it was clear, save for a band of grey cloud covering the sun. Although the sun was still visible behind it, something strange had happened to it. A piece of it seemed to have been eaten away. It was no longer perfectly round, but a broad crescent, as if it were the moon starting to wane.

"What has happened to the sun?" she asked. Nurse looked upwards. She looked for a while without speaking, puzzled.

"Perhaps it's the cloud. Perhaps a piece of cloud is covering the sun."

But they could both see it was not. As they watched, the sky darkened more, almost to indigo. Behind them, in the west, a reddish glow appeared on the horizon. Maybe a storm was coming, thought Aelfled. She looked again at the sun. Behind the clouds she could see that the crescent shape of the sun was growing thinner. Fear gripped her. The sun was going. The sun had gone wrong.

Suddenly she and Nurse were both running, running back along the path leading to the minster, flowers falling from their baskets unheeded. As they ran, a wind suddenly got up, gusting in their faces. Aelfled forgot about Nurse. She wanted to find Mother Hild. Mother Hild would hold her close and explain what was happening.

But when she reached the minster, there was a crowd of folk round the cross outside the church, talking and pointing at the sky. She couldn't see Hild anywhere. She pushed through the crowd, trying to see if Hild was among them, but something strange was happening to the light that prevented her. The stone cross looked as if it were made of some metal, bronze or silver. Every detail of the carving stood out, lightless but distinct. People's faces had the same metallic appearance, so that she couldn't recognise them. The crowd of men and women standing around the cross, the huts, the church behind, all took on an unreal glow, as if they had been suddenly translated from the ordinary world into some purgatorial place, motionless save for the wind that tossed their clothing about.

"Mother Hild!" she screamed, again and again. The metal people took no notice; they were crying out and wailing too. The sun was almost gone; there was just a tiny sliver of gold remaining. It was growing colder and colder, as if night were falling. Crows rose up from the fields, flying towards the woods in confusion. Aelfled could no longer think or understand; there was only fear.

She saw a dark circle of the sky detach itself and slide towards the last remaining sliver of the sun. Like a black shield the circle entirely blotted out the sun. At the same moment, a wall of dark shadow burst across the horizon at incredible speed, bearing down upon the headland. The air was split apart with screams of terror from all the helpless watchers as it engulfed them. No-one doubted that the end of the world was upon them. Aelfled stumbled over to the woman closest to her, trying to cling to her, but the child's sudden assault made the woman lose her balance. They fell to the ground together.

Yet the darkness swept on without destroying them, and in its wake Aelfled saw to her amazement that stars were shining in the sky as if night had fallen. Where the sun had been was a ring of fire, with tongues of flame leaping out into the darkness. A crown of silver light surrounded the disc of blackness that had been the sun. A new awestruck terror took hold of her. It was the Eye of God, she understood; it was God's All-Seeing Eye, gazing down at her, Aelfled, seeing into her heart and knowing all her thoughts. She tried to pray, but panic robbed her senses of all recollection. Nothing came to her lips; she stared, mesmerised, unable to move or speak. Her lungs were crushed within her chest so that she could only breathe in short shallow pants. The pearly shimmering light of the Eye was at once overwhelmingly beautiful and terrifying in its power.

Then, as suddenly as it had come, the vision vanished. There was a flash of brilliant yellow light. The stars faded from the sky and the dark wall of shadow fell back and rushed away eastwards. Light began to return. Aelfled was too spent to feel relief. The woman beside her started to struggle to her feet, but Aelfled lay motionless, shocked to the soul by what she had witnessed. When Nurse found her at last, she had to wrap her in a cloak and carry her to the infirmary.

When Aelfled opened her eyes, she saw Mother Hild looking down at her. At once Aelfled started to cry.

"I couldn't find you! I couldn't find you, and the sky went black!"

Hild sat down beside her and took the child in her arms, letting her sob till she was done. She stroked back her yellow hair.

"It's over now." She kissed her, and Aelfled felt the warmth and safety of her arms. If only she had found her before! Hild would have prayed special prayers, would have protected her.

"It's over," said Hild again. "Now drink this."

Aelfled drank. The herbs were bitter but comforting in the warm ale. She looked round the infirmary. Everything was as it always had been. Sunlight came through the open door, and the air was soft and fresh.

"I saw . . . Mother Hild, I saw . . . ," and she stopped. How could she tell Hild about the Eye? It was too fearful to speak of.

"We'll talk about it later," said Hild. "Rest now. See if you can sleep a little."

When she got up the next day, she was wary. She looked out of the hut at the sky, but it was a dull day with lowering cloud. It was a relief. When she and Nurse went over to the hall to eat breakfast, she held Nurse's hand tightly and sat close beside her at the table. The bread and milk tasted sweet and good. It felt as if she were tasting it for the first time. Her heart rose. She was alive! God had not struck her down after all. She was here at the table with Nurse and her sisters.

Later, Hild sent for her, to the infirmary. She felt her pulse and looked at her tongue.

"That's fine. You can go to lessons."

But Aelfled lingered.

"Will it happen again?"

Hild shook her head.

"No. It is given to few people to see what we have seen. Even though you suffered, it's a gift. You have seen God's majesty and power directly, so you will never doubt it."

Aelfled thought of the dark shadow sweeping across the sky and saw again the silver outline of the Eye. She would never doubt it.

"The astrologers call it an eclypsis. The moon moves across the face of the sun for a time, blotting out the light. It is a sign from God."

Aelfled stared at her. "A sign of what?"

"Of our wrongdoing. The sun and moon are part of God's ordering of creation. If the order is disturbed by our wrongdoing, it shakes the movement of the heavens. No-one can say what it foretells."

No-one could say, but everyone was speculating. Frightening rumours spread around, of an outbreak of a yellow plague in the south, of children born with no fingers on their hands, of a spotted blight that was destroying the barley. The ordinary people went to seers for amulets, and even some of the nuns secretly wore one for protection beneath their robes. Hild ordered extra prayers to be said at all the offices, asking for God's deliverance from war, pestilence and famine. Another story spread that it was a special year, 664. If you added the numbers together, it made 16, and 1 and 6 made 7. It was the mystical number of the Apocalypse.

Hild had her own fears. Two days after the eclypsis, she took clean parchment from her writing closet, and mixed ink. She sat at her desk, head bent, and started to write in Latin.

> *To Oswy, most Christian king and overlord of Northumbria, our greetings in Christ.*
>
> *Since by heavenly signs and portents Almighty God has made known to us His displeasure, I write to entreat that the Church abstain for the present time from all convocations that might tend to discord.*
>
> *Even as I, having been baptised by our holy Father Paulinus into the Roman Church and taught the Word of God according to its customs, was then received by blessed Aidan into the religious life within the Celtic rite, so may the Church within your kingdom continue peaceably to drink from all springs of truth without division.*
>
> *The Synod that you, most honoured Lord and King, have proposed to the Church, we can now see to be ill-omened. The late eclypsis was an augury of great import in the heavens, which presaged conflict in the earthly kingdoms. We should take heed of such an augury and do nothing that might engender discord. Even as Father Aidan saw no reason to prefer one tradition above the other, let us follow his example and live peaceably together in communion.*
>
> *Therefore as your sister and counsellor in God, I beseech you most earnestly to suspend this Council and trust in God's righteousness alone.*

She sat back and re-read it. She knew already the political undertow of the Synod and had little faith that Oswy would take notice of her fears. But nevertheless, she would do what she could. She leaned forward again, and signed,

> *Hild, by God's grace Abbess of Whitby.*

CHAPTER 17

"I SOON MAKE THEM CRY"

June 664 AD

Aelfled watched the ships as they crossed the wide bay, their brown sails filled with the wind. She knew that they carried Mother Hild's visitors from the north. One of them was her Aunt Ebba, whom she had never met. She was an abbess like Mother Hild. All the others were men, a bishop and abbots and other important people. Later in the day, she caught sight of them climbing up the steep hill to the minster. Her aunt looked quite old and the others had to help her up.

The next morning Mother Hild called for her to her room.

"Our guests have arrived," she said. "Your Aunt Ebba, Bishop Colman from Lindisfarne, Abbot Eata and Father Cuthbert from Melrose, and Father Cedd. You will greet them with me."

"Yes, Mother."

"I want you to stay and listen to what we are discussing. You won't understand everything now, but you will later on."

When the guests arrived, she stood beside Mother Hild and greeted them politely. Her Aunt Ebba was small and smiling and exclaimed at how like her father she was! Then she kissed her and gave her a little gold bracelet. Aelfled was overjoyed.

Then they all settled down on the benches and started talking. At first she played with the bracelet, seeing the dim glow of the gold reflected on her skin. Hild glanced at her.

"Are you listening, child?"

"Yes, Mother."

They talked on and on. She tried to remember a story of Nurse's to tell herself, but she kept forgetting what happened in the middle. She thought about her mother and imagined going up to the great hall on the royal estate to see her when she came for the Synod. Her mother would give her cakes, and she might see her new sister-in-law Audrey. Audrey always told her how lucky she was to be a nun, how she wanted to be one too. Which was strange, because she was married to her brother Edfrith. After a while it was difficult to think about anything, because her bottom was getting sore from sitting on the bench for so long. She had a little wriggle to help it.

"Stop fidgeting!" said Hild.

It was a relief when it was time for None. But as soon as the office was finished, they went back over to Hild's room to start all over again. One of the visitors walked beside her. It was Father Cuthbert, the tall monk from Melrose.

"Are you good at riddles?"

"Yes!"

"I'll tell you one. You can solve it while we're talking. If you can guess this one, I'll tell you another."

"What is it?"

He stopped beside her and bent down to whisper it in her ear. His rough brown cheek was close to hers.

"When I am alive, I do not speak. Anyone who wants to can take me captive and cut off my head. They bite my bare body. But I do no harm to anyone, unless they cut me first. Then I soon make them cry."

"Say it again."

"Once more. Then we must go in."

She listened hard while he repeated it. As they went into the Chapter room, she gave Father Cuthbert her nicest smile.

After that she started to look forward to the sessions. Father Cuthbert told her a new riddle before each one, and if she was able to solve it, he would pull out a little prize for her from his pocket, an apple or a curious whorled shell. Sometimes he had to help her a little bit. She sat on the hard bench wrestling with her riddle. She made little faces to him to try and get his attention, but he never looked at her then. He was serious and grave like the rest of them. Not outside though. He liked to laugh, and when he did, it made her want to laugh too. She watched him when he talked with the other guests. He didn't lose his temper or shout like her king-father did.

Nurse always told her that the king loved her, that she was the most precious thing in the world to him. But when he came to Whitby and she was taken to see him, he never showed any sign of it. He sat on his big chair covered in furs staring down at her as she kissed his hand. All she could see of him when she was kneeling in front of him was his thick leather belt studded with silver, pulled tight over his purple tunic. If she looked up, she saw his beard and straight mouth half covered by the hair of his moustache. She couldn't tell if he was smiling or not. Sometimes he would mutter a blessing and pat her head with his hard strong hand. Like a dog, she thought. He never picked her up or hugged her like her queen-mother did, and he never brought presents for her. He didn't care about giving me away, she thought. He just wanted to get rid of me.

Everyone told her that cousin Hild was her mother in God, so why shouldn't she have a father in God? She would have Father Cuthbert. Her father in God.

After one of the sessions in the Chapter house, Aelfled sat in the school room with Sister Bertha. They were practising writing. She could write in Latin, although she didn't understand all the words. She would turn them round in her mouth while she carefully traced out the letters. *Credo in unum Deum, patrem omnipotentem, factorem coeli at terrae.* She liked the way Latin changed an English sentence into something succinct and formal. She worked on one sentence at a time, using a stylus to practise on a wax tablet. When she was confident of all the letters, she would copy it onto parchment, using a quill pen, cut short for her small fingers. For the capital letter at the start of the sentence, she was allowed to use a fine boar's bristle brush and red ochre, to interlace a pattern of climbing leaves into the letter. When the parchment was finished, it would be a present for her queen-mother.

"Bertha," she said, when she had successfully completed the last letter of her sentence and was sitting back to wait for the ink to dry, "why do they talk about Easter all the time?"

"It's complicated," said Bertha. "You'll understand when you're older."

"Do you understand it?"

"It's all about what day of the moon you use to calculate the date. There's a right way to do it and a wrong way to do it, that's all you need to know. And if you don't hurry up and get the next sentence done, it'll be getting on for Christmas, never mind Easter."

Bertha doesn't know, she thought. When the afternoon office was finished, she ran up to Father Cuthbert as he left the church.

"Father Cuthbert, would you like to see the pigs?"

"Yes! Where are they?"

"I'll show you. There's a bucket of apple peels outside the kitchen we can give them."

They walked together to the kitchen, he picked up the bucket, and they set off towards the farmland that lay behind the minster. She had to trot to keep up with his long stride. It was a bright afternoon, with a strong wind over the headland driving the clouds across the sky. Sunlight flickered in and out. They passed Mother Hild's herb garden and caught a glimpse of her inside the infirmary, bending over a sick woman. Then the track led them away from the minster buildings, towards the fields and the stables.

"Father Cuthbert, why do you all talk about Easter all the time?"

He slackened his stride and looked down at the hazel-blue eyes turned up towards him.

"When's your birthday?"

"November 29th."

"Does it come on the same day of the week every year?"

She thought about it. "No."

"Sometimes it's on a Monday, sometimes it's on a Tuesday, or a Wednesday . . . is that right?"

"Yes."

"Christmas Day is like a birthday. It's always the same date, whatever day of the week it is. But Easter Day is different, because we know that our Lord Jesus rose from the dead on a Sunday, and Sunday is a special day because of that. We can't celebrate Easter on a Monday or a Tuesday or any day, except a Sunday. So we have to work it out in a different way. Agreed?"

"Yes. Bertha says there's a right way and a wrong way."

"That's how some people see it. But no-one knows for sure. We talk about it to try and find the truth."

They reached the pig pens. They were made of rough wattle fencing and the pigs stuck their snouts through, eager for the peelings. Aelfled took handfuls of peels from the bucket and let them snuffle them up from her hand. Cuthbert leaned over and scratched their dark bristly heads. Aelfled pulled him over to a shed full of straw with a closely fenced run.

"Look. Piglets. She had them three days ago."

The piglets were stripy black and grey, with tightly curled tails and soft pink snouts. When the sow saw the bucket, she lumbered to her feet, scattering the piglets off her teats. They ran squealing round the pen.

"That one's the runt," Aelfled pointed. "Garth says he hasn't got much strength, because he was born last, so he can't push for his food like the others."

She threw in the peels, and the piglets rushed wildly towards them while the sow shoved them out of the way with her snout. The runt staggered over to the side of the pen and stood uncertainly.

"I'm like a runt," said Aelfled. "My brothers and sister get all the fine food, and I get pushed out the way. They go to feasts, and they wear linen clothes with gold embroidery on them."

"That might be true, about the feasts and clothes." Cuthbert paused, considering. "But you're not pushed out of the way. You have something more precious that they will never have."

"What?"

"They only have one family. You have two. You have your brothers and sister at court, but you have all the sisters and brothers here as well. You have two families to love you."

She looked up at him. Father Cuthbert made you feel better, she thought. He was kind and understanding. And he was much younger than her king-father. She took his large hand and held it as they walked back to the minster with the empty bucket.

CHAPTER 18

THE KEYS OF ST PETER

664 AD

The first thing Enfleda noticed when she and Oswy entered the minster's great hall for the start of the Synod was Connal. Instead of sitting on the dais with the other members of the king's family, he had positioned himself on the left, with the papal envoy and his party. She felt a spasm of tension constrict her belly. He stared at them as they took their seats, his face flushed. Wilfrid and the other Catholic clergy sat with him.

Oswy gave no sign of displeasure. He bowed to the assembly and seated himself without a word. The hall was packed. Rows of benches along the front and sides provided seating for the senior or infirm clergy; for the rest, there was standing room along the back—monks, priests and clerics of every rank. Enfleda settled herself on her royal chair and tried not to look at Connal. Edfrith was beside her; his straight young body felt reassuring. Audrey leaned forward and smiled at her.

The hall was large and well-built, with long straight roof beams, two good hearths and casements at either end. But it was very plain. The walls were whitewashed, with no hangings at all or decorations. Only a crucifix in the centre. Hild had strong views about simplicity and poverty; she had been trained by Aidan. Hild was Enfleda's cousin and had lived at her father Edwin's court, but she was ten years older than Enfleda. They had never been close. It wasn't just their age. She found Hild intimidating—she was so capable, so energetic and learned. She made Enfleda feel weak and stupid. It wasn't Hild's fault—she was always pleasant and affectionate towards her, but it didn't make any difference. And now she was Aelfled's spiritual mother.

Aelfled was sitting beside her—Hild erect and attentive, in her light brown habit and white veil, and Aelfled in the same, poor sweeting. Such plain clothes. Still, she was safe here. She would never be married off to a remote princeling for the sake of some short-lived alliance. Or suffer the anguish of childbirth. It was a kind of freedom.

For now, Aelfled was kicking her legs to and fro just slowly enough not to attract Hild's attention. She was so like Oswy; the same upcurved lips set in a slight smile, the same wide-apart eyes and clear forehead that gave her an open, guileless look. She knew that beside her, at this moment, Oswy would have the same clear face in spite of his advancing years. He was 52; an old man, some would say, but behind that seeming openness his mind was still a constant fever of schemes and calculation. The debate in the Synod would go on for hours, but the churchmen might as well save their breath, in her view. The final decision was the king's, and she was certain he had already made up his mind. He hadn't discussed it with her, but she had grown used to following the workings of his mind. There was Connal to consider, and Oswy's alliances with the Catholic kingdoms of the south.

There were prayers and invocations and psalms and Oswy gave the opening address.

"We all serve one God. We all hope for one kingdom in heaven. So on earth we should be as one also, and not differ in how we celebrate the sacraments. Our task at this great meeting is to hear the arguments for both traditions regarding the celebration of Easter, and to decide which is truer. And I call upon you, when we have made the decision, to loyally accept it one and all."

Of course it was about more than Easter. It was about the whole governance of the Church. Northumbria had been converted by the missionaries from the great Irish monastery of Iona, and Iona continued to oversee Church appointments. Catholic Easter would mean Catholic governance.

Colman, the bishop of Lindisfarne, was to speak first. A white-haired and venerable father of the Church, he was simply dressed in a white linen alb and black cope, with his silver bishop's cross about his neck. An Irishman who spoke Latin fluently, but still stumbled with English. Abbot Cedd from Mercia stood beside Colman and translated, sentence by sentence. It was tedious and Enfleda's attention started to wander. She'd heard the arguments often enough, as had everyone in the hall. The Ionan Church followed the traditions of St Columba and his followers. They took their authority from John the Evangelist, Christ's beloved. He had celebrated Easter on the fourteenth day of the moon, if it were a Sunday, or the nearest Sunday to it. And so on. Enfleda was half asleep by the time he was finished, but there was a general mutter of agreement and approval around the hall.

The papal envoy, Agilbert, was to speak for the Catholic side. More translation, thought Enfleda. She could hardly bear it and the day was only half started. But Agilbert spoke only for a few minutes, in his heavy Frankish accent. He had spoken at length with Father Wilfrid, he said, and was satisfied he was well qualified to present the arguments. Father Wilfrid would speak in English. There was a little stir in the hall. The standers at the back craned forward to see the new speaker.

It was like the sun rising, thought Enfleda as Wilfrid came forward onto the speaker's dais. Like opening the casement in the morning and seeing the light stream in. The brightness she had seen in him all those years ago had not faded. It had grown stronger. He was strikingly handsome now, dressed in a long dark red tunic, richly embroidered at the collar with gold thread. A gold chain and cross hung round his neck, and his light cloak was fastened with a jewelled shoulder buckle. It would shock the clergy, of course. The Irish tradition was all about asceticism and plainness. But why not? Why should a man of God not celebrate His glory in his dress? The Roman Church never forbade it.

Wilfrid was already speaking by the time she brought her attention to his discourse. He started into a critique of Colman's view and a summary of the conclusions of the Council of Nicaea. She was taken by surprise by his eloquence. His language was clear and brilliant, the words skilfully chosen, as if bubbling up from a spring within him. He was able to sustain his train of thought without hesitation or stumbling, so that as he continued his argument gathered an irresistible logic. Enfleda felt as if she was understanding for the first time how essential it was to follow St Peter's nineteen-year lunar cycle, how every country in the world except the North understood these things, how stubbornly ignorant its opponents were.

She looked over at Connal. He was rapt, half-smiling, his gaze fixed on Wilfrid. A shock of apprehension passed through her. He loves him, she realised.

Wilfrid was reaching his conclusion.

"Easter is observed by men of different nations and languages at one and the same time in Africa, Asia, Egypt, Greece and throughout the world, wherever the Church of Christ has spread. The only people in the whole world who stupidly contend against the whole world are those Irish men and their partners in obstinacy the Picts and Britons, who inhabit only a part of these two remote islands in the ocean."

Goodness, thought Enfleda. There was a ripple of disapproval through the hall. She glanced at Colman, hoping he hadn't understood. But Colman immediately responded in Gaelic. Cedd translated,

"It is strange that you call us stupid, when we uphold customs that rest on the authority of so great an Apostle, who was considered worthy to lean on the Lord's breast and whose wisdom is acknowledged throughout the world."

Wilfrid didn't hesitate.

"Far be it from us to charge John with stupidity, because he literally observed the Law of Moses at a time when the Church followed many Jewish practices . . . "

He was off into another learned discourse on developments in the early Church. He seemed oblivious to the offence he had given. He doesn't understand feelings, thought Enfleda. He doesn't understand people. Or doesn't bother to. He only understands with his head. And suddenly the insight made her fearful. It will cause conflict, she thought. She half turned to look at Oswy. He gave the slightest widening of his eyes, expressive to her alone. He has seen it too, she knew. He was close to Colman and held him in high respect.

Wilfrid was winding up his latest discourse. "It is quite apparent, Colman, that you follow neither the example of John, as you imagine, nor that of Peter, whose tradition you deliberately contradict."

Cedd winced as he translated into Gaelic. This time Colman did not trouble to reply.

"Even if your Columba was a saint potent in miracles, how could he take precedence over the blessed Prince of the Apostles? Did not our Lord say, 'Thou are Peter, and upon this rock I will build my church, and I will give unto thee the keys of the kingdom of heaven'?"

Oswy unexpectedly rose to his feet. He had seen his opportunity. He addressed Colman directly in English. "Is it true, Colman, that these words were spoken to Peter by our Lord?"

"It is true, Lord."

"Was a similar authority given to Columba?"

"No."

"Do you both agree that this is true, that Peter was given the keys of the kingdom?" He looked from one to the other for assent. "Let this resolve the issue then. When my death comes, I don't want to be turned away at heaven's door. If Peter holds the keys of the kingdom, we must obey his words and follow his traditions."

He paused. The hall was suddenly silent. Everyone understood that the king had made the decision.

So it was Rome, thought Enfleda. As she'd expected. No matter that Colman was his friend and confessor. No matter that the Irish Church had given him and his brother shelter in exile, had nurtured and taught him. She had learned long ago he would sacrifice any allegiance for the sake of his kingship. But she admired him too, admired his quick-wittedness in seeing a way to cut through all the discussion, to justify what he was certainly going to decree anyway. She stole a quick look at Connal. She expected to see him exultant, but he was scowling and flushed. Had he wanted Oswy to oppose him?

"So," Oswy concluded, "let us all be agreed. Give me your voices. Do you all assent to follow the teachings of the Apostle Peter and to celebrate the festival of Easter in accord with the Catholic teaching?"

There was a pause, a hardly discernible moment of silence heavy with revolt. Then the hall responded to their king and overlord:

"We do."

Not Colman. Not his monks. They sat in silence.

It was all over. Everyone started to move and stretch and the air grew loud with talk. Enfleda watched as her daughter Aelfled jumped down from her bench and ran over to the prior from Melrose. She had clearly taken a fancy to him. He was young and had the strong straight stature of a fighting man. Another warrior turned priest, she thought, and as she thought it, Wilfrid crossed the hall to speak to him. The young prior swung Aelfled up in his arms, laughing with her. When he turned round and saw Wilfrid, he dropped her back to the ground and bid her greet the abbot. But Wilfrid ignored her and immediately started talking to the prior. Aelfled tugged impatiently at his sleeve.

"Aelfled!" Enfleda called out. The little girl turned, saw her mother and with a last look at the prior, ran over to her open arms. She held her daughter close, comforted by the innocence of her small sturdy body. Oswy came over and sat heavily in the chair beside her. He looked old suddenly; whey-faced and exhausted. They sat together silently for a moment. Seeing that he was low in spirits, Aelfled leaned helpfully towards him.

"Would you like to hear a riddle?" she enquired.

A sudden fit of irritation flared up in Oswy. His face reddened and he started to his feet. Aelfled shrank back into her mother's arms, fearing he was going to strike her. For a moment he stood staring at her, holding himself in check.

"We've heard enough riddles today," he muttered. He strode away without another word.

CHAPTER 19

THE ROAD TO LINDISFARNE

664 AD

Suddenly Wilfrid was at his side. Cuthbert was conscious first of his Frankish perfume, of a sweet smell of calamus and some musky incense he couldn't name. Wilfrid's fine linen shirt lay softly against his throat; the gold clasp on his shoulder shone with dull light. Cuthbert felt his own coarse woollen habit, his sweaty undershirt. Wilfrid caught hold of his arm, ignoring Aelfled who was tugging at the same arm.

"My dear brother!" He clasped Cuthbert's hands in his, smiling at him. "I'm so glad you're here! What a great day!"

There was no personal triumph in him, Cuthbert saw. He was innocent, as if he had no idea of the outrage he had caused.

"You've been loyal to your abbot, but there is nothing to hold you back now! No, and for that matter, not Eata either." He paused, drawing Cuthbert a little closer. "Of course, you'll need to be properly consecrated. The Irish consecrations aren't acceptable. But that won't be a problem."

"You mistake me, Wilfrid. I have no desire for position."

"Desire? What do our desires have to do with it? We are called to serve the Church."

"We understand that differently."

Wilfrid's face was close to his, and Cuthbert saw some of the animation drain from it. His heart tightened with regret. He knew Wilfrid wanted him and some part of Cuthbert's soul hankered for his brotherhood too. But in his deepest self he could not give in. There was a rigour in himself he would not betray.

"Can you be stubborn still, after all that has been said today?"

"So much has been said today. I need time to reflect on it."

"But it is decided!"

Cuthbert turned away.

"You're not ready to change yet, that's all. It will come. When you're ready, come and see me." Wilfrid left him and walked away, towards Prince Connal and the Roman clerics. Cuthbert caught a glimpse of Connal staring at him, his dark eyes burning.

Compline was finished, and the great silence of the night hours had begun. There would be no more speech till the morning. No more discussion. He walked wordlessly with Eata and the other monks to the guest-house. Even in the silence, the shock was still palpable between them.

He slept but seemed to wake almost at once. He found himself on Dere Street, walking bare-foot like a pilgrim. He saw that the Street no longer ended in Northumbria or the kingdoms of the south, but that the waves of the sea had parted to let it through. It passed onwards to Frankia, and he knew that from there it would continue all the way to Rome. He saw a great company of horsemen dressed in gold and scarlet riding down the road towards him. Their horses danced and skittered as they snuffed the air, the riders held their banners aloft, and Cuthbert saw that Wilfrid rode at their head, dressed more gorgeously than the rest in cloth of gold. They urged their horses forward into a gallop, with loud cries and halloos. They were heading directly towards him. He called aloud but they seemed oblivious to his presence. He tried to scramble off the road but there were thorns and briars growing so thickly he couldn't push through. The horsemen were upon him, so close that he could see the sweating flanks of the horses and their glaring eyes. The horse closest to him reared up, so that its hooves were lifted high above his head. In the seconds before they descended he glimpsed Wilfrid's face staring down at him. Then the hooves pounded down upon his head and he fell unconscious to the ground.

He woke gasping for air, still caught in the dream, and pressed his hands to his head, astonished to find himself alive. In the low dormitory he could see the dark forms of the other men sleeping peacefully in the stillness of the night. "Christ have mercy," he muttered. The words cracked in his throat. He got up and went into the hall, taking a pitcher of water from the table and sluicing cold water over his head. He slipped on his boots and stepped outside, breathing in the fresh chill of the night. A light wind blew across his face. The stars were diamond bright in the sky above him, tiny gleams from the heavenly light beyond. The night presence calmed him. There was a faint glimmer of light in the east; it would not be long till Matins.

He saw again the dream image of the rearing horse, of Wilfrid's staring face. Was it a warning? A premonition? Why did Wilfrid cause such turmoil in him?

The tradition of Cuthbert's vocation was founded on poverty, on the turning away from all worldly possession and temptation. Without that discipline, how could the soul be open to God? How could Wilfrid with all his wealth and finery know God? How could he speak of God's will? Surely his words were false! A sudden surge of anger sent his hand involuntarily to his sword hip. He found himself clutching at the woollen cloth of his habit and smiled at himself. He heard Boisil's voice in his head, as clearly as if he were beside him. "Don't judge people," he said. "Leave judgement to God." He bowed his head and submitted.

In the morning Colman called a meeting in the hall. There was no royal party this time, no Catholic clergy. Colman spoke in Latin, in formal ecclesiastical phrases that gave an added weight to his interdiction. The hall had an intense listening stillness. Colman's face was pale, but his eyes were fiery coals.

"Beloved sons and daughters in God, I come to take leave of you and of this most blessed land. I was sent here from Iona to uphold the authority and traditions of the holy Saint Columba and his teacher Saint John the Divine. The king has chosen to set those aside and to place his Church under the authority of Rome. I grieve that he has been misguided, and I pray that God will lead him back to truth. I have told him that I will resign the see and return to my homeland. I invite all of you who may so desire to follow me."

The hall grew quieter still. Colman lowered his head and wept without restraint or shame. Many in the hall wept with him, and his monks from Lindisfarne gathered close to him. They would follow him, for sure. When his tears were spent, he continued,

"Anathema on the cunning words that have so deceived the king! And on the falsity dressed up in finery that has blinded him! May he be preserved from judgement, and may God bring about the downfall of false prophets!"

Cuthbert felt Eata beside him, contained and silent. They had suffered the same loss at Ripon, but the shock was greater now. That loss had wounded them, but they had believed the conflict was over their monastery alone. Now it was revealed as the first skirmish in a wider war. Colman was leaving, as they had left Ripon then, but what of the rest of the Church?

As Colman ended his farewell, a young deacon hurried towards them. His eyes were bright with excitement, and he caught hold of Eata's hand in his eagerness. "Will you go? Will you leave with us?"

Eata held his hand for a moment, then released it. "How could I leave? I swore my vows to Aidan to be a witness to our people."

The young man was dashed. He turned to Cuthbert. "You, Father Cuthbert?"

Cuthbert shook his head.

"What is to become of Lindisfarne?" Eata asked the deacon. "Aren't you from there?"

"We'll found a new Lindisfarne in Ireland, greater than the first! Join us!" urged the young man.

Eata shook his head. "Madness," he said. "It's madness."

Looking across the hall, they saw Hild making her way towards Colman. For a shocking moment they thought she meant to join him. But after she had embraced him, she moved away and went to stand on the dais and prepared herself to speak. The clamour in the hall subsided.

"Dear brothers and sisters in Christ, I grieve as we all do for our Father Colman's going. His love for us will live forever in our hearts." She paused. "But let us not be divided. Although the king has chosen to accept the authority of Rome, he was baptised and raised in the traditions of the Irish Church. I am certain he has no wish to change our traditions or our rule."

Hild would accept the decision, Cuthbert understood. Although she had been trained by Aidan, she had been brought up in the Roman Church. She understood the wisdom of both traditions. Hers was the voice they needed. But Eata leaned towards Cuthbert.

"It's too soon. They're too hot to listen."

"The king has betrayed us!" someone yelled. Another voice joined in till the hall was in uproar again. It was shocking to see Hild so unheeded. Cuthbert felt Eata move away. Suddenly swift, he crossed the hall to her side and, taking her arm, helped her away.

"Mother Hild cried yesterday," Aelfled told him. They were walking down the steep pathway that led from the minster to the harbour below, to see the royal ship being readied for sailing. The king and queen would leave on the noon tide.

"She cried in front of everybody."

"Did you comfort her?"

"I didn't know what she was crying about."

"No."

"Did you cry?" She was intent on his face and forgot the steepness of the path.

"Watch your feet now!" He caught her hand before she fell. "Why! That was close, little sister!" He laughed till Aelfled started laughing too, and they stumbled down the slope together, still laughing. Then Cuthbert heard someone shout his name. He pulled Aelfled to a stop beside him and turned, to see a servant of the king scrambling down the hill after them.

"You are to wait upon the king in the Abbess's hall, prior. Abbot Eata is there already."

He stood astonished for a moment, before he could respond. He let go of Aelfled's hand. "Thank you. I'll go at once." He looked down at the child. "Could you—please?" he asked the man. "The princess Aelfled would like to see the king's ship." Ignoring Aelfled's scowls he handed her over to the servant and turned back towards the minster.

In the hall he found the king seated with four of his young retainers standing behind him. Eata stood before him like a plaintiff. Cuthbert went to his side, still out of breath and mud falling off his boots. It was the first time he had stood so close to the king. He saw a trace of Aelfled's innocent face in his wide forehead and clear eyes. More than a trace of her scowls too.

"Good. We have found you at last." He glared at Cuthbert for a moment to register his displeasure at being kept waiting, before turning to business.

"As you know, Colman has chosen not to accept the decision of the Synod. He is mistaken, in my view." Mistaken. Oswy hissed the word like a menace. "It will make no difference to what has been decided. But he has made a request of me to which I have agreed for the sake of our past friendship." He paused, looking at the two men. "Because, Abbot Eata, you were one of the twelve Northumbrian boys chosen by Aidan, Colman has asked that you take charge of the monastery at Lindisfarne."

He took a long draught from his drinking vessel and set it down heavily on the table. "He wants you to preserve Aidan's inheritance." He leaned forward, appraising the abbot. "I am willing to grant the request. It'll need a strong hand. I advise you take your prior with you."

Eata moved his head slightly in assent. Oswy continued, "I'm going to appoint a new bishop to take over from Colman. Tuda. He's sound. He'll be based at Lindisfarne, but you'll have authority over the monastery."

The king stared at them for another moment, then turned away and started to speak to one of his men. The audience was over. Eata bowed deeply; Cuthbert, bewildered, had to be nudged into doing the same. Eata pushed him towards the door.

Once outside, Eata glanced at him, then gestured to the path that led away from the minster. "Let's take a walk," he said. A path led past the huts and north along the headland. As they walked the hubbub of the Synod faded into silence. A grey mist was starting to blow in from the sea. In the stillness, Cuthbert felt the agitated beating of his heart.

"Are you willing to come with me?" said Eata. Cuthbert stopped and glanced behind him. He couldn't answer yet. Eata stood beside him, waiting. As the mist grew thicker, even the edge of the headland was obscured.

"Colman wants Lindisfarne to continue in the spirit of Aidan. He knows that means accepting the Synod's decision. In his heart he must think it possible."

"What's possible?"

"A middle way. A uniting of the traditions. But there'll be a lot of opposition on Lindisfarne."

Cuthbert thought of Wilfrid. "Come and see me when you're ready," he had said. He could go to Wilfrid and become a senior cleric in the new order. He could travel with Wilfrid, have a monastery of his own to command, build new churches. But as he thought it, he knew he would not. He would go with Eata. Of course he would. His heart steadied.

"I'll come with you," he said.

CHAPTER 20

ABSENCE

664 AD

Father Cuthbert and the abbot stayed on after her queen-mother and king-father left and spent hour after hour shut away with Mother Hild. This time Mother Hild didn't tell her she had to sit and listen, although she wouldn't have minded. She could have played the riddle game with Father Cuthbert. But as it was, she hardly saw him till he was getting ready to leave. She was called for from her lessons, to join Mother Hild in the hall where the farewells were taking place.

All the senior monks and nuns were there, as well as Mother Hild, all talking together with the abbot and Father Cuthbert. She could hear him laughing. When he saw her, he came towards her.

"Are you going now?" she asked.

"Yes. It's time to say goodbye."

She looked up at him. Suddenly she couldn't think of anything to say.

"I have something for you," he said.

He opened the leather pouch attached to his belt and pulled something out. She thought it might be like a riddle prize, a special shell or two fat hazel nuts. But this was different. It was a little cross, whittled out of a single piece of wood. The four arms curved out symmetrically from the centre and flared wider at their ends. It was pine wood, and still smelled of its aromatic oil. She held it close to her nose, smelling it. It felt smooth and polished. When she turned it over, she saw there were carvings in the centre of the cross on both sides. They looked like letters, but different from any she knew.

"What are they?"

"Runes."

"What do they say?"

"That's for you to find out. Keep it safe."

She nodded, holding it tightly to her. The abbot had finished embracing Mother Hild and the others. They were starting to move towards the door.

Cuthbert put his hand on her head and said a blessing for her. When he had finished, he bent down and kissed her forehead. Then Mother Hild and the abbot were beside them, and the abbot gave her a blessing too, and everyone went out to bid them farewell. They walked with them as far as the path down to the harbour, and then watched them as they wound their way down to the ship waiting for them at the quayside. By the time they were on board it was too far away to see them distinctly, but Aelfled thought she saw Father Cuthbert turn and wave. A brisk westerly wind filled the wide sail and the ship moved swiftly over the water of the bay and out to sea.

For a day or two after they left, Aelfled felt blessed and holy. She kept the little cross beside her bed and held it while she said her prayers. She was becoming a holy nun, she felt. But at breakfast on the third day a thought came like a serpent within her. Father Cuthbert had gone away and hadn't said anything about coming back. If he would, or when he would. All of a sudden she understood the truth. He wasn't coming back. He had gone and she was all alone. He had betrayed her. She pushed away her bread and milk half-eaten.

"What's the matter?" asked Nurse.

"I'm not hungry." A salty tear ran down her cheek and she licked it away. "I don't feel like eating."

Her low spirits continued over the next few days. She was unusually quiet and took no interest in her lessons. During the offices she couldn't bring herself to sing. After a while Mother Hild sent for her. It was time for harvesting herbs for drying, and she wanted Aelfled to help her. She had baskets ready for both of them. They went off together to the herb garden to pick sage and lavender. It was one of Aelfled's favourite tasks. She loved the aromatic smell that filled the air as they cut the herb stalks and lavender stems. It was a fine afternoon, and the beds were full of the sound of bees working the flowers. She rubbed the lavender between her fingers and held it to her nose. She looked at Mother Hild, in her brown robes and fresh white headdress, working steadily along the row of herbs.

"Mother Hild, could I go and live at Lindisfarne for part of the year?" Mother Hild laughed.

"You would have to cut off your hair and wear boys' clothes if you did. It's not a double minster like Whitby."

Aelfled stared at her. "Aren't there any nuns?"

"No. Just monks."

"Why?"

"That's how Father Aidan arranged it. He started with a monastery, and on Lindisfarne it has stayed that way. He trained me as an abbess, so that a convent could be founded, but land was given here for it."

Aelfled went on picking lavender stems in silence, till she could no longer hold back another question. "Will Abbot Eata and Father Cuthbert come and visit us again?"

"Not for a while. They will be busy when they go to Lindisfarne. But there will be Church councils and other gatherings. It will be up to the new bishop to decide where they are held."

Hild straightened up from the bed and looked out to sea, as if half expecting to see a distant sail. "Soon you will be old enough to visit the court at Bamburgh. Lindisfarne isn't far away from Bamburgh. Perhaps you will see them then."

"Will I? Will I visit Bamburgh?"

"Yes. When your mother invites you."

Aelfled felt her spirits lift. She would go to Bamburgh and eat feasts and see Edfrith and Audrey. Father Cuthbert would come and see her. She put her basket down and ran over to Mother Hild. Mother Hild put her arms round her and held her tight.

CHAPTER 21

IN CHAPTER

664 AD

As he came out of the Lindisfarne infirmary, Cuthbert took a deep breath of the dawn air. It was a relief to stand for a moment in the cold wind, to see the clouds moving across the sky, to feel rain on his face. He muttered a prayer for the suffering of the man inside. Tuda, their new bishop, was still alive, but after a week of fever and foul skin eruptions, his body was wasting. His feet and hands were turning black; the stench of decaying flesh was nauseating.

This outbreak of the plague had brought new and dreadful symptoms Cuthbert hadn't seen before. He didn't fear for himself; God had spared him through the faith of his brothers, and it could not touch him now. But he knew there was no possibility of recovery for the bishop. He was too weakened to survive, his spirit scarcely clinging to a body already half-destroyed. All they could do was try to lessen his suffering and pray it would purge his spirit so that he would enter heaven already purified.

There were outbreaks of the plague all over the country; half the monks at Gilling had died, and many more of the lay people. Tuda's death wouldn't be the first. But it would cast a longer shadow over the turmoil at Lindisfarne. After Colman's departure, it had taken time to consecrate the new bishop. Tuda had hardly been two months on the island before the sickness took him. Was it a sign of God's displeasure, as some would surely say?

He would not think of that now. His body was aching for sleep after the night vigil in the infirmary. Cuthbert looked round for the monk due to relieve him at Tuda's side. There was no sign of him. He set off to the man's hut to remind him.

He reached the hut and looked inside. The monk's name was Hereward, he remembered. The man was seated, apparently in contemplation. Cuthbert waited a moment till he should finish.

"Brother Hereward, you are waited for in the infirmary."

The man acknowledged him with a movement of his head but made no move to rise.

"The bishop needs your help," Cuthbert prompted.

"Tuda is not our bishop."

"It's not the time for arguments. He is a dying man."

"Let his own attendants wait on him."

Cuthbert hardly knew the man. He and Eata had taken up the positions of abbot and prior at Lindisfarne only months ago. There was no bond of loyalty between them and these Lindisfarne brothers, no understanding. But what understanding could there be of such stubbornness?

"Where has this hardness of heart come from?"

The man sat sullen, refusing to look at him. Like a child with the sulks, thought Cuthbert. He could order him to do it, but what was the point?

"I see you are refusing to move. I'll return to the infirmary in your place."

He straightened up, took a breath and walked back to the infirmary. It took a momentary effort to go back into the stench of the sickroom. When he did, he saw that Tuda's suffering was over. His pale face was rigid, eyes staring in death. One of the priests he had brought with him was saying the prayers for the dead over him. Cuthbert dropped onto his knees beside him, and reaching over, closed Tuda's eyes and prayed with the priest. The familiar words flowed through him, although he was so tired he was hardly conscious of what he was saying.

They buried Tuda the following day in the monks' cemetery on Lindisfarne. His corpse was already decaying; there was no time for ceremony. Eata sent messengers to Bamburgh to inform the king that he had lost his bishop and would need to consider a new appointment. It would all take time—a suitable candidate had to be found, who would not cause offence to either the Irish or the Catholics. Usually a new bishop would be sent to Canterbury for consecration, but the plague had carried off the Archbishop too. The pope would have to choose and consecrate a new archbishop first. It could take months. Years.

After the interment, Cuthbert and Eata walked together, past the crag that loomed over the bay to the far tip of the island and the open sea. Waves broke on the rocks in a sudden spray of white surf. Beyond the shore, the water stretched away to the horizon, the grey water stippling and darkening under the gusty wind. It was still a wonder to Cuthbert, to live so close to the ocean. He understood, now, why the Irish monks chose islands. Here, you were at one remove from the world. Close to the infinity of God.

"Aidan used to come up here," said Eata. "It was his consolation, when all our arguments and fights got too much for him."

They stared out. Not far from the shore there were scores of gannets circling over the water, turning to dive with wings drawn back and plummeting fast into the water. They moved with the shoal of fish beneath, diving again and again. Then dark shapes became visible among the birds.

"Look!" said Cuthbert. The shining black forms of dolphins rose out of the water and plunged back with an upward flip of their tails, joining the pursuit of the shoal. The two men watched the dark line of arching backs cutting through the waves. The creation was all joy, Cuthbert thought. Why did men mar it?

Eata bent down and picked up a stone, running his fingers round the hole worn through its centre. "Do you know what one of the brothers said to me today? He said that I should be ashamed of betraying my teacher Aidan. He said this to my face, I who am his abbot."

"What did you say?"

"I was furious. When did I last feel furious with one of my brothers? I felt insulted in my office, that he should dare to speak to me like that. Then I realised I should be grateful to the man. How else would I have seen my own pride? I thanked him and gave him my blessing."

They both laughed.

"He didn't know Aidan, or he wouldn't have spoken like that. It didn't worry Aidan if there seemed to be contradictions or differences. They were our limitations. He believed it was all contained in God's mercy, if we could but see it."

Cuthbert was silent. It seemed impossible that the brothers would share such a vision. Impossible that the bitterness and anger would ever be over.

"Don't meet evil with evil," said Eata. "Christ has taught us that. We have to hold steady."

Cuthbert realised that he spoke the truth of himself, that Eata held steady and always would. Whatever it cost him.

The next day, during the afternoon work period, Cuthbert saw the monk, Brother Hereward, who had refused to help him. He stood with a little group of his brothers, so intent on their conversation they didn't notice the prior approach.

"Time for work, brothers," Cuthbert remarked.

Reluctantly they dispersed, with glances at one another as if to make an assignation for further whispering. Hereward turned aside, and as he did so, glanced back at the prior. The spiteful malice in his gaze caught Cuthbert off guard. He felt it physically, like a blow to his body that made him wince. When he looked back, Hereward had turned away. He hardly knew the man, and yet such hatred. It wasn't personal, he knew. He would almost rather it were. Hereward saw him through the glass of his beliefs and grievances. They were like a new pestilence, he thought, that spread through the blood vessels to the heart itself. Love dried up and all that was left was recrimination and hatred.

He walked on, down to the infirmary, and pulled the dirty blankets off the bed where Tuda had lain. They would have to be burned. He carried them down to the shore and set a fire on the stones with pieces of driftwood and dry seaweed. When it had grown strong enough, he threw the blankets on. He stood watching the flames leap up through the cloth, poking and pushing with a stick till it was burned to ashes.

Every day, as their prior, he met with the brothers in Chapter. At Melrose the meetings were the heart of the community's life. The brothers could talk about any difficulties they were having, conflicts were brought into the open and practical matters sorted out. Everyone understood that Chapter was to be conducted in a spirit of charity. Not here. The wounds of Colman's departure were still raw. The debates raged on, with angry denunciations of the Roman position. The arguments were picked over again and again, and any intervention he made was met with raised voices and hardly restrained criticism.

Even practical matters caused conflict. Many of the younger brothers had left with Colman to found the new monastery in Ireland. With lower numbers, it was difficult to cover all the tasks of the monastery. Cuthbert would do the work of two, but the brothers refused to take on any extra duties. Quarrels would break out between them. He had never known such ill-will in a community. It oppressed him like a dark cloud over his spirits. He could impose discipline and forbid discussion, but he knew it would only break out elsewhere.

He came to a decision. Each morning, he required silence of the community for the first part of Chapter. During that time he spoke to them about the Roman teaching on Easter, on Christ's resurrection and the changes to the Rule they were now required to accept. He went on to give orders for the work for the day. The brothers were then at liberty to speak. The attacks and arguments would start all over again. He made no attempt to respond but concentrated himself fully on his own state, on being himself in charity, so that he could bear witness to the spirit of Chapter. He begged the Holy Spirit to strengthen him. When he felt he could endure no more, he got up and left the meeting. The following morning he returned and set it before them again. And again.

He was working in the infirmary one afternoon when Brother Hereward came to the door. His manner was changed; he was shaking and agitated.

"Father. Forgive me. I am . . . I cannot say . . . I must come . . . "

Cuthbert saw that sweat was running down his face and neck. His skin was pale with a hectic red flush high on the cheeks.

"Come in, brother."

Hereward burst into tears and staggered forward to take his hand.

"Forgive me, Father! Will I die?"

"All of us will pray for you. Don't be afraid." He took the man's arms and took him inside. He sat him on a bench and called for a brother to help. "Bring hot water and cloths!" The monk came, caught sight of Hereward's feverish face and started to back away. "God save you! Just bring me water. And the herbs we used for Tuda."

He stayed with Hereward through the afternoon and night. The same sores and boils that had afflicted Tuda erupted on his skin, and fever burned him. All night Cuthbert sat with him, putting poultices on the sores, helping him drink, washing the sweat from his body. Day came, and he knew it was time for Chapter.

When he entered the hall there was a new silence. He felt fear in the room. "Brothers," he said, "you know our Brother Hereward lies sick of the plague. Please pray for him. And I need someone to help me."

There was no argument now. No reproaches. Two brothers came forward, and together they turned back to the infirmary. At last, he felt the beginnings of a brotherhood with his monks.

CHAPTER 22

THE CUB SNAPS AT
THE OLD WOLF

664 AD

"Drink it," Enfleda said. "And do what you're told in future."

"It's horrible," Aylwin protested. "The other boys don't have to have it."

"Do you want boils all over your body and your tongue to turn black? Drink it. You too, Edith."

The little girl watched her brother, and when he finally swallowed down the infusion, she tried too. The bitter yarrow was too much for her, and she stopped with a face.

"Look," said Enfleda. "I'll drink a bit, and you can drink the rest."

She swallowed a gulp and gave it back to Edith. The physician stood beside her, watching.

"Every morning, my lady. They must take it every morning."

"Yes. I'll make sure they do."

Aylwin put down the beaker. She took him in her arms and gave him a hug.

"There. It wasn't so bad, was it?"

He was six years old now, and so strong and brown and sturdy after a summer in the hills that she couldn't imagine sickness taking hold of him. But after the plague deaths on Lindisfarne she was taking no chances. She had the physician make up infusions for the children to take, and the halls were smoked every day with juniper and bunches of wild thyme. So far, there had been no outbreaks inland. They were safer here, at Ad Gefrin, and she persuaded Oswy to delay their return to Bamburgh. There was no hurry. He had a new bishop to find, but it could wait. After the upheavals over the Synod he was ready to take his ease and watch his tithe stores filling up.

Aylwin ran off to find his friends in the village. Enfleda took Edith's hand and looked round for her nurse.

"Can we go to the river? Can cousin Audrey come with us?"

"Yes. Go and find her. And Nurse. I'll wait for you."

It would get Audrey out of chapel. Audrey adored Edith and would do anything she asked. Why not have one of your own, Enfleda felt like asking her. Audrey was 27, had been married to Edfrith for more than three years, and there was not a whisper of a pregnancy. But it was hard to stay angry with Audrey. In some ways she was an ideal daughter-in-law. She got on well with everyone, never tried to interfere with Enfleda's running of the household and didn't gossip. And, in spite of her saintliness and disregard for her appearance, she was good company. Enfleda could confide in Audrey, as she would not have done with her women; Audrey was a royal princess of the blood. Like herself, she had been married off when she was scarcely 16. Although she was now married to Enfleda's son, there were scarcely eleven years between them. They could have been mistaken for sisters, rather than mother- and daughter-in-law.

As Enfleda waited outside the hall, she saw three horsemen arrive at the gate. The guard called servants to take their horses and the three men hurried across to the hall. Oswy was inside, she knew. He would receive them.

But by the time Edith came back, with Nurse and Audrey holding a hand each and swinging her along, the news, whatever it was, had been delivered. She could hear Oswy shouting in the great hall. Audrey's face turned pale. She was afraid of her father-in-law.

"Come on," said Edith, tugging at them.

"All right," said Enfleda. "We'll find out what's happened soon enough."

The hall was humming with rumour when they got back. It seemed that Oswy and Edfrith were already in council with the senior commanders of the guard. Clearly, this was something more than a summer cattle raid. Nurse took Edith away and Enfleda sent a servant to find one of the messengers who had brought this news. She took Audrey with her and went to her private rooms.

It was Connal, she understood, as soon as the man began to speak. There was an inevitability about it—not in the particulars of what he'd done, but the principle—so that she felt no surprise. Only a familiar, cauterising sense of dread. She had known it would come, sooner or later.

It seemed that the prince had received the news of Bishop Tuda's death not with grief, or even with polite regret, but with a sudden outburst of crazy laughter and shouting. Wilfrid was at his side when the news arrived, and the messenger reported that everyone had seen Connal turn and embrace him without restraint.

"At last!" he had cried out, according to the messenger, "At last! God has made straight the path! You will be bishop!"

Enfleda interrupted the messenger to ask what Father Wilfrid had said. But the man had taken no note of that. Audrey leaned forward, pale face tight with anxiety.

"Father Wilfrid—I'm certain he would think only of the Church, of his vocation."

Audrey had fallen under Wilfrid's spell at Whitby. She couldn't bear him to be blamed. Wilfrid would have regretted Tuda's death, she was sure. But all the same he might have seen it as the will of God. And himself as His instrument.

The prince had taken it on himself to immediately appoint Wilfrid as Bishop of Lindisfarne, the messenger told them. At once Enfleda understood Oswy's reaction. Everyone knew that such an appointment was the prerogative of the king alone. It seemed that Connal had not even troubled to consult Oswy. He would have known that his father would never appoint Wilfrid, she thought. Although Oswy had accepted the Roman Church in principle, when it came to appointments he still favoured men from the Irish tradition.

Connal had sent the news out under his own seal to all the Church leaders in the kingdom, the messenger told her.

It was a deliberate, public flouting of Oswy's authority. Connal must have been seized with madness. Was he blinded by his love for Wilfrid? Or was it, as they were whispering in the hall, a declaration of war?

But the messenger hadn't finished. She turned her attention back to him. With the Archbishop dead of the plague at Canterbury, Wilfrid had chosen to be consecrated in Frankia. He had already set off, with many retainers from Connal's household. Neither he nor Connal had troubled to seek Oswy's permission.

When the messenger had been dismissed, Audrey was red with agitation.

"Father Wilfrid doesn't seek his own glorification. He's not a vain man. He's not self-seeking. He wants only the glory of the Church."

"But it blinds him, Audrey. Connal is using him."

Audrey stared at her, uncomprehending. Audrey was so innocent. She wanted to see only goodness. How could she conceive of the treachery hidden in Connal's heart?

In the afternoon Oswy called the household together. She sat beside him in her royal chair, her gold circlet on her head. She was afraid, but since the news of the morning, anger had been growing in her like a building storm. She felt herself severe and unyielding beside the king. He wore a dark leather tunic studded with silver, a rich purple cloak and gold rings round his neck and arms. His hair was white, but he was still a powerful figure. At this moment, with his kingship under threat, she sat with him to demonstrate their strength and majesty to the household. The kingdom was held in their hands; they would not waver.

From the corner of her eye, Enfleda saw Audrey, sitting next to Edfrith. She looked distraught, with red eyes and anxious fingers pleating and re-pleating the cloth of her gown. She must wish she were safe in a convent far away, thought Enfleda.

Oswy rose from his chair and stood, legs akimbo, and glowered down at his household.

"You have heard the news that Prince Connal has attempted to appoint Abbot Wilfrid as bishop. He has exceeded his authority. He might wish for Wilfrid's appointment, but the choice is mine. The appointment will go to Father Chad."

Oswy's jaw was clenched so that his words had a kind of drawled menace. He stared over the heads of the gathering to the open doors beyond.

"I have sent word to the churchmen revoking Abbot Wilfrid's so-called appointment, and to Prince Connal. I have ordered him to recall Wilfrid at once, and to return him to his former position as abbot. If Prince Connal obeys my orders, it will be an end of the matter."

The "if" hung in the air for a long moment.

"In the meantime, the reeve will start organising the household to leave for Bamburgh as soon as possible. My warriors will leave with me tonight."

Before he left he came and saw her privately. He lay heavily on the bed, letting out a deep sigh. She sat on the end of the bed, watching him. He was getting old. When he got to Bamburgh, his body would be stiff and painful after the ride, he would have to be rubbed with oil before he could sleep. How could he lead men into battle? He sat himself up on one elbow and looked at her.

"I have yielded to him again and again. This time it has to come to question."

She nodded.

"The cub is snapping at the old wolf. He may find the wolf still has some bite left in him."

"What will he do?"

"The council thinks it will be war."

"Let your warriors fight, Oswy. You are too old for battle."

"I have to lead them. Edfrith is too young. He has not fought. And how should he fight against his own brother?"

"How should a father fight against his own son?"

Oswy didn't respond. They sat for a few moments in silence. Then, turning to the wall he bowed his head and started to weep. She sat without moving. She had no comfort for him. They were not her tears; how could she weep for Connal, who had become the enemy of her house? But Oswy might weep indeed, to be so betrayed by his son and his first-born.

It took the messengers six days to return from Deira. By then the household had returned to Bamburgh, and the fortress was being provisioned. Aylwin had cried to leave Ad Gefrin, but now he was enthralled with the camp developing on the flat ground below the castle rock. Every day brought another war band, too many to house in the castle. The soldiers put up tents with poles and hides and tethered their horses in grazing lines near the dunes. At night there were camp fires and a roar of singing and laughter as they drank good ale. Aylwin was not allowed to join them. He had to watch from the gatehouse.

"When will there be a battle?" he wanted to know.

"Ask your father. There might not be a battle. It won't be here in any case. They are gathering here, that's all."

Audrey wanted to know as well. She came to find Enfleda, her eyes and nose red and tears dripping off her chin.

"Edfrith won't talk to me. He's with the soldiers all the time, as if war was about to break out."

"Yes."

"It can't be! We can't let this happen!"

"Maybe it won't happen. All Connal has to do is obey his father and recall Wilfrid."

"But Wilfrid—why should he not be bishop?"

"He's been a fool. He shouldn't have accepted the appointment from Connal."

"It was for love of the Church."

Enfleda felt irritation rising up in her.

"Connal wants the kingdom, Audrey. All of it. He is testing Oswy. If he has his way, what do you think will become of Edfrith? Of Aylwin? Of us? We'll all be fugitives or worse."

"No! No! It can't be so!" The tears streamed faster off her chin till the neck of her gown was damp.

Deira, Enfleda thought. Trouble always came from Deira. She saw herself again, younger than Audrey was now, pleading with Oswy for her kinsman Selwin. "He is kin, you must talk, it is a misunderstanding," she had told him. Just as Audrey pleaded with her now.

She was certain it would be war. She didn't shrink from it. This was her war; for her sons, for her husband. She didn't want a truce with Connal. She wanted war, at any cost, that would stamp on the head of the serpent in her Eden. He could be banished. Or deposed. But he must be gone. She still felt the old dread, that Oswy would be killed, that Edfrith would be killed, that all would be lost, but this time her anger was stronger than the dread. For the first time she understood what men felt, what gave them the courage to stand in the shield wall.

When the messengers returned, they were taken directly to the king. The whole fortress was on tiptoe, waiting for the news. When he came out into the hall with his bodyguard, she knew before he spoke. His face was as hard as the black rock of the castle.

"Prince Connal has raised his forces. He is camped at Catterick. We will march tomorrow."

CHAPTER 23

NEW YEAR

665 AD

ᴜʜɪᛏʙʏ

It was like a riddle, but a bad riddle where everyone else knew the answer except her. Today, on New Year's Day, she would find out what it was.

When Aelfled had first noticed the change, she thought it was just a mistake. It was during the part in the offices when there were prayers for the rulers of the world. "Especially," the Cantor would say, "for Oswy, King of Northumbria, Connal, Prince of Deira, and all the family of the king." She always listened to that part of the office, because at that moment everyone was praying for her, as part of the royal family. She stood in a dignified way, to acknowledge all those prayers for her safety and righteousness.

One morning she heard the Cantor say, " . . . and especially Oswy, King of Northumbria, and all the family of the king." At first she wasn't sure what was wrong. Next time she listened more carefully. Then she realised. Connal, Prince of Deira, had been left out. Her half-brother was missing. The next day and the day after it was the same.

"Why have we stopped praying for Connal Prince of Deira?" she asked Bertha.

"Have we?" Bertha had replied. "I hadn't noticed."

"Don't you listen to the prayers?"

"Of course I do. I just didn't notice that."

When she went to do her spinning with two of the older sisters, she tried again. While she was preparing her pile of fleece, she asked them, "Why have we stopped praying for Connal, Prince of Deira?"

"Because he was a wicked, sinful ... " The other sister looked up quickly from her distaff and gave the speaker a sharp look, which Aelfled saw clearly.

" . . . and because he's just a prince. We never should have been praying for him, and now we've stopped."

The other woman leaned over.

"If that pile of fleece gets any higher, you'll be spinning till midnight. Let's get your thread started—like this, look."

It was the same whoever she asked. If Father Cuthbert had been there, he would have told her. It was one of the good things about Father Cuthbert. He answered questions properly. But he hadn't been back to Whitby since the Synod. There was plague and the bishop had died on Lindisfarne and nobody was travelling anywhere.

In the end she asked Mother Hild.

"You're right. We have stopped praying for Prince Connal. It is part of the doom this evil year has brought. It has set brothers and sisters against each other and fathers against sons. When the year is finished, I'll explain to you what has happened."

Aelfled heard the bit about fathers against sons. Perhaps Connal had quarrelled with their father. She had seen for herself what a bad temper her father had. She remembered how Connal had sat on his own, at the Synod. He had dark hair and eyes and looked full of fire. Although he was her half-brother, he hadn't talked to her. Not once.

Last night she had reminded Mother Hild of her promise, and now she stood in Mother Hild's room. It was New Year's Day, and she would get an answer at last.

BAMBURGH

Enfleda felt the silk between her fingers. The quality of it was wonderful, crisp and smooth. It had been dyed in different shades of red, from a dark orange through to scarlet. It filled her with a kind of exultation; it was so beautiful. Imagine a gold necklace set against such colours! She held the fabric to her cheek. They could stitch panels of it into a gown, so that it would move with the linen.

She had intended to give it to Audrey as a parting gift, and perhaps she still might. But what a waste it would be if she never wore it. Even now, when she was to have her own kingdom, Audrey took no interest in her appearance. It doesn't matter what you want, Enfleda had told her. It's expected of you. People will think Edfrith has no regard for you. Audrey had smiled, her sweet but now-tragic smile, and said nothing.

She would decide in the morning.

Oswy had been generous to Edfrith. He had given him some of his best horses, warriors for his bodyguard, and a whole chest of gold—coin, rings, ornaments. Edfrith would need to be lavish when he arrived in Deira. Most of the Deiran nobility had remained loyal to Oswy, but they would expect gifts from their new prince.

Oswy had returned from the campaign with grief like shutters on his face. She knew better than try to talk to him. She'd got it all from Edfrith.

Connal's revolt had petered out. The Deirans had little interest in a war over a bishop; when Oswy arrived with his war-hardened troops, most of the Deiran fyrd melted away. But not Connal. He wouldn't submit. He gave battle with the loyal warriors of his household and they fought to the end. Oswy had given orders for Connal to be taken prisoner, Edfrith told her. But they couldn't get near him. He fell with his men.

Should she have grieved for him? He had been her step-son. She had tried to love him. But when she heard the news, she felt nothing. Only pity for Oswy. She had tried to find out how Edfrith had taken it. He was so tall now she'd had to crane her neck to look at his face. Even then she could mostly see his beard. She wanted to see his expression. Had he seen

Connal die? Was he pleased to be his father's heir? It was impossible to know what he felt. Oswy was calculating, but his emotions could burst out, and she had learned to understand all his moods. But her son, her first-born who had been closer to her than her own soul, was a stranger to her. He would be Prince of Deira now and heir to the kingdom. Wasn't it what she had wanted? Wouldn't her love for him be fulfilled when he ruled? Yet still she felt an aching in her heart when she looked at him. She thought of Aylwin. She would never let him go as she had let Edfrith go. Never.

COMPIÈGNE

There was a sharp frost on New Year's Day. Inside the cathedral, the stone walls held a damp chill that penetrated the very marrow of the monks' bones, and they thought of the New Year feast that awaited them, of the warm red wine they would drink. But Bishop Wilfrid, dressed in the heavy vestments of his new office, felt neither cold nor appetite as he raised the paten of consecrated bread high over the altar. This was the only food he sought now. He had sworn to say 40 masses for Prince Connal's soul, and with each one he felt himself become more remote from earthly attachments.

At first, he had felt sudden stabbings of anguish whenever he remembered Connal. He saw again the intense dark gaze reaching into his soul, crying out to him. At such moments he would take a draught of incense into his nose and mouth to cleanse his thoughts, if he were in church, or splash cold water over his head. God had showed him his error. He had taken from him what he loved most to show him his unfaithfulness. Put not your trust in kings or princes, the psalms reminded him, but in the Most High who is always your protector.

He prayed now for Connal's soul and for his eternal rest, and the monks mumbled obediently behind him. Why would they feel anything for a prince of a distant northern kingdom they'd hardly heard of? And should he himself not wash his hands of it, now that Oswy had banished him and appointed Chad in his stead?

But Oswy could not undo what God had sanctified. He had been consecrated as bishop to the Northumbrians in this very church, borne aloft to the altar on his episcopal throne by six of his fellow bishops. His consecration had been witnessed by all the brethren of the Church, and no earthly king could undo it. God's purpose for him had not changed, he was certain. It was God alone who would bring about the fulfilment of his vocation and the undoing of the heresies that contaminated His Church in Northumbria. Connal had given his life to affirm that vocation. Wilfrid would not betray it.

LINDISFARNE

Cuthbert watched the red disc of the sun slide up from the sea's edge on the horizon and grow into a perfect and glorious whole. It was unblemished, with no clouds in the pale pearly sky. It appeared to him like a New Year covenant of forgiveness, a sign that the dreadful augury of the eclypsis had ended.

He had climbed over the rocks to the small isle before dusk the evening before, taking only some water with him. He stood and knelt in prayer through the long hours of the winter night. The stars wheeled over him in a distant silver cloud, and a new moon hung low in the sky. In the hours before midnight the tide flooded in over the rocks and surrounded the isle with gleaming water, ripples glittering in the moonlight over the deep darkness of the sea. It was an isle beside an island; a tiny hump of grass and rock next to Lindisfarne that stood stark and bare out of the water at low tide and became a true island for five or six hours at each high tide. In the autumn Cuthbert had built a retreat cell there. He had started to yearn for solitude; to stand before God alone, stripped of everything, like the Desert Fathers. It wasn't an escape, a turning away from his brothers. It was only here, where his heart could be empty of everything but God, that he could become a means to help them.

It was bitterly cold through the night, and his body was chilled to the bone. Sometimes he walked up and down to loosen his joints and tucked his frozen hands into the warm cloth of his habit. The water he had brought with him started to freeze; he put the bottle close to his body as he knelt and took small sips when he rested between rounds of psalms and prayers. When the moon set, he lay down on the hard floor of his cell and slept for a few hours, till the ache of hunger woke him.

The brothers would celebrate on New Year's Day, but he would maintain his fast till dusk. He was doing penance for the monastery, to expiate the sins of the old year and to pray for the souls of the men who had died of plague. There had been so much suffering. So much strife.

Now, in the cold dawn, listening to the unearthly crying of the seals hauled out on the sands of the island, he felt his heart rise with the glowing sun. It was a new dawn, a new year drawing him closer to Christ's coming again. Even in his penance, he rejoiced.

PART 4

THE ENEMIES OF GOD

670–78 AD

CHAPTER 24

THE BOWER HALL

670 AD

They had moved Oswy to the private chamber at the back of the hall. The door stood open, to allow warmth from the hall fires to enter the room. She had ordered extra hangings to be placed on the walls to keep the icy February draughts at bay, and his bed was covered in furs and blankets. But it was still cold. When Enfleda sat with him, she wore her fur-lined cloak and held it close around her. She stayed with him, hour after hour, watching him. Candles burned all through the long night, casting a sallow light on his face. His cheeks and lips were sunken, so that his long bony nose stood out more prominently. He looked like a beak-nosed salmon caught in a net, his body twitching and jerking restlessly beneath the covers as though trying to break free. Nights had merged into days while she sat here, watching him struggle and sink back again, enmeshed in fevers that left him weak and exhausted.

It felt like a bad dream from which she would wake up soon, and Oswy too, and they would drink a cup of warm wine together and laugh at their imaginings. It could not be. After all his struggles, she had come to believe that he was invincible. He had fought for his kingdom all his life, all their married life together, and now his grasp was secure. What could shake him? True, his hair was a shock of white and his face was worn like leather, but his mind was still as cunning and vigilant as ever. He sat every morning in his hall as he had always done, consulting his reeves, hearing plaintiffs, receiving guests.

But now a different enemy was laying siege at his door. When he had ridden out with his dogs on a bright January morning to hunt deer in the Kyloe hills, she had caught no whiff of fate in his traces. But the day had turned stormy, and he had come home late, soaked through and frozen. Still, she had thought nothing of it. She had seen him soaked often enough before. But two days later the fever started, and with it the terrible pain in his limbs that made him scream aloud. She brought physicians, made them smoke him with strong herbs and rub his tormented body with oils. Sometimes it seemed to bring relief, but it was only a truce before the next onslaught of the enemy. With every bout he grew weaker and a little more of his strength ebbed away.

It was as though he had already entered purgatory, Enfleda thought; had started the suffering he must endure to purge his soul of the sins of his kingship. She had a gold altar cross placed on the table beside him and had his mass priest wait on him constantly in case he wanted to make confession. But he would not let go. Not yet. When he was lucid, in the respite between the fevers, his mind still worked restlessly. He would send for his reeve or his commander and give new orders. She felt the world would stop without Oswy.

Yesterday, letters had come from Theodore, the new Archbishop of Canterbury.

"You must wait," she had told the messengers. "He's better in the mornings." Now, with the men waiting behind her in the hall, she looked at him. He seemed to be sleeping, his eyes closed, his hair streaked with sweat. "No," she thought at first. "Let him rest." Then his eyes opened, and he looked at her.

He saw that it was Enfleda his wife in her fur cloak standing in the doorway with her gaze upon him.

"What is it?" His voice was grown so faint, she had to strain to hear him.

"There are messengers from Theodore." She waited for his response. He nodded slightly. "Yes."

She let the two men enter. They bowed deeply and stood back from the bed, their eyes not yet accustomed to the dim light. The first one started to speak. "Most royal king, Archbishop Theodore sends his greetings in Christ. He has bidden us bring his letter to you." The man unrolled a parchment and looked uncertainly at Oswy.

"Read it to him," Enfleda said. He started to read the long formal invocations. Oswy shook his head and glanced at her.

"Just tell him what the Archbishop wants," she interpreted. The messenger lowered the parchment.

"Most royal king, it concerns the priest Wilfrid, formerly Bishop of Lindisfarne. The Archbishop believes that Wilfrid was consecrated bishop through a true and catholic consecration under God, such that no man can set aside but God alone. He asks that in obedience to God you allow Wilfrid to take up the office to which he has been called."

Oswy did not stir. There was a long silence. The noises of the hall drifted into the room; a man dropping a load of logs beside the hearth, the reeve shouting at the servants moving a table, the distant sound of laughter. Inside the sickroom the candle flames jumped suddenly in the draught. The messengers glanced at each other, uncertain if the king had understood.

She watched him, waiting. His eyes opened again and caught hers for a moment.

"Get a scribe," he said, so softly only she heard him. There was a sudden scurry of activity to find a scribe, to fetch quill and document. The scribe, breathless, had to bend close over the bed to hear what Oswy wanted him to write. Then the servants must help the king to sit upright for a moment, so he could take the quill and sign. He beckoned to the messenger to take it. The man took only a moment to read it and show it to his companion. Enfleda saw that Oswy must have agreed to the request; the men were all bows and smiles as they backed out of the room, uttering cordial wishes for the king's recovery. Oswy held himself alert till they were gone. Then he let his head drop back against the pillow, exhausted. She could see drops of sweat gathering at his forehead. She dropped to her knees beside him and took his still-hard cold hand. He had done it for Connal, she was certain. He had made his peace with Connal.

In the evening the physician came long-faced to find her. "He may not last the night, my lady." She understood him with one part of herself, but another part wanted to scream at him, you fool! You fool! How can he not last the night? Has he not lasted last night and every night? Fool, fool, fool!

"I'll go into him now," she said.

Another bout of fever had taken hold of him. His face was stark-white, eyes staring. Spasms shook his body, making groans rise from deep in his belly, though he was unconscious. Sometimes inaudible words moved his mouth as he sagged down after a spasm. She felt a frenzy rising in her. She slipped across the bed and took hold of his shoulders, half shaking him.

"Oswy!" she screamed at him. "Oswy! You are the king!" But his eyes stared beyond her, distant, as if he were already on another shore. She started to weep violently, her tears running down his chest. She clung to him with all her strength, to hold onto him, to pull him back to herself. She would not let him go. She would not. In her arms his body shuddered and twitched. At last the priest bent over her and pried her arm from his shoulder.

"The last rites, my lady. He must have the last rites."

She let herself be pulled away, till she was slumped on the bed beside him. Through her tears she saw the children had been brought, Aylwin staring round-eyed at his father and Edith crying. All the men and women of the king's household were crowding into the room. The priest took the sacred oil and anointed Oswy's forehead, then took the holy bread and placed it on his lips. By the time he had finished the prayers Oswy's body was still. There was a long waiting moment. Then the women started to wail, the air suddenly broken apart with their keening. The mourning for the king had started.

✝

He had wanted to be buried at Whitby, at the royal minster he had founded. As soon as he lay dead, preparations started for the voyage. One ship would carry the king's body with his bodyguard. There would be another for her and the children and her attendants; two more for the household. It took days to make ready, with servants pestering her for orders and the halls in uproar with people arriving every hour to mourn the king. When at last his body was set in the ship in all its funeral state, she half expected it to be set alight and pushed out to sea, as the heathens did. Somehow it would have been a fitting end for Oswy. But there were no flames, only a dark-red sail hoisted high above his coffin as the hearse-ship made its way out to sea. She and the children were boarded, and soon they were flying after him, their pale sails streaming out like a bird's wings over water.

She had dreaded the idea of taking his body to Whitby, dreaded that her last journey with him should end like the first, stumbling seasick and bedraggled onto the shore. But God sent them a spell of quiet weather, and after the clamour and uproar after his death she found the voyage a respite. In the empty sea, her mind stilled by the monotonous rhythm of the oars, she felt as if she was crossing over into the other world beside him.

When the funeral rites were over, she sent Edith and Aylwin back to Bamburgh. She stayed on at the royal estate at Whitby. She wanted to hear the 40 masses that were to be said for Oswy's soul. After that the weather turned stormy and kept the ships in harbour. Although she missed the children, she found she was in no hurry to return to Bamburgh. There would be changes to be made and she didn't want to think about that. Not yet. She needed to get used to life without Oswy. She liked the steady rhythm of life at the minster; the offices, the work, the regularity of it, was comforting. Sometimes she would sit through Matins or Compline, hardly hearing the psalms and prayers but held by the kindly presence of the sisters around her. They were gentle and solicitous. She liked to sit in the infirmary, watching Hild with her oils and tinctures. The bitter aromatic odours were like a purge for her thoughts. She forgot her old reserve and talked to Hild constantly about Oswy. Aelfled would come and sit with them too, listening and nodding. She was a grown woman now, near enough, and shapely beneath the plain habit. She looked at her mother with an enquiring gaze, as if inviting confidences. It was easy to talk to her. She was still her child, in spite of all the absences. Not like Edfrith.

At last, in the mild days of early June, she and her household sailed for home. As they drew close to Bamburgh, she saw a small party waiting on the beach. She had scarcely been lifted down from the ship before Aylwin was flinging himself at her.

"We saw your sails! We saw them from the rock! I knew it must be you!"

She hugged him, laughing. He would be a youth soon, but he still had the open spirit and eagerness of a child.

"Why, look at you! You'll soon be as tall as me!"

"I will, and look, my new belt, I can hang a knife from it."

"Where's Edith?"

"She's here too."

She saw her daughter half-running along the beach, and for a moment thought she was seeing Aelfled again. How like they were, for all the three years between them! But Edith didn't have to suffer poor Aelfled's habit. She was dressed like a princess in fine blue linen. Her shining hair was braided round her face and her lips were as red as her cloak. Enfleda's heart lifted with joy at her children. It was good to be home, after all.

"Bishop Wilfrid is here," Aylwin told her as they walked towards the castle. "He's been staying for ages. When can we go to Ad Gefrin?"

"Edfrith says we have to wait till Bishop Wilfrid goes," Edith said.

"It's boring when Bishop Wilfrid's here. There's prayers all the time."

"And sermons," Edith complained. "It's not fair because I have to go, but Audrey says Aylwin's not old enough."

"Can we go to Ad Gefrin now you're here?"

The two children were dancing round her, and it was hard to take in what they were telling her. "I've hardly arrived," she declared. "You'll have to wait till I get myself settled. Then we'll see."

But after the joy of the children, her spirits soon fell. Everything seemed to have changed. Although she was in no mood for laughter, the bower hall was strangely quiet. There were long periods of prayer in the morning and evening, not just in the chapel but here, in the hall. Audrey's women were very modestly dressed, with full head veils and covered necks and chests. It made her want to wear her loveliest, richest gowns, to rub the perfumed oils into her body that Oswy loved. These women seemed as quiet and mousey as Audrey. When they sat with their spinning or embroidery there was no chatter and gossip, no singing. No-one jumped up to dance the length of the hall and back. It was Audrey's household now.

She remembered her mother, all those years ago when Enfleda had begged her to come with her to Northumbria. "I'm not going to live in another queen's hall," she'd said, and Enfleda had thought her heartless.

Audrey had changed too. She was filled with new determination and purpose. She was constantly at Bishop Wilfrid's side, absorbed in his conversation, nodding earnestly. Her plain angular face had taken on a radiance that made her almost beautiful. Aylwin had been right. There were a lot of prayers, and every day the household had to gather to listen to Bishop Wilfrid preach to them. Audrey and Edfrith sat on their royal chairs, and the bishop stood between them, glancing at them from time to time when he wished to give a point special emphasis. He had acknowledged Enfleda, but formally and without warmth. It grieved her to think of their original closeness. Clearly, he had not forgiven Oswy for his banishment.

Enfleda sat with Edith cuddled close beside her and whispered to her when she started to wriggle with boredom. But Enfleda found it impossible to be bored by Wilfrid. He spoke with such eloquence and energy that she found herself compelled to listen to him. And to look at him. Although he was still as handsome-featured as she remembered, two deep lines had cut their way between his eyes. When he paused in his discourse, he would frown for a moment as if to give more weight to his utterance, and the lines would furrow deeper. For a moment he would look utterly forbidding. He kept a large household, and always had half a dozen retainers with him, strong men with swords in their belts. He disliked question or interruption, she noticed. If another of the clerics in Edfrith's household spoke, he would pick at his garments, brushing off specks of dust with no pretence of listening, waiting till he should take the floor again. There was a hard edge to his preaching now. He spoke often about "the enemies of God". At first she thought he must mean the heathens. But soon she realised he meant the other churches. Churches or priests who hadn't accepted the new dating of Easter, or who revered relics belonging to Celtic saints, or who had not been properly consecrated. Members of such churches were heretics. Heretics were the enemies of God, and must be driven out of the kingdom, at the point of the sword if necessary.

Enfleda was shocked. Bishop Aidan would be horrified, she thought. She watched Edfrith, to see how he would react. His face was impassive. Why was he letting Audrey do this? Why was he allowing Wilfrid to take over his household and deferring to Audrey's judgement as if he was still a fifteen-year-old? It would affect his reputation, she thought. Audrey was running the kingdom, and he was not even man enough to get her into bed.

The day before Bishop Wilfrid left there was a ceremony in the great hall. There was to be a land grant, and a table had been set out with a scribe in attendance and the parchment ready for signing. But when it was time to make the gift, it was Audrey who rose to her feet.

"We make this gift to our beloved bishop in Christ, Wilfrid," she said, voice clear and certain, "for the building of a holy and Catholic Church to the greater glory of God, and for this purpose we give him our estates at Hexham extending to the River Tyne and all the pastures, woodlands and easements contained there. And we give it into his possession for the Holy Church in perpetuity, to enjoy all its tithes and revenues."

Enfleda knew the estate. It lay south of the Tyne, west of the Roman bridge at Corbridge and close to Dere Street. It would give Wilfrid a new centre in the heart of Bernicia. It was conveniently linked to Ripon and to York. He had already started to rebuild the church in York, she'd learned. He would base his bishopric there. Not on Lindisfarne, with its troublesome monks. His ambition was clear, and it was even clearer that the Queen of Northumbria would support all his desires. She is in love with him, thought Enfleda, a fury of bitterness filling her as she watched Edfrith; silent, sidelined, impotent.

Once Wilfrid had left, she found herself as eager as the children to leave for Ad Gefrin. She was oppressed by the close spaces of the fortress and the dreariness of Audrey's household. Her women were complaining, too, that they were not given enough room in the bower hall and that the other women were unfriendly. There would be more space and freedom at Ad Gefrin. She told her steward to start preparations for their departure. But within hours Edfrith had come to see her, in her private apartment.

It was the first time she had been alone with him since her return. She felt his tall straight body as he embraced her. He was strong, for sure; a warrior like his father. She held him close till he started to shift uncomfortably. She looked up at him, at the smooth young skin of his cheeks above his bristly beard, at the light watchful eyes and their fair eyelashes.

"Edfrith. My dear son."

He stepped away from her. "Mother, Audrey has asked me to speak to you."

"Could you not speak to me without her asking?"

"It is about a particular matter."

She decided to wilfully misunderstand him. How else could she remonstrate about Audrey's failure to produce an heir?

"A particular matter? Gracious, Edfrith—you don't need to speak to me about that. You need to speak to her. To Audrey. About her duties." She saw his cheeks colour deep red, but his expression didn't alter.

"It is about your household, mother. Now that you are no longer . . . now that your situation has altered, Audrey and I feel you no longer need a full household of your own. There is not space in the hall. Audrey's women can take care of your needs."

It was her turn to feel her cheeks grow hot. "No. No, they can't. I require my own women."

"Of course, we understand that you'll want to keep on your close attendants. Audrey is willing for you to keep three or four at least."

"Three or four?"

"She does ask, though, that your people do try and fit in with the household. Of course things are not quite the same."

Enfleda felt herself about to burst apart with rage. That her own son should so betray her! She wanted to spit and scream and tear at his clothes.

Instead she felt her mouth open and heard herself say, "She need not trouble herself about the behaviour of my women. I do not mean to live at court. I will live with my own household on the royal estate at Whitby."

She had no idea that such a decision was in her thoughts, but as soon as she said it, she saw it was right. Taken by surprise, Edfrith was thrown off course.

"But, mother . . . the children . . . Aylwin. He is my heir. He must stay at court."

"Do you not mean to have an heir of your own?"

Now it was war between them. Edfrith bit back, "Aylwin will remain at court. Edith may choose for herself where she goes. For now."

"No," she said, losing all her pride at once. "At least, he must come and visit me. I must see him often. He is too young to be taken from his mother."

"Too young?" said Edfrith staring at her. "Too young? I was six years old when you sent me to Mercia."

Enfleda broke down. That he should so reproach her! Tears started to run down her face. "It broke my heart! You were my son! I would never have let you go! Don't make it happen again!"

He stood silent for a long moment. At last he stepped forward and took her in his arms. He held her till the sobs had ceased.

"Go to Whitby, mother. It'll be better. But you can come to court as often as you want. And Aelfled too. I want my family here." He kissed her head, and ducked away, back to the great hall and his wife.

Before she left, she took him aside. She had an idea for him.

"It's about Audrey. One thing. I promise I will say nothing more after this."

He listened warily, watching her.

"Audrey has great faith in Bishop Wilfrid. She would walk on hot coals, if he gave the word. Get him to help you, Edfrith. Next time he visits. Get him to counsel her to fulfil her marriage duties. I swear she will, if he tells her to. Offer him gold—land—anything he wants."

Edfrith's face went slack with indecision. She took his arm and pulled closer to him. "You must, Edfrith. A king needs children. He needs heirs. Doesn't the Church say that is the purpose of marriage? She is betraying her vows to you."

"I'll think about it."

"It's not too late. I gave birth to Aylwin when I was older than her."

"I'll think about it, mother."

"God bless you, my son. May you prosper."

CHAPTER 25

HIS INWARD PART

672 AD

*For indeed, nothing is more fugitive than the heart, which
deserts us as often as it slips away through bad thoughts.*
Gregory the Great: Book of Pastoral Rule

Aelfled had decided last winter that she was ready to take her vows. She
had always known she would be a nun. She had grown up in the minster.
It was the air she breathed, the pulse of her very being. Latin came as easily
to her tongue now as English, and she could write both in a fine hand. She
knew the psalms and the offices by heart, and most of the gospels. The
other girls and women in the novitiate chafed at the hard routine of the
day, but she found it easy. Why wait any longer? She told Hild and asked
that Father Cuthbert come to consecrate her.

But Cuthbert sent word that it would be midsummer before he could
come. Well, she would wait.

In the meantime, her mother had returned to Whitby. Enfleda had
decided to make the royal estate her home, and she was constantly sending
for Aelfled with one request or another. When Aelfled was a child, she had
longed for her parents' visits, longed to be allowed to visit the palace, to sit
on her mother's lap and eat cake. Now it seemed she was walking up and
down the valley two or three times a week. The household was quieter,

but her mother still lived like a queen. She loved music and dancing, and there was always wine and rich food.

"Should I eat there?" she asked Hild.

"Yes, you should eat. But don't put anything on your plate that you wouldn't eat here. Be moderate."

It was only months till she would make her vows, till she would commit herself to a life of poverty and obedience. Her vocation was strong within her, yet visiting the palace stirred up desires that confused her.

"It's not easy," Hild said, as if reading her mind. "You're called to live in two worlds. You have to know in yourself which world you belong to. You have to know that in your heart."

Her mother's arrival had opened a new door. Through it Aelfled saw the other world of her family, a bright fierce world of intrigue and conflict. It shocked her with its violence, but it also stirred desires that shook her calm existence. When she embraced her mother and smelled the odour of her perfumed oils, she tried to remember her vocation. But she had only to touch the lovely silk of Enfleda's gown, to gaze at the intricate tracery of gold and pearls in her necklace, to find herself seized with longing. It was a temptation, she told herself. A trial. Perhaps she needed more time, to become stronger in her vocation. But Father Cuthbert had been asked already. She couldn't put him off. He would be here in a few months.

Sometimes fantasies overtook her of becoming a queen like her mother, with a gold crown on her forehead and a prince at her side. Once she asked Enfleda,

"If I had still been a princess, who would I have married?"

Enfleda considered.

"Into Mercia, most likely. King Wulfhere has no heir, but he has a brother, Athelred. He's a Christian. I heard some talk that Edfrith might go after him for Edith, although she's too young yet. So yes, it might have been Athelred."

"How old is he?"

"Oh, goodness—younger than Edfrith. Edfrith played with Wulfhere when he was a hostage in Mercia, and they were the same age. Athelred must be your age."

Her own age. A prince and a Christian. She felt a bitter pang in her heart. Enfleda saw it and laughed at her. "Don't mourn for it. It brings nothing but suffering and grief. Your father died in bed, but few kings do. If I had my life over, I would choose your path."

Would you, thought Aelfled. Would you?

Through her mother, she heard of wars and alliances at court, of the treacherous Picts, who were pushing for new territory at the borders of the kingdom, of her brother King Edfrith taking an army against them and driving them back. She tried to imagine her brother with a chain mail tunic and helmet, riding amidst his standards at the head of an army.

"He'll defeat them," said her mother. "Our army is too strong for the Picts. A victory will win him respect. From the Picts and from his own warriors. Audrey doesn't have to tell him how to do that."

Audrey was a constant refrain in her mother's conversation. Audrey, and Wilfrid.

"God forgive me that I was ever so deceived by him!" she would say. "He has brought nothing but trouble to our family."

She was visiting her mother when the news about Audrey came. The messenger was brought into the hall where they were sitting. They had just finished the noon meal, and her mother was cracking nuts, looking for diversion. She was pleased to see a messenger and offered him ale. But he was ill at ease, in a rush to deliver his message.

"The king has sent me. It is about the queen, my lady."

"Yes?"

"The king offered Bishop Wilfrid much gold and treasure to use his influence with the queen. To convince her of her, ah, duties in the married state."

He paused.

"Yes," prompted her mother, pleased, "yes, and what then?"

"Bishop Wilfrid accepted the king's gifts and agreed to speak privately with the queen. However, his counsel—ah . . . "

"His counsel what?"

"My lady, they were alone."

"Someone must have heard."

"It seems the bishop counselled her instead in praise of the virgin state, my lady. Afterwards he went with her to Coldingham . . . "

"Why to Coldingham?"

"To the convent at Coldingham, my lady. He himself consecrated her a nun."

"A nun?" screamed Enfleda, sending the bowl of nuts scattering across the table. "How can she be a nun? She's a married woman!"

"The bishop—ah—annulled the marriage."

"Annulled the marriage? At Coldingham? Ebba allowed this?"

The messenger said nothing for a moment. He was red-faced and sweating. With a final effort he concluded, "She and her companions have gone to Ely, my lady. To a convent there she formerly endowed."

It was a lightning bolt, a shock that struck her mother at first speechless. Then there was a storm of fury and reproach, at Wilfrid, at Ebba, at Audrey herself that seemed unending. Enfleda went to her chamber, she threw herself on her bed, beat at the pillows. She would not eat. Aelfled had never seen such a passion of emotion. She stayed with her mother, saying little, waiting for it to burn out. While she listened to her mother's reproaches, she thought of Audrey; kind Audrey, who had always been a loving sister to her. She might never see her again. She was a queen, the highest in the land, and she had given it all away to be a nun. Aelfled wished she could see her, could ask her, had it been hard? But as she thought it, she knew it was not. Audrey was not like her mother. She cared nothing for feasting and finery. But didn't she care for Edfrith? For his family? She was his closest companion. His wife of 12 years. How could she leave him? How could Bishop Wilfrid counsel her to do that? He has bewitched her, her mother said. In her heart Aelfled thought it was true.

Enfleda left for court within the week.

"Edfrith needs me," she said. "He won't know what to do without Audrey. He needs a woman's voice."

While she was gone, Father Cuthbert came, with two of his brothers for company. When they walked through the minster gates, she remembered how she had run towards him as a child, eager to seize his hand and beg him for riddles and stories. Now she stood demure, waiting for him, but she felt the same delight. There was a lightness, a warmth about him that made you forget your troubles. He took her hands and blessed her.

Before her consecration, the formal catechism had to be undertaken. Cuthbert would prepare her for it, and Hild lent her chamber for them to use. Aelfled sat on the bench at the side of the chamber, and Cuthbert stood by the small lectern that Mother Hild used as an oratory. On it a small book lay open before him. The casement was open to give light, and she felt the morning air on her cheek. She had sat in this chamber more times than she could number, but she felt as if she were sitting here for the first time. As if she was learning only now what she was about to undertake. Her mind was taut. Suddenly Father Cuthbert seemed like a stranger to her. His face was still and serious. There was no laughter now, no jokes and riddles. He spoke a short prayer and started the catechism.

"These are counsels," he said, "for those who desire to become perfect." He waited.

"I desire perfection," she responded, her voice almost a whisper.

"The Holy Church counsels us to take from our lives all that may hinder our souls.

So that we may not love riches, we vow ourselves to poverty.

So that we may not be led astray by desire, we vow ourselves to chastity.

So that we may not look for worldly power, we vow ourselves to obedience."

Each of the counsels struck her heart like the reverberation of a heavy bell, sending tremors through her being. They had always been there, waiting for her, but now they made such a clangour within her she wanted to stop her ears. She felt panic rising inside her.

"These are the vows you will make before us all," Cuthbert continued.

He had made them, she thought. He spoke the words easily, intimately, as if there were nothing fearful about them. Like Audrey, who seemed to long for them. Why didn't she? A gust came through the casement. Suddenly words burst out of her, as if blown out by the wind.

"Father Cuthbert, what if I can't? What if I can't keep them, like Audrey couldn't keep her marriage vows? What if I break the promise?"

There was a long moment of silence. She felt her heart beating hard in her chest. She couldn't look at Cuthbert. When he spoke, his voice was no longer in his formal catechism tone. He spoke to her directly.

"It wasn't an accident that your father gave you to God," he said. "It was your destiny." She looked up at him, caught with surprise.

"A daughter is like the inward part of a man. Your father was the king; he had dominion over the earthly kingdom. But through you he gave over his inward part, his soul, to God. It was his covenant with God and you are his inheritor."

He paused.

"You were born from a mortal mother but raised by Hild, your soul's mother. For your house, for the Idings, you are destined to be the link between the earthly powers and the spiritual."

Aelfled was quite still. The turmoil in her mind had gone. Cuthbert's words were like an announcement to her. What he was saying did not appear to her as his opinion, but rather as the expression of a truth about herself that she knew but hadn't recognised till now.

"It isn't easy for you. The vows seem fearful now, but you must look in your heart. Trust in God." He turned towards the door. "We'll talk again tomorrow."

Two days later she took her vows in the minster church. The familiar space seemed heightened and lofty, the air still, as if she were moving in a dream. She was aware of the presence in the church of her brothers and sisters, but she felt detached from them, as if she alone were present.

When she reached the altar, she saw that Cuthbert was waiting for her. Hild sat in her abbess' chair against the wall. She prostrated herself before the altar, knowing only the cold earth of the floor. When it was time for her to rise, she knelt before the altar. Cuthbert took both her hands. She felt his strength and understood that she could use it to steady herself. She felt nothing but the rise and fall of the breath in her chest and the touch of his hands. Bit by bit, she let go of her fear.

"Do you desire perfection in Christ our Lord?" he asked her.

"I desire perfection in Christ our Lord," she responded. The litany continued. She spoke out her vows in a clear strong voice. When it was finished, Cuthbert said the prayers of consecration over her and anointed her forehead with oil.

Afterwards Hild held her close with tears in her eyes. All the brothers and sisters gathered around to embrace her and suddenly the solemnity was over, it was all rejoicing and laughter. She remembered Cuthbert's words when she was a child—"you have two families to love you"—and she felt her heart suddenly full of love, more, as if it were overflowing with love towards her spiritual companions. A lightness filled her. She had passed through the valley of the shadow and come forth unscathed.

CHAPTER 26

An Altar to Saint Gregory

672 AD

Before his departure, Cuthbert went to make his farewells to Hild. He found her with her sisters in the infirmary, standing with a lay woman, plainly dressed in a rough woollen gown stained with mud. Her face was full of distress. He made to withdraw, but Hild called him back.

"You should hear this," she said.

The woman turned towards him, her cheeks dirty and tear-streaked. Words poured from her. She was British, he realised. He could understand little of what she was saying, though her anguish was evident. He put a hand on her shoulder for comfort.

"What does she say?"

"It's about her son."

The woman nodded, and clasping at Hild's robe, fell to her knees before her. Hild bent down and spoke to her as best she could. Then she turned to Cuthbert.

"She has travelled over from the west, where her village is. When her son was young, she and her husband took him often to visit the monastery where the Irish monks were."

"Was it Ripon?"

"Yes."

Did he recognise her, he wondered. He had often travelled out from Ripon on preaching journeys. He remembered visiting British settlements in the hills.

"Then her husband died, and she stopped taking the boy, because he had to do the work of his father. But last year new monks came through the village looking for novices. They took him away to the monastery, but he was unhappy. Their prayers were not like the British church, and he was roughly treated, as if he were a slave. So he ran away, back to his village. A few weeks later, armed men came looking for him. His mother hid him in the house of another woman, but they found him and dragged him away. The priest went to the monastery to plead with them, but they drove him away with drawn swords in fear for his life."

Hild paused. "She has come to ask me to intercede on her behalf for his release."

She took the woman by the arm and helped her up, speaking gently to her. Cuthbert watched the woman's face, seeing her become calmer. Hild called one of the nuns and gave her instructions to take the woman to the guest-house.

He was shocked. How could such a thing happen in Christ's name? He wouldn't have believed it if he hadn't seen the woman with his own eyes. Was Wilfrid running the monastery by force? He turned to Hild.

"It must be some warrior, some retainer in Wilfrid's service, who has gone beyond his orders", Cuthbert said. "Surely Wilfrid is unaware of this."

"It's not the first. Two weeks ago a man told us armed men had come to their church and destroyed the relics of their saint, because he wasn't canonised by the pope."

Cuthbert thought of Wilfrid at their church at Ripon. Of the angels not authorised by the Holy See. Even then, Wilfrid was determined to wipe out any deviation. No wonder, then, if he opposed the British now. Their Church was far older than the Saxons. They had been converted by Ninian centuries ago and held firm through all the years of heathen rule. But they were used to governing themselves; they had always refused the authority of Rome. Wilfrid would be determined to bring them to obedience. But to use force? To act with such brutality in Christ's name? How could he countenance that?

"What will you do?" he asked Hild.

"I'll write to Wilfrid. I will set out the objections to holding a novice against his will and ask him to release the boy. But I don't expect him to listen to me."

She tucked her hands into the sleeves of her robe and started to walk up and down the room.

"Wilfrid is setting up his bishopric as a second kingdom. He wants to make the Church great through force." Her walk quickened as she grew more agitated. "It's wrong. Aidan brought Christ's word to our people through love and example. He didn't need armed men."

What has happened to his heart? Cuthbert thought. Wilfrid was capable of love. He, Cuthbert, had felt it. Known that in some way Wilfrid loved him. Certainly he had loved Connal. But now he had become heartless.

Hild was still talking, becoming more impassioned.

"Wilfrid may think he is bringing the Roman Church to Northumbria, but he is wrong. It has been here all along. The spiritual father of our kingdom is Saint Gregory."

Gregory. Cuthbert remembered the story—the pope who saw the golden-haired English slave boys in the market place and took them for angels. *Non Anglii sed Angeli*, he said, when told the boys were Angles. He sent missionaries to the kingdom of the angels; Paulinus, who had baptised Hild, and Queen Enfleda too, in the waters of the glen at Ad Gefrin. When King Edwin was killed, the new religion was lost till the Idings re-conquered the kingdom. But they had sent to Iona for their missionaries, not to Rome.

"I am having a new altar erected in our church," Hild told him. "To Saint Gregory. Whitby will bear a witness to the first foundation of the Northumbrian Church, so that everyone understands that it was so. And understands that there is no contradiction between the two traditions, between Gregory's teaching and Aidan's."

Hild took a book from her lectern. "Listen to this! It's Gregory's Dialogues. Listen to what he says."

She read him sections, her clear voice eloquent with enthusiasm. She spoke Latin flawlessly. Cuthbert had trouble following it all, but it was not hard to grasp the outline of Gregory's message. Priests and the religious were to live simply, without possessions. There was to be no finery, no vain dress. They were to give away anything they owned to the poor, and to hold any necessary possessions in common. They were to be dedicated to the care of their congregations. It was an utterly different version of the Roman Church to Wilfrid's. That was the point. Cuthbert nodded.

"He speaks with the same tongue as Aidan."

"You see? Here at Whitby, and with you and Eata at Lindisfarne, we will bear witness against this so-called Roman Church of Wilfrid's, with all its talk of heresy and schism."

Cuthbert understood Hild's ideas, supported them, agreed with them. But they didn't touch him. It was definition and counter-definition; debate over traditions and teachings. That was Wilfrid's domain, where Wilfrid would always win. There needed to be another kind of witness. A Christ-like witness of total sacrifice. He had no idea, yet, how it might come about. He sensed again the connection between himself and Wilfrid, a connection that might once have united them. Now it was driving them apart into pure opposition, as if they were separate poles of magnetic force.

CHAPTER 27

THE CONSECRATION
OF RIPON

675 AD

It was three years since Wilfrid's treachery. Enfleda had certainly not forgiven him, but in her secret heart she admitted that it had been for the best. Because Wilfrid had annulled the marriage, Edfrith had been free to marry again. They'd found a princess for him, a girl who had fallen head over heels in love with him. Wasn't that what he needed, after all those years of Audrey shutting him out of her bedchamber? And her new daughter-in-law, Ermina, was years younger than Edfrith. There was no more of Audrey's managing ways. Ermina hung on Edfrith's every word.

And Edfrith was reconciled with Wilfrid now. He was going to the consecration of Wilfrid's new church that everyone was talking about. So was Aylwin, and most of the nobility of the land, it seemed. There would be a three-day feast. Hild thought that Whitby should be represented, but she was sick with a coughing ailment she couldn't shake off. She felt too weak to go; would Enfleda go in her place? Enfleda had been happy to accept.

Now she stood in Wilfrid's great church at Ripon. It was like nothing she had ever seen before. It was built of great blocks of stone, cut and evenly shaped, mortared together and roofed with lead over timber beams. At the entrance was a great sandstone arch carved with intertwining vine leaves and images of the apostles. A massive oak door stood beneath it. Once inside, there were stone colonnades along the centre of the hall, with broad aisles to either side. Above the colonnades the walls rose up to the roof, pierced with arched windows filled with coloured glass. Light filtered through them in blues, greens and reds onto the smooth paved floor below. The high altar was set in a semi-circular apse at the far end of the church; torches were fixed to the walls behind the altar so that the gold vessels that stood on it shone and glistened.

Wilfrid had sent for masons and glaziers from Gaul, Enfleda had heard. No local craftsmen could have built it. In spite of the bitterness she felt towards the bishop, she was astonished and inspired by its magnificence. Standing in the lofty, light-filled space with the smoke of incense rising, she wanted to drop to her knees in awe. It was as if, entering the church, one was transported into another realm, where the majesty of God was close enough to feel.

During the consecration, lines of monks dressed in white processed through the church, chanting the psalms in the Roman manner. Bishop Wilfrid stood before the altar, magnificently robed in an alb of gold and purple, his mitre on his head. The church was filled with all the nobility of the land. When everyone prayed together, the walls of the church rang with the sound. Who could deny the power and greatness of God?

But afterwards, when the feast started, it was not the power and greatness of God everyone was talking about. It was Wilfrid's wealth. Apart from the church itself, there was the monastery's great hall, where the feast was held. It was bigger than the king's hall at Ad Gefrin. A forest of oaks must have been used to build it. The walls were whitewashed and covered with tapestries brought from Gaul, as if English stitching would not serve. And there was the feast itself; a feast three days long to celebrate the consecration. To celebrate Wilfrid's power, some whispered. There were more than two hundred seated in the hall alone, Enfleda estimated, with their attendants and servants to feed as well as Wilfrid's household. He must have an army of cooks and bakers. It far exceeded the king's Christmas feast.

During the celebrations, when the women were in the hall, she sat at one end of the high table with her attendants. Aelfled hadn't come with her. She had excused herself; with Hild still ill with fever, she was needed at the minster. But Edfrith and Aylwin were here. Her two sons, seated either side of Bishop Wilfrid. Edfrith didn't look as if he was enjoying the bishop's company. He stared down the hall, scarcely speaking. It was clear that there was no love lost between them. But on the other side Aylwin made up for him, chattering to both his neighbours, laughing at the scop, emptying cup after cup of mead. He was only 14, she thought. He would soon be very drunk. She watched her two sons. She loved them both, but how different they were! Aylwin was as guileless and open-hearted as Edfrith was reserved and remote. But Edfrith loved his younger brother. He trusted him more than any of his warriors; already he had made him Prince of Deira. Did he see him as his heir? What would his new wife think of that?

Her new daughter-in-law sat on Edfrith's other side. Ermina was absorbed in picking over the sweetmeats in front of her. She found an especially tasty morsel and nudged Edfrith. When he turned towards her, she held up a piece of honeyed hazelnut pastry towards his mouth. He let her stuff it in, chewed for a moment and then bent over and kissed her. She had never seen him behave like that before. He was still besotted with her.

Her under-dress was cut so low that it was hard not to stare when you were close to her. If you weren't distracted by her jewellery. Ermina had arrived from Kent with a dazzling dowry—gorgeous necklaces of gold and cornelian, brooches studded with garnets and moonstones, veil bands trimmed with silver and gold—and she loved to be arrayed in it. She seemed like a child still, Enfleda thought; a passionate wilful child with her wild lips and black-rimmed eyes. She adored Edfrith. But could she carry an heir? Her first pregnancy had ended in miscarriage. They had married her too young in Enfleda's view. They were eager for the alliance and feared that Edfrith would look elsewhere. Just because a girl had started to bleed didn't mean she was ready for childbirth. Please God she wasn't damaged.

The feast went on and on. There were scops chanting the praises of the bishop and his wealth, boys singing canticles, harpists, dancing. The serving folk filled and refilled the cups of mead and wine and the noise in the hall grew more raucous. She would withdraw soon. On a distant bench at the far end of the hall, sitting among the churchmen, she caught sight of Aelfled's favourite, Prior Cuthbert, alongside his abbot. He was nearing middle age now, but he still had the upright bearing of a warrior. His kind face was grave, and he shook his head when the servant offered to fill his cup. There was a stillness about the two men, as if they were separate, untouched by what was going on around them. Of course, she remembered. Abbot Eata had been forced out of Ripon by Wilfrid all those years ago, when Wilfrid first became Connal's favourite, and maybe Cuthbert was with him then too. What must they feel, returning now? Wilfrid had demolished their wooden church. There was not a trace of the original church to be seen. She stared at the two men, and suddenly found herself wanting to sit with them, wanting to be held in their stillness. Perhaps she was turning into a nun.

The climax of the feast came on the third day. Wilfrid would conclude the ceremonies with an address to all the company. He stood on the dais, with eight of his retainers holding a ceremonial canopy over him and his steward at his side holding documents. First, he announced, he would read a charter of title of the lands which the kings and nobles of the land, for the sake of their souls, had granted him. As the list went on, her astonishment grew. Some were whole districts—the lands next to the Ribble, the lands around Dent. His estates made him one of the greatest land-owners in the kingdom. No wonder he announced the gifts, lest anyone should change their mind and take back their land. By the time he finished, there was a stiffening in the hall.

He took the next document from his steward. "We have continued to wage war against the enemies of God," he declared. "Let it be known that these following are the lands where we have driven out the schismatic priests and monks of the British and other peoples who cling to the heresies of the Ionan Church. They have deserted these lands, fleeing the hostile sword in the hand of our nation. We will not halt till we have uprooted all the poisonous weeds planted by the heretics of other nations."

The same talk of the enemies of God. It made her uncomfortable. She knew Hild hated it, hated the idea of Christians using violence against each other. Aidan would never have countenanced it. Wilfrid continued, listing areas she hardly knew, on the borders of the kingdom to the west and north. As he read through his list, a movement in the back of the hall caught her eye. She saw that Prior Cuthbert and Abbot Eata had risen to their feet. There was a shiver of tension through the hall. Without a word, they bowed to the company and left. Had Wilfrid seen them go? He paused for a moment and spoke to one of his retainers. He looked round the hall. No-one else moved. He continued to read.

Back in the guest-house she found Edfrith by the women's apartments, waiting for Ermina. She would ask him, she decided.

"Why such a war on heretics, Edfrith? There's never been such a thing before."

"That's Bishop Wilfrid for you."

"Where do all these people go, that he is driving out?"

"Ireland. Dal Riata. Pictland. Back to the Ionan Church."

She felt a familiar movement of unease in her belly. "Have a care, Edfrith. It could be dangerous if it stirs up resentment."

He was quiet for a moment, considering. "You may be right. I have spies in Pictland. They have told me . . . "

Before he could finish, Ermina came out of her apartment, and seeing Enfleda, rushed towards her. She was upset, words tumbling over each other as she spoke. Enfleda quickly learned that it was the first list, not the second, that had upset her.

"It's wrong, Mother, isn't it? He's acting like a king! Look at all the land he owns! And all the men—his household is bigger than ours! It's wrong." She glanced at Edfrith. He raised his eyebrows slightly. Ermina didn't wait for Enfleda to answer.

"Aren't they meant to vow themselves to poverty?"

"That's monks. Not bishops."

"Anyway, a bishop isn't meant to be richer than the king. He's building more palaces like this at York and Hexham too.

"They're churches, Ermina. Not palaces. Wilfrid is building for the Church in our kingdom. To the glory of God."

"It's for his glory. Look at the way he struts around in his finery, with a dozen retainers to help him whenever he wants to lift a spoon." She stamped her foot and burst into tears. "You're too good! You don't see it! All your thegns want their sons to serve Wilfrid, not you!"

Edfrith took her in his arms and held her tight against his chest. "Don't worry," he said, looking down at her wild tear-stained face. "You'll always be first in the land. For now, Wilfrid can do as he likes. It won't be forever."

CHAPTER 28

Blessed are the Meek

675 AD

There'd been no need for consultation. They had risen together as if from one impulse. Once outside the hall, they stood close to each other for a moment without speaking. Their servant came out of the hall after them, hurrying towards them. "Is anything amiss, Father?"

"It's all amiss," said Eata. Then seeing the man's dismayed face, he put a hand on his arm. "No, no—not with you. But we'll leave straight away. Bring up the horses and load the packs."

"What about provisions, Father?"

"It doesn't matter. Some bread. Whatever there is."

Cuthbert felt himself and Eata united, like warriors at one in the shield wall. It was, in some grim way, a relief. There had been so much to disquiet them since they'd arrived in Ripon. Now this proclamation had swept away any last doubts about Wilfrid's intentions. He was making war on the British Church. Even on the Celtic Church of their own tradition. There was no attempt at discourse, at communion in Christ's name. Rather, he was using his position as bishop not to evangelise but to persecute; to crush opposition to his version of the Church with unrestrained violence. Wilfrid made no secret of it; and now his proclamation made all his guests complicit in his action. Cuthbert and Eata had to leave. Had to. Whether he was their bishop or not.

As they started back towards the guest-house, another man pursued them. They realised that it was one of Wilfrid's retainers, richly dressed and with a sword belt round his waist. "Abbot Eata!" he bawled.

Cuthbert glanced at Eata. The abbot seldom gave way to anger, but Cuthbert saw his face flush. He turned to wait for the man. The retainer stood in front of them, legs apart, blocking the path to the guest-house.

"Abbot, Bishop Wilfrid requires you and the prior to return to the hall. He wishes you to hear the remainder of the proclamation."

"Thank you for bringing us this message." Eata turned away. The man took his arm, insistently. "You are to return, on your obedience." Eata looked at him, then lifted the man's hand from his arm. There was a long moment of tension. The abbot was in his forties now, but he was still formidable. The strength of his gaze was too much for the retainer. The man stepped back.

"Take the bishop this message from myself." Eata looked hard at the man. "You are to tell it to him in the words that I speak it. Listen carefully." He paused for a moment. "Tell the bishop that I am his obedient servant. But he must be reminded that when I entered the Christian faith, I was sworn to Bishop Aidan, who first brought this kingdom to Christ. As heir to his wisdom I will support nothing that causes division or dissension in the Church."

"But you are to return."

"Repeat the message for me." The man hesitated, then turned back to the hall without a word.

They looked after him before walking on towards the guest-house. The man's boorishness was an ugly taste of Wilfrid's methods. Cuthbert was still half-shocked. An image rose up in his mind of the chapter-house at Lindisfarne. He saw himself as he had sat there the day before he left for Ripon, in tranquillity, at peace at last with his brothers. Had it all been for nothing, all the struggle after the Synod to accommodate, to heal divisions, to bring about a new vision? Could it survive Wilfrid's onslaught? He had made his version of the Church powerful indeed. Cuthbert thought again of his dream after the Synod. He felt the flailing hooves reared up above his head, saw again Wilfrid's face looking down on him, blank and staring. Had it been a prophecy? Wilfrid was riding roughshod over the Church, trampling down all opposition. How were they to resist him?

Before they reached the Street, Eata reined his horse in. He turned in the saddle to look back at Ripon, just visible still in the distance.

"Fourteen years? Or fifteen?"

"Fourteen. It was the year that Boisil died." Cuthbert felt grateful Boisil had not lived to see this. It would have broken his heart. He and Eata looked back, over the once-familiar countryside. "We'll say the office here," said Eata, slipping his feet from the stirrups. Cuthbert dismounted, and their servant held the horses while they said the afternoon prayer, as a last blessing over the monastery that had once held them. When they were done and remounted, Eata turned in the saddle towards Cuthbert. "Prayer," he said. "What else is there? What else can we do?"

As they rode away, Cuthbert remembered Ripon as it had been, in the two years they had spent there. There'd been no whisper of these troubles, back then. No word of division. When they first came to Ripon, there was only joy and hopefulness. They believed that Christ's word would grow, that it would bring light to all the country. During their years there, the monastery had become a centre for all the settlements and villages nearby. As well as the monks, lay people came to live and work with them. Now, it seemed, there was not a familiar face left. Only kings and princes and the great men of the kingdom.

Cuthbert felt as if the light had gone out. In Ripon. In himself. Wilfrid's will was bent hard against them. His Roman Church was like the Street, rolling forward straight and hard, no matter what lay in its way. Hills were flattened, curves were straightened, rivers were bridged; all that was particular or different was crushed beneath its path.

Sooner or later, he thought, Wilfrid would come after Lindisfarne.

They would ride to Tynemouth and stay at the monastery there for a few days before taking ship to Lindisfarne. They camped the first night and rose early to say Lauds. As they rode on, the journey settled into the rhythm of the Rule, saying the prayers and psalms together as they rode. They felt their spirits collected, as if they were returned to themselves by the Rule. The tension steadied.

At nightfall on the second day the weather started to close in with driving rain and mist. Eata sent the servant on ahead to see if there was a village where they could take shelter.

It was near dusk before he returned for them. They turned off the Street, down a village track to a settlement. In the dripping darkness, they could see light from the huts and smoke from the hearth fires. Doors opened to the travellers, and there was welcome and warmth. Their sodden cloaks were taken for drying and the horses led away to oats and shelter. Cuthbert found himself lodged with a family, the children bright-faced in the firelight, and the man and his wife eager to welcome him. They sat him at the table with bread and a hot bowl of stew at his elbow. He faced the family across the bench.

"A story!" demanded a curly-haired small boy.

"Let the Father eat!"

"A story! A story!"

Cuthbert filled his mouth with food and swallowed. He took a few mouthfuls more to gather his wits, the children watching him. He smiled at them, laid down his knife and began.

"This is the story of the Prophet Jonah who was swallowed by a whale."

In the morning the rain had abated, though long drips still ran down the thatch. The children were sent outside to play, so that Cuthbert could say the morning office. When he was done, he saw that Eata was waiting at the door.

"The alderman of the village has asked us to preach for the village." Cuthbert nodded. "The Beatitudes," said Eata. "It'll be a consolation for us as well as them."

The alderman set the doors of his hall wide open, so that if anyone couldn't get inside, they could stand and listen. Cuthbert and Eata stood in the centre of the hall, and a woman of the village sang a hymn for them in her high clear voice. Then Cuthbert started the recital of scripture. The abbot would speak on the text.

"Blessed are the poor in spirit," he started, "for theirs is the kingdom of heaven. Blessed are those who mourn: for they will be comforted. Blessed are the meek . . . "

The familiar words seemed a kind of declaration. Cuthbert continued to the end of the passage.

"You are the light of the world. A city that is set on a hill cannot be hid. Neither do men light a candle, and put it under a bushel, but on a candlestick, and it gives light to the whole house."

As he spoke, the words struck him with a sudden force, as if they were a particular and urgent revelation to him. A city set on a hill. A light to the whole house. He sensed that there was an exhortation in the text, directed to him alone, that he did not yet understand. He lost awareness of his surroundings and stopped speaking.

As he stood speechless, the congregation started to shift, puzzled. Eata touched his shoulder. He came to himself sufficiently to conclude the recitation, the words coming to him without effort. He was present as before, but he knew his state had changed. He heard Eata starting to preach, expounding and explaining. The people in the hall were still, listening, the faces turned towards him grave and attentive. There were both men and women, the women with their heads decently covered; youthful faces still smooth and fresh, old faces that had known affliction, weatherworn and lined. He felt a profound love upwelling in his heart. He

knew it as Christ's love within him; as His love for His people. An inkling
of what he was called to do entered him.

After they had returned to Lindisfarne, he asked Eata's permission
to go into retreat, on the little isle off the shore of the main island. The
state he had entered on the journey had not left him, but he needed to
understand it more clearly. The restless spring tides moved about the isle,
slapping on the black rocks of his retreat and sending spray arching over
his hut. When the night was clear, he saw the sprinkled stars in splendour
above him. The cold night wind turned his hands numb and stiffened his
knees so that he could hardly stand by dawn. He fasted for days at a time,
drinking only water. He had to be certain his heart was pure, that there
were no wiles of the Devil deceiving him.

He dreamed one night that the tiny isle was a ship and that he sailed on
the sea. It was night-time, and darkness was all around, on the waves and
in the sky. He was borne away, out into the fearful gloom of the ocean, and
sailed all night long, till his ship reached the shadowy cliffs of an island. It
drew so close he feared the ship would be driven in against the rocks and
shattered into pieces. As the dark cliffs towered above him, he knew he was
come to Inner Farne. He heard the howling of the demons that afflicted the
island, and he trembled. High above him a single beam of light glimmered
in the darkness, no brighter than a candle flame. It wavered and flickered
in the wind, till it seemed it must surely be drowned in the night, but then
it shone again. A candle that gives light to the whole house, his dream-self
remembered. His ship passed into a small haven at the side of the island
and was beached upon the sand. He knew there would be no returning.

He stood before Eata in the abbot's room, in the half light of a dreary
afternoon. When he had finished speaking, the abbot got up from his seat
and walked to and fro, reflecting. Cuthbert waited. He was in obedience
to Eata in rule and from the heart. He was content to wait for his decision.

"Father Aidan used the island for retreat once or twice. You know that. His hand is over it." He considered. "Prayer," he said. "And witness. Yes?"

"Yes."

"For sure, they will know that you are there. The king looks on Inner Farne every time he rides out of his gate." He laughed but was soon sober again.

"It is a great calling, but it will be the harshest of trials. We must be certain that you can endure it." He stood still, turning it over in his mind. "You should continue to be part of the community, even in solitude. You'll need help. You must have a proper cell and high walls. And a guest-house, so that men can visit you."

Cuthbert nodded. Eata looked at him. "They say it is inhabited by demons."

"Yes."

Eata sighed. He thought of Cuthbert when he was a novice, all those years ago. Had he really changed?

"You must test yourself first. Over the winter. Retreats on the small isle, or in the hills, and I will visit you. You're certain now, but I must be certain too, that it won't be past enduring, or turn your wits."

So it was agreed. As autumn turned into winter, his trial began.

CHAPTER 29

ABSENCE

676 AD

Aelfled walked along the beds of the infirmary's herb garden, looking for the first fresh shoots piercing the dark soil. Along the edges of the bed were aconites, their bright yellow like tiny gleams of sunlight. Dog's mercury sprouted along the fence, and the curled leaves of hawthorn were breaking. A blackbird started to sing, clear and musical. She bent down and picked the tops of the mint, bright green and pungent, and the first tender plantain leaves. How fresh and alive they were! She would make an infusion with honey for Hild. She felt her spirits lift. It had been an endless winter. So much snow, and then puddles and mud on all the paths for weeks after it melted. For all their efforts the damp and cold had worsened Hild's illness. She grew thinner and the coughing seemed to shake and rattle through her whole body. What would life be without Hild? In the dark endlessness of January such thoughts had snared her, but not today. Today the air spoke of spring, of life returning and the sun. Hild would get better in the spring.

When she had prepared the infusion, she took the cup to Hild's chamber. She was lying on the day-bed they had made for her. She suffered night sweats that left her exhausted in the morning hours, but she refused to be an invalid. She saw her visitors in her chamber. In spite of her weakness, she was still the abbess, still part of the life of the community.

This morning she was animated, Aelfled saw as she entered. Her eyes were dark with fatigue, but they glittered in her pale face. Her cheeks were flushed.

"Look!" she said, "we have a visitor."

At first she saw only her mother, sitting in her customary place on Hild's chair in the corner. Then she saw that Abbot Eata was standing in the shadow at the back of the room, smiling to her. At once she was delighted. Is Father Cuthbert with him? she wondered.

"We've been waiting for you to come," Hild said. "Eata has news for us."

She set the cup by Hild's bed and went over to greet the abbot, asking after his journey and his health, and did he have company? But Hild was impatient to begin, so she settled on the bench to listen. Eata smiled at her and began.

"It concerns our prior at Lindisfarne, or rather, our former prior. Father Cuthbert. He asked that when I was next to visit Whitby that I would tell you the news."

When Abbot Eata finished speaking, Aelfled sat quite still. She felt as if everything had stopped. As if the flow of life through her body was suspended, so that it would need a great effort to speak. She glanced at her mother, sitting in the corner on her chair, hoping she might object. But although Enfleda's expression was politely attentive, Aelfled saw she was distracted with a lock of hair that had slipped under her veil across her eyes. She poked at it with a finger, trying to shove it back under. Clearly the news had not affected her. In a rush of irritation Aelfled found her voice.

"No," she said. "It's impossible. He can't."

Abbot Eata was a tall man, still upright despite his years. He made Hild's chamber seem too low; his head was barely an inch from the ceiling. Aelfled looked up at him, trying to see his expression, but his face was in shadow. He said nothing. It was Hild who replied.

"Why not? It's his calling. His witness to our people."

Enfleda had rearranged her veil to her satisfaction. She got up from
the chair and went over to Hild, leaning over the day-bed and propping
her up so she could talk more easily.

"Can you imagine," Enfleda said, shaking the pillows. "Out there in the
middle of the sea with only the gulls for company? I'd go mad in a week."

"He can't," said Aelfled again.

"Well, he's not going for ever, surely."

The abbot bent his head deferentially before he contradicted her. "He
does mean to, my lady. Yes. To spend the rest of his mortal life in retreat."

To her dismay, Aelfled felt tears starting to fill her throat and eyes.
She turned her head away, clenching her hands together inside her robe.
What was wrong with her? She was 21 years of age, a grown woman. She
already held office as Hild's deputy. Yet here she was, ready to cry like a
child. Father Cuthbert had abandoned her. Again.

The abbot turned and spoke to her directly. "He's not disappearing. He
will be present to us in a different way." His kindness made it worse. What
if she wept before them all?

"I wouldn't have given my permission if I thought there was any wish
to abandon the people. But that is not his intention at all. Rather, what he
is doing is for their sake."

Aelfled rallied herself. "But Abbot Eata, he is a teacher. He is always
travelling and teaching. The people need him."

"It's still a teaching. A witness, as Mother Hild says."

Hild nodded.

"For one thing, on Inner Farne he will be constantly before the king
and his household. Every time they look out to sea, when they are at
Bamburgh, it will remind them."

They were all silent for a moment, thinking of the long sandy shore at
Bamburgh. Inner Farne rose up out of the sea opposite the castle rock like
a whale rearing out of the water. In some lights it seemed close enough
to swim across, though in reality there were two or three miles of deep
water between the island and the mainland. Eata was right; Cuthbert was
not trying to hide himself away in his retreat. There were other islands of

the Farnes that were more distant, that one could scarcely glimpse, that he could have chosen.

"Remind them?" asked Enfleda. "What of?"

"What do you think?"

"To be thankful for a dry bed at night?"

Eata laughed.

"And for a mead cup! He'll have nothing like that I suppose. What will he eat?"

"The monks will take him food. But he means to grow crops on the island so he can feed himself."

"But what's the point of it?" Aelfled burst out in spite of herself. "How can he help people if he becomes a hermit?"

"We'll find out."

Aelfled stared at Eata, half-hating him.

"There are ships," he added. "He's not sworn to solitude. He's building a guest-house for his brothers. Men can visit him."

But not women, Aelfled thought. They won't let women go out there. She felt sick.

Then Hild started the little tuss-tuss of her coughing. It worsened till little drops of sweat lined her forehead. Aelfled went to the door and called to a sister. A final spasm shook Hild's body, and suddenly there was bright blood at her lips. Enfleda took a piece of linen and wiped her mouth. Hild lay back on the pillows, exhausted. Aelfled stared at the red blood on the linen. Was she to lose both of them at once?

Two nuns arrived with warm water and cloths. Abbot Eata bent over and kissed Hild's hand before withdrawing. Aelfled waited till he was gone, and then slipped out of the door. She knew she should stay and help, but she couldn't bear it. She needed to be alone, to think. She escaped into the cold spring sunshine outside the hut, but then, there was Eata standing a few yards away. He had waited for her. She had no wish to speak to him. Somehow, she felt he was to blame. But she couldn't flounce off like a novice in a tantrum. She would have to speak to him. She glanced up, and found he was looking at her, waiting to speak.

"Don't think Father Cuthbert will stop taking care of you because he is on Farne," he said gently. "He'll still be with us."

Tears came to her eyes again. She would not look at him. "I need his guidance," she said. "I need to see him, to be counselled by him directly. He promised my father."

"It will make no difference. He'll know when you need him."

Would he? How would he? She stared at Eata. How could he be so calm? How could he let this happen? She had a sudden movement of pity for him. Eata and Cuthbert had been abbot and prior together for 15 years. First at Melrose, then Lindisfarne. Everyone thought it was an unshakeable brotherhood; Eata the just, Cuthbert the friend and counsellor.

"Won't you miss him, Father?"

Eata didn't reply for a moment. "Our own wishes are of no account in the religious life," he said. "We are bound to serve God's will, not our own." He paused. "But yes," he said. "Yes, I will miss him."

CHAPTER 30

INNER FARNE

676 AD

A long spit of rock opposite the seaward end of the island stilled the swell of the ocean. The tide carried the boat through into calm water. The men rested the oars for a moment, staring through the water at the green seaweed swaying below. The April sunshine was sweet on their arms. "Here?" they asked him, and he nodded.

They beached the boat on the small sandy beach between the sloping rocks of the island's shore, pulling out tools and provisions and piling them up above the tide line. When they were done, the men took bread and leather bottles of ale from their bags and lay back on the sand to rest from the voyage. Cuthbert left them on the beach and climbed up through the marram grass onto the land above. He stared about him.

Above the shore the land was level for a couple of hides before it sloped upwards towards the cliffs at the landward end. Rough grass covered the thin topsoil. The new growth was not through yet, but last year's dead seed-heads swayed and rustled in the breeze. A ragged hawthorn in a hollow was breaking into bud. Waves hissed on the rocks. The distant snatches of voices from the beach below scarcely breached the stillness. The wind blew, and all around him the sea stretched away to the mauve edge of the horizon. He felt like the first man, surveying his domain.

He worked with his brothers for the rest of the day, digging turf for a cell on a ledge of land above the beach. He would sleep there and shelter from the worst of the weather while he built his hermitage. There was nowhere else; no sheltering caves, no friendly trees. They'd brought planks with them to roof the cell and piled it with turf to keep out the rain. A few days' provisions were stacked inside: bread, onions, ale, cheese. The brothers worked with him till the light started to fade and the ebbing tide sent the boat drifting north on its mooring. They clambered back into the boat, relieved to be sailing back to the monastery, to the familiar world. The last rope that bound him to the world was cut away. His solitude was complete.

He woke in the night, at the accustomed hour for the night office. His body was chilled from the damp ground. He pulled the hood of his habit up over his head and stooped through the low entrance of the makeshift cell. For a moment he thought he must have slept until dawn, it was so light outside. Then he saw there was a full moon. The pale light glittered on the sea, and lit up every stone, every tuft of rank grass. The air was frost-cold, with a light wind blowing. He reached into the cell for his cloak, wrapped it tightly round him and walked towards the other end of the island, till he stood on the cliffs at the westward side. The gleaming waters stretched away to the mainland, scarcely two miles away across the ocean. He could see the long ribbon of sand stretching for miles along the shore, glowing in the moonlight. Behind it a shadowy landscape of dark forests and pale fields rose away from the coast. The fortress rock of Bamburgh stood stark and black above the dunes. Beyond it, the sea widened into a vast shining bay stretching all the way to the stony tip of Lindisfarne. More distant still, the hump-back line of Cheviot and its rounded sister hill were visible, dark and mysterious. All that was familiar, known, was made strange and spell-bound in the moonlight. He looked up at the milky skies, covered with the shining brilliance of a thousand stars, and at the moon in her pale magnificence. An exaltation took hold of his spirits, till he was aware of nothing but the light and the silver rocking of the sea beneath the cliffs. The night wind sang in his ears. He fell to his knees on the soft turf.

When he was next aware of himself the night had grown darker. The wind was stronger and clouds obscured the sky. He was suddenly exhausted, overwhelmed with the fatigue of the previous day. He got to his feet and stumbled down to his cell. Within moments of lying down on the ground he was asleep.

In the morning he roused himself for Prime. Then the realisation rushed upon him. He had spent the night staring at the moon. The night offices had gone unsaid. Shame filled him. His first night, and he had failed his calling. He saw that the demons of the island were more subtle and beguiling than he had imagined. He would do penance. He would remind himself, night and day, that he was here to bear witness. He remembered Eata's words. "You'll need high walls."

The building went on through the spring and summer. He grew accustomed to the shrieking of the seabirds nesting on the cliffs and the sudden whirring flight of puffins with a beak-full of sand eels. He had chosen a site at the seaward end of the island, a few feet back from the shoreline near the harbour. The ground was low-lying, with some shelter from the higher land behind. It looked out to the immense emptiness of the ocean, broken by the distant shadows of the other islands. Terns swooped down on him, wanting the land to make a scrape for their eggs, but he chased them off. There was to be an outer wall, circular as far as the land would allow, and within it, a cell divided in two. One side would be his living area, with a hearth for cooking and a pallet to sleep on; the other, his oratory, with an altar and a wide door he could open for light.

It proved to be hard, back-breaking work. With no trees on the island, the build had to be done with stone, patched together with turfs. Nor was it like the yielding sandstone on the mainland, he discovered. It was black whinstone and hard as iron. The brothers brought out a mason to help

him. The man showed him how to look for tiny cracks and fractures in
the rock, where he could tap in the blade of a sharp splitting tool. Once in,
he swung his mallet down hard on the tool again and again, till the rock
split apart. Even so, it was stubborn. He tried lighting a fire against the
rock, piling up wood till the heat cracked it. But supplies of wood had to
be brought over, and he needed them for his own hearth. So he became
cunning and skilled with the splitter, coaxing great stones down from
fissures in the cliffs to make his walls. The brothers were astonished. Word
spread that he was helped by angels. It was impossible, the brothers said,
that he could have shifted such stones alone. Whenever the weather and
tides allowed, two or three of the brothers would row over to help him,
full of wonderment as the hermitage grew out of the rock.

He started to dig out the land within the enclosure, looking for water.
There were seeps and dewponds on the island, but as summer came on he
feared they might dry out. He needed water close to his cell. He listened
as he dug, listened inwardly and watched. Rain-water falling on the island
would seep down through the soil, he reasoned. It would find its way
through the rock and run down to the lowest end of the island, where his
cell was. There would be water, if God would guide him to it. At last he
felt certain enough to ask the brothers for help. He showed them where
he wanted to dig. They would need to hack through the rock beneath the
topsoil, as deep as they could reach. It was arduous, exhausting work,
taking turns with picks. At last they had made a deep cavity, feet down
into the rock. One of the men put his hand down to the bottom. He held
it up for them all to see. Water was dripping off his finger nails.

Next morning they went to look. Their well was brimming with water;
clear, good water. One by one, they scooped up handfuls of it; they drank
it, they washed their heads in it. It was certainly a miracle. God had given
water.

Sometimes storms swept across the island with such spiteful fury
it seemed as if they were trying to tear him off the land, to fling him
headlong over the cliffs into the roar and thunder of the waves. It was
impossible to continue working at these times. Even filling his bucket from

the well was beyond him; the wind came at him like a malicious demon, snatching the bucket from his hand and sending it rattling across the stones, or if he managed to hold it close, gusting so fiercely that he would stumble and slop the water down his habit. He kept to his cell, lasting out the fury of the storm. When the winds dropped at last and the scoured land lay spent and still, the island held him to itself again.

As he grew familiar with all its moods, Cuthbert became secure on Inner Farne. A certainty grew in him of his solitary calling. It was not, as he knew his brothers thought, that angels appeared beside him or that God sent messengers to inform him. But it was no less miraculous. Here, in the solitude of the island, his contemplation deepened. As his heart opened into closeness with Christ, he found His love constant within himself. He felt the pain and turmoil that continued with Wilfrid's persecutions, and he prayed constantly for the people of all the Church. He prayed over the small world of the island too. He grew familiar with the elements around him, the birds who were his constant companions. He knew they heard his voice, and he heard theirs.

When the turf was cleared from his first field, he dug it over to plant barley. The rooks who lived on the island watched him, heads sunk back into their chests and feathers ruffled out against the wind, patient. As soon as the barley went into the ground they were on it, long beaks digging the grain from the soil. He called out to them at once, remonstrating. "Why are you eating my grain? Do you need it more than I do? Has God given you permission to take it?"

The rooks paused, looking up uneasily. The pecking ceased; after a while they hopped away sideways with a show of disinterest. He knew they had heard him. Next morning they returned. One of them had a lump of fat in its beak. They spread out their wings on the ground, lowering their heads, and dropped the fat on the ground before him. He blessed them and picked up the fat as they flew off. He sowed the crop again. When the bright green shoots pierced the soil and waved in the breeze unmolested he laughed aloud.

He had other visitors. One morning, returning to his cell, he saw an eider duck was making her nest in its shelter, snugly tucked in against the rough stone and turf. He watched it grow, day by day. The outer part was shaped with dry grass and seaweed. Then she plucked down from her own breast to make the soft lining; the tenderness of it touched his heart. When it was ready she settled down to lay her eggs, day by day, large pale green eggs nestled in the down. She paid no attention to his comings and goings, but visitors disturbed her and she would run off the nest at their approach. When his brother Edward saw the nest, he stooped down to pick up the eggs. Cuthbert reproved him; "Put them back," he said. Edward stared at him and returned them to the nest.

When the clutch was complete, she started sitting, her mottled brown and white feathers like the earth beside her, only the brightness of her dark eyes giving away her presence. When he prayed in his cell he knew she was there, a few feet away, holding her vigil. Hour after hour, motionless, they were together.

On a day of blustery winds the ducklings hatched out, tiny dark balls of feather that scuttled wildly to and fro till she shoved them under her wings with her broad bill. When all the cracking and breaking had died down, she ran her beak around the nest to make sure that the hatch was complete. Then she set off on her sturdy webbed feet, down the slope towards the beach with a trail of ducklings behind her, blown and buffeted off course by the wind, dashing back behind their mother's upturned tail and sheltering breast. They skittered across the sand till the waves caught them, and in a moment they were bobbing up and down on the heaving sea, tiny fragile slips of life.

Each day he watched them coming up out of the water onto the sloping yellow-lichened rock by the beach, not alone now but in a nursery of other ducks and young. When a black-backed gull swooped down for a duckling, the mothers herded them close and fought together. The ducks took care of it. The drakes, resplendent in their black and white plumage and long striped beaks, kept to themselves, riding the waves offshore.

There were other predators too. The fishermen had been used to avoid the islands for fear of evil spirits. Now, emboldened by his presence, they came ashore looking for eggs. The ducks huddled close in to their young instead of flying away; it was easy for the men to grab them and twist their necks as the ducklings scattered frantically in all directions. Cuthbert saw what was happening too late to prevent them; they were back in their boat with their spoils when he reached the beach. He tried to herd the ducklings back to safety, but they were terrified and fled from him. He sat on the shore and wept. Human blindness and brutality reached even here.

But this was his kingdom, and here he was master. He gave orders to the brothers. They must tell the fishermen that the eider ducks were under his special protection. They were blessed birds; they plucked the down from their breasts for the sake of their young, like the pelican who fed his brood with his own blood and was the image of Christ. They must not hunt them or harry them during the breeding season. It was his special decree, and they would have his blessing if they followed it.

When he heard about the decree, the king laughed, but he made it law for Cuthbert's sake. Cuddy's ducks, the fishermen called them.

CHAPTER 31

THE GIRDLE

676 AD

Aelfled slipped out of the bower hall at Bamburgh and pulled a cloak around her. She would go to the church for a while. It was such a commotion of stitching and fitting in the hall, and her admiration was all used up for now. Tomorrow her sister Edith would marry Athelred of the Mercians, and her mother was in a frenzy of packing and preparation. The bridal gown was still to be finished, and all the linen and clothes that she would take with her into Mercia had to be packed up. Aelfled felt her senses overtaken with the softness of silk against her skin, the wonderful indigo blue and deep vermilion of the gown, the garnet and gold of Edith's jewellery. She needed the austere winds of the North Sea to blow it all away. She took in a deep breath or two.

Edith was beautiful, her long fair hair braided up around her face, her skin like cream and roses, her lips painted red. Her eyes were so blue, so innocent, but Aelfled saw the fear that lay in their depths. She remembered her own terror before she took her vows. She had promised herself to God; there was no doubt of God's goodness. But Athelred? She had seen him in court, in the hall with Edfrith. Would she have wanted to make vows to such a man? He was of an age with Edfrith, and they had known each other as children, when Edfrith had been hostage in Mercia. But there seemed to be little warmth between them now. Athelred was often morose;

when he was introduced to Aelfled he had avoided looking at her directly and muttered into his beard. She saw his eyes were small in a thickset face, with a fleshy nose and a clipped brown beard that concealed his chin. Not a handsome man, and perhaps, not a kind man. He was more animated when he was drunk and would burst into loud bursts of laughter in the middle of conversation.

But her mother seemed to have no reservations. She sat beside him whenever she could, her face turned up towards him as if he were fascinating to her. She talked to him about his court, exclaimed at his stories, and used all her charms to win him over. Aelfled was surprised at her mother's queenly skills and felt her own inexperience and awkwardness. She could think of nothing to say to Athelred. But what did it matter? She was a nun. No-one expected it of her.

She found herself close to the church, but instead of going inside, she went over to the cliff wall and stared out to sea. Stared at Inner Farne. Cuthbert was there, just a few miles away. So close she could almost see him. She strained her eyes, but the cliffs rose up at the landward side of the island, screening him from view. For sure, he would have his hermitage on the far side, away from prying eyes like hers. Nevertheless, it was comforting; comforting to stand here and feel him close. The same wind that whipped her veil across her face was blowing on him. Did he know what was happening? she wondered. "Pray for her," she asked him, "pray for Edith."

She heard a little cry behind her. She turned and found her sister-in-law behind her. Ermina came and clasped her hands.

"Why, what are you doing up here? Your hands are frozen! Come inside, we will have some wine brought up." She turned to the two women with her. "And some cakes! They have made so many delicious cakes for tomorrow! But we'll try them now, no-one will miss them."

She tugged Aelfled along with her to her rooms. "It's so exciting, isn't it! Doesn't Edith look beautiful?" She stood on tiptoe to hiss into Aelfled's ear. "But what do you think of Athelred? I don't think Edfrith really likes him. Poor Edith."

They went inside, to her chamber hung with bright tapestries and benches covered with furs and cushions. How different from when Audrey had been here! It had been as plain as a Whitby cell in those days. Now it smelled of frankincense and roses.

Ermina gave her a cup of wine and raised her own cup towards her.

"Dearest Aelfled! It's so lovely to see you. If only we could always be together, you and me and Edith! We could have such times together! And look, here is the cake! What do you think?" She stuffed a piece into her mouth. "Mmm! How nice." Then she leaned forward confidentially.

"The abbot from Lindisfarne will marry them. I told Edfrith I couldn't abide to have the bishop here. He would have brought all his retinue as if he were a king himself. And the Mercians would have wondered at it. It's wrong, isn't it, sister? You don't wear rich clothes and bring a great retinue. Religious people are meant to be poor. Wilfrid is almost as rich as the king!"

Aelfled wanted to laugh, but she held her expression as grave as she could manage. Ermina leant forward and took another cake. "Have one! They're so good! The physician says I must eat well so that I grow strong. He says I wasn't strong enough to hold the baby last time. Do you think I will, next time?"

"God willing, sister."

"Edfrith doesn't mind. He says it doesn't matter whether there's a next time and that Aylwin will be his heir anyway."

Outside, Aelfled heard her mother calling. She went to the door.

"You're in here! You're to come, both of you. Edfrith wants us all."

Ermina clapped her hands. "Gift-giving! That's why he wants us!"

On the table in Edfrith's chamber there was more wine and sweet bread made with raisins and cinnamon. Aelfled remembered how she had longed for such treats when she was a child, dreamed of being at court and feasting every day. Now she was here, with all her family about her. She felt a slight giddiness; perhaps it was the wine she'd drunk. Edith, she saw, had drunk more than her. She was sat forward on Edfrith's own chair, flushed and excited. Aylwin leant over the chair, teasing her and making her laugh. They seemed to shine together like the sun, her little brother and sister.

Edfrith called the family together.

"Tomorrow our beloved sister Edith will leave us to become Queen of Mercia. You are a peace-weaver, Edith, and a light for the kingdom. But tonight you are still ours, and we have gifts for you."

It was the custom. Bride gifts. Edfrith would give her the bride price to take with her to Mercia, but he gave her also a beautifully wrought golden bracelet set with quartz stones as a remembrance. From her mother there was an embroidered silk undershirt for her bridal chamber. Ermina gave a necklace of amber, Aylwin an ivory board game with intricate figures. Edith received her gifts with cries of delight, embracing each one of her family. Last of all Aelfled had a little figure of the Virgin for her, carved from smooth elm-wood. Edith hugged her and held her for a moment.

"Pray for me, sister," she whispered, and for a moment all the high spirits were lost and she held Aelfled tight.

Afterwards, Edfrith came to speak with her. "They've grown up together, Aylwin and Edith. They'll always have that closeness. But you and I have hardly known each other. I want that to change. I need good counsel."

She smiled at him. It was true, that they hardly knew each other, and yet he was familiar to her. He was like a different version of herself.

"Yes. I should like that." She thought of what Father Cuthbert had told her when she was a child. "You have two families to love you." It was true. This was her other family, and it seemed that they did, after all, love each other.

The illness started within hours of the ship leaving Bamburgh. At first Aelfled thought the giddiness she felt was seasickness. The movement of the ship became a torment for her, where every rise and fall caused nausea to radiate through her body. She thought vomiting might relieve her, but though she clung to the gunwales, the sickness seemed locked inside her. At last she could no longer hold herself upright and sank down onto one of the benches. They laid her down, but it gave her no relief. The awful giddiness in her head became unendurable. She groaned and cried out, longing for the journey to be over.

But when at last they came to harbour, and they carried her off the ship, her condition worsened. Aelfled was no longer conscious of where she was, or what they did with her. Fever burned through her, and sudden shooting pains in her limbs. She was consumed with suffering as if there were no world outside it, but only the anguish of her body. Once, the fever lessened and in a brief moment of clarity, she knew that her forehead was being anointed, and that someone was trying to open her mouth for the host. She heard prayers being said close to her ear. She understood that she was dying and prayed to God to take her quickly. Then she was aware of the world no longer, only of darkness and pain.

It was two days later, they told her, that the fever left her. She woke and saw a shaft of sunlight on a whitewashed wall. I am in the infirmary, she thought. I am alive. She gazed at the roof beams above her and saw that a sparrow had flown inside. He preened his feathers and cheeped loudly. She smiled. He was alive too! Alive! Indescribable joy filled her. She was going to live.

But her joy was short-lived. At first they thought the weakness in her limbs was caused by the fever. She would soon gain strength, they told her. But as the weeks passed, and her health and spirits returned, still she couldn't stand. It was worse than weakness. If her legs had been weak, she could have still staggered a few paces, she knew. But they wouldn't work at all. She couldn't stand, couldn't walk. She had to drag herself along the floor with her arms, her legs trailing behind her. She had to be carried into the church. She tried to force them to work and had two servants support her so that she could practice walking again. But the legs flailed and dangled uselessly beneath her, her feet knocking against the path. She was a cripple.

One morning she woke early, determined to learn to move by herself, to pull herself along with her arms. She slid onto the floor and started to drag her body to the other side of the hut. It was exhausting. The legs were like a dead weight, sullen and resisting. How could she spend her life like this? Despair filled her. At that moment, an overwhelming longing rose up in her like a prayer.

"If only Father Cuthbert were here!" she thought. "If only he were here, he would help me!" She dropped her head to the floor and wept.

A week later she was lying in her cell when one of the sisters put her head round the door and asked permission to enter.

"A messenger came this morning from the north. He brought a gift for you. He said it was from Father Cuthbert." She paused, pulling something from within her habit. "Here it is."

She put a leather pouch into Aelfled's hand. Aelfled lifted the leather flap and peered inside. It was cloth of some sort. She pulled it out, a length of finely woven white linen. She stretched it out to its full length, wondering.

"Did the messenger say any more?"

"He said the holy father knew of your illness. He has blessed the cloth. You should bind it round your waist and wear it day and night to relieve your trouble." The sister looked at her, bright-eyed, excited.

Aelfled stretched over and squeezed her hands. "God bless you!"

"Will you put it on? Shall I help you?"

"In a moment or two. I want to look at it first."

When her sister had left, she took the linen and buried her face in it. It was soft and sweet. She fancied she could feel his touch in it. She stretched out the cloth to its full length and wrapped it round her body, tying it like a girdle. She could feel its support against her skin.

She wore it for two days and nights before she felt the first movement: tingling and pins and needles in her feet. She found she could move them, just a little, to and fro. After a few more days, her calves started to ache and twitch. She bent down to rub them and felt sensation. At last it spread up through her thighs, so that as she lay on her bed she could lift first one leg, then the other. The muscles were wasted away, and her first steps were tottering. But she could move. She could walk. She knew she was healed. More than that. She knew Cuthbert had heard her.

CHAPTER 32

DEPOSITION

678 AD

*In all conditions he bore himself with unshaken balance, for
he kept throughout the same countenance, the same spirit.
At all hours he was happy and joyful, neither wearing a sad
expression at the remembrance of a sin or being elated by the
loud praises of those who marvelled at his manner of life.*

Anonymous Life, *Book 3*

Cuthbert was bent over in his vegetable garden, pulling up pea holm and
stripping off the last of the peas, now hard and wrinkled in their pods.
A good crop that would see him through the winter. He tossed the pods
into a basket and piled up the browning holm. It would be useful for a
fire or two. The soil was becoming more friable after a couple of years
of cultivation. It had been difficult to work; underneath the top layer of
spongy peat there was clay, heavy and unyielding. He had dug in seaweed
over last winter. The kale was growing strongly, shiny green in the autumn
sunlight, and the onions sat fat and brown, half out of the soil and ready
for harvesting. He gave thanks to God for His bounty, for feeding him as
He had fed Adam in his Garden.

He was rich in time now. The building work was done, and he had only
to work his crops. He told time by the rhythm of the island. The movement

of the tides and moon were his calendar, as familiar now as his own pulse. Even when the skies were clouded he knew the measure of the day. Against the days and seasons he set the counter-rhythm of the offices, rising in the night and the pre-dawn and marking morning, forenoon, afternoon, evening. He had been a monk for quarter of a century or more, and he no longer had need of timetables or books. He knew the New Testament and much of the Old by heart and the Psalms, many hymns, prayers. When he had completed an office, he continued, sometimes for hours, in contemplation of the Gospels and Christ's life, or calling on Christ's name directly. The cool darkness of his oratory was the grave of his senses. He knelt, hour after hour, on the hard ground before the altar, where the silver cross gleamed before him like a lode star in the night. He had neither hearth nor fire in the oratory. In winter the winds pierced every crack between the stones till his knees were frozen to the ground and his fingers refused to tell the beads. If he were fasting, he hardly had strength to pull himself upright, and he had to clutch the door frame till the blood returned to his stiffened limbs. He offered up all his body's suffering and weakness to Christ. When he went out from the oratory into the island, the light dazzled him. The vastness of the sky and ocean stretched away into immensity, beyond the tiny scrap of land that was his habitation, his small foothold on the earthly world half-drowned at the door of the heavens.

Sometimes he was besieged by phantoms; slender laughing women at the door of his hermitage, lifting cups so close to his lips he could smell the honeyed fragrance of the mead; half-drowned sailors clinging to the rocks who beckoned him into the ocean; crawling demons who clutched at his habit when he went to draw water. Memories assailed him too, so vivid that they seemed real; Wilfrid, magnificent in his bishop's cope, luring him back to the world with power and office. Aelfled, a pigtailed little girl again, knocking and knocking at his door. Aniel, radiant as an angel, her smiling face turned up to him in a cloud of red-gold hair. Sometimes tears ran down his face, or cries broke from him. He paid them no heed. He knew he was assailed, knew that he suffered, but he did not regard it. His gaze was single.

He felt other currents too, not phantoms but reverberations of the mortal world. Sometimes the sight took him and he saw present or future things as if in a waking dream; sometimes it was no more than a dread, an apprehension. Two months since, a comet had appeared in the sky. It rose, not at night but at dawn, so bright it could still be discerned at noon, with a fiery tail like a column of fire. It filled him with foreboding. In its fiery magnificence, it made him think of Wilfrid.

This autumn morning, with sunshine gleaming through the clouds, he felt expectation. Perhaps it was the movement of the season. He looked upwards. The first skeins of geese were starting to fly south across the island, their straggling formations like smoke among the cloud. The island was turning towards winter. As he turned back to his work, a movement on the sea caught his eye. A boat, setting off from Lindisfarne. He watched for a few moments, the boat no more than a far-away smudge on the sea's face. He gathered up his basket and tools and set off back to the hermitage to stow them in the store. Then he went down to the guest-house to make ready.

When the boat was close to shore, he saw it was Eata come to visit him. Overjoyed, he hurried down to welcome him and his companions. The monks had brought food with them; they would cook over the hearth in the guest-house, while he and Eata talked together. First, Eata said, he would take a walk round the island.

"My legs are stiff from the boat. I'm growing old!"

Cuthbert looked at him. His fair skin was more webbed with wrinkles now, the ring of hair around his tonsure turned silver. But he was the same to Cuthbert; the same essential Eata. Unfaltering. The rock.

Cuthbert gave him his arm and walked with him till he felt Eata's legs become steadier. Arthritis, he thought. It must pain him when he kneels. When they got back to his cell, he fetched a bench and set it outside in the sunshine. Eata smiled. Cuthbert sat beside him, and for a while they sat together without speaking.

After a while Cuthbert asked, "How are the brothers?", and they talked about Lindisfarne, about the brothers and all the affairs of the monastery, till they were settled. Then Eata said, "The news I have come to tell you is about Wilfrid." He paused. They were both still for a moment.

"He's made many enemies since you left. His war on so-called heresies angered the Irish and the Picts. Even Archbishop Theodore felt he'd gone too far. Eventually the king persuaded Theodore to move against him. He and the king brought a formal charge against Wilfrid. He was accused of fomenting dissension and division in the Church, as well as other matters. Theodore deposed him from the bishopric, and the king confiscated all his estates."

"The Archbishop deposed him?"

"It was at the king's behest. But Theodore also wanted to curb Wilfrid's influence. Wilfrid had petitioned the pope to create a new archbishopric at York for himself. Theodore felt his own power would be challenged."

Yes. Wilfrid would have had unassailable dominion over the north. But clearly it was not to be. Suddenly, it seemed, it was all over. All Wilfrid's ambitions for a great empire of the Church. The war on heresy.

"What's happened to Wilfrid?"

"He appealed against the charge. It was heard at York last week."

"And?"

"The appeal was refused."

Cuthbert imagined Wilfrid's standing trial, all impassioned defiance, utterly convinced of God's support for his cause. It was astounding news. He struggled to digest it.

"Who will be bishop in his place?"

"Theodore plans to divide Northumbria into three separate sees—Bernicia, Deira and Lindsey."

Cuthbert understood. Theodore meant to make sure there was no more talk of archbishoprics. No more powerful bishops standing against him. A new inkling entered him.

"Will you be a bishop, Eata?"

Eata nodded. "Bernicia."

They were silent, sitting together in the sunshine on Cuthbert's bench with the sound of the sea in their ears and the wide sky above.

"It's a mercy. You'll be a fine bishop. It'll heal the wounds."

Eata sighed. "God willing. At least I'll be based at Lindisfarne."

"And the others?"

"Bosa and Eadhaed. Both men of our tradition. Bosa was trained at Whitby. All three of us were chosen by Theodore. He has no interest in continuing Wilfrid's wars on heresy. He wants to settle things down. He can see the people could turn against the Church altogether."

"What about Wilfrid?"

"He's in prison."

"Dear God!"

"The queen wanted it. She wanted him dragged down for everyone to see. When his possessions were seized, she took a gold reliquary he treasured and wore it round her neck at court to humiliate him. It was shocking. Not good for the Church either."

How strange it was. That he'd known nothing of it. For years now he had known Wilfrid's presence within himself, had felt his will tugging at him like the drawing of a magnet. But now he was aware of nothing. Wilfrid had let go. All his will now must be bent against Theodore and the king. He would look for help from the pope, no doubt. And he would fight them to the end.

"God forgive her. And spare Wilfrid."

"He'll be all right. Now the appeal's been heard, he'll be banished. He'll go to Frankia maybe."

Was it over? No, he thought. Wilfrid would never give up. Never let go.

Then a fear entered him. Had Eata come to ask him to return? To serve as abbot at Lindisfarne when he became bishop?

Eata saw the question in his eyes. He laughed. "No. I came to tell you, that's all. Your work's here. The people look to you as their special friend with God. You're a light to them. You've become a miracle-worker too, by the way. I hear all kinds of stories."

They smiled. It was true, though, thought Cuthbert. It was a kind of miracle. To be given this life here.

"May God make it easy for you. The bishopric, I mean."

Eata said nothing. They sat in silence together, listening to the wind. At last Eata stood, stretching his legs. "Let's see what our brothers have got on the hearth."

In the month of August 678 there appeared a star known as a comet, which remained visible for three months, rising in the morning and emitting what seemed to be a tall column of bright flame. In the same year a dispute arose between King Edfrith and the most reverend Bishop Wilfrid, who was driven from his diocese.

Bede: Ecclesiastical History, IV, 12

PART 5
MANY ISLANDS IN THE SEA

684–88 AD

In 679, the ninth year of his reign, King Edfrith fought a great battle near the river Trent against King Athelred of the Mercians, in which Edfrith's brother Aylwin was killed. The latter was a young man of about 18, who was much loved in both kingdoms, since Athelred had married his sister Edith. This gave every indication of causing fiercer strife and more lasting hatred between the two warlike kings and peoples, until Archbishop Theodore, the beloved of God, enlisting God's help smothered the flames of this awful peril by his wholesome advice. As a result, peace was restored between the kings and peoples, and in lieu of further bloodshed the customary compensation, wergild, was paid to King Edfrith for his brother's death. The peace thus made was maintained between these kings and these peoples for many years.

Bede: Ecclesiastical History, *IV, 21*

CHAPTER 33

COQUET ISLAND

684 AD

Aelfled sat at the table with parchment in front of her, quill resting over the ink. In moments of indecision, she had a habit of sucking both lips tightly in together, which made her look for a moment like a child again. Then she would shrug her shoulders, her lips would part with a little sigh and her face come back to rest. If she had not been a nun, she might have been thought beautiful, with her white skin and eyes that were halfway between blue and hazel. But she seldom had the opportunity to see her own face, and in any case, she was not vain. She was proud of other things; her reputation as a scholar and her skill as a physician.

But though she had been abbess for four years now, when she sat here, in Mother Hild's room that was now her room, she still expected to look up and see Hild's familiar presence at the door; still half believed she was only away on a visit and would soon return. In her heart she felt that Hild was still the abbess; that she, Aelfled, was just standing in for her. When there were upsets in the novice house to deal with, or a difficult visitor, she asked herself, what would Hild do? And the answer would come to her, as clearly as if Hild stood beside her. She knew her brothers and sisters felt the same; they were all dedicated to continuing Hild's inheritance. She couldn't have managed otherwise. When her mother came to live at Whitby, she was supposed to help with the running of the minster, the estates in particular. As a queen, Enfleda had been shrewd and careful with the running of the royal estates, and Hild had asked for her help. At first she had been eager to help. But after Aylwin's death Enfleda had lost interest in everything. When the reeve spoke with her, she couldn't concentrate on what he was telling her. She would stare into the distance, lost in her memories. These days the man came to Aelfled instead when he wanted a decision.

Would it help her mother to see the new chapel? To know that Aylwin's soul would be constantly remembered before God? Or would it still, even after five years, still prove an unbearable reminder?

She paused, waiting for Hild's voice. She would start the letter, she decided, and see what would come to her.

> I, Aelfled, Abbess of Whitby and servant of Christ, send greetings to my beloved brother, Edfrith, king of Northumbria, and to Ermina your queen.
>
> I rejoice that, as directed by the blessed Archbishop Theodore, peace-maker and counsellor to our house, the mass chapel in York to the memory of our brother Aylwin is now complete, and I will attend the consecration.

Here she paused. This was the difficulty. Edfrith had also, of course, invited their mother Enfleda to attend the consecration.

But would it be wise? Would it stir up the grief all over again? After Aylwin's death, she had feared her mother would go mad. Enfleda had lost all restraint. The least mention of her precious youngest son would set her sobbing afresh, tearing her clothes and flinging herself on the floor. Hild had tried to counsel her, to pray with her, but by then Hild herself was so weakened she could scarcely speak two sentences without gasping for breath. Edfrith had come to see his mother, but she would only scream reproaches at him. She blamed him. How could he have gone to war with Athelred, only two years after Edith married him? Why had he not given

Aylwin a bigger bodyguard? And more, on and on. Edfrith's face had set hard and he left her. It had been a year before he returned to Whitby.

Edith wouldn't be coming to the consecration either. She would fear to provoke Athelred, her husband. She had suffered more than any of them, Aelfled thought. To lose her beloved brother at the hands of her husband's army—what could be worse than that? Although the wergild had been paid and the rift patched up, Mercia was their enemy.

So there would be no Edith to help with her mother. Only Ermina. That was the trouble. These days, Enfleda said whatever came into her head. She couldn't stop herself from reproaching her daughter-in-law. Where was the new heir for the kingdom, she would ask. She, Enfleda, had born four children. Why had she no grand-children? Did Ermina think herself too great for childbirth?

And Ermina would shriek insults and cry to Edfrith to rebuke his mother. The hall would be full of gossip for days.

She turned back to the letter. Hild would agree with her decision, she felt.

> *For our beloved mother, being advanced in years, the journey is too*
> *arduous and cannot now be undertaken. I will leave the care of the*
> *minster under her direction.*

There was another matter she was hesitating over. Edfrith often told her she was his adviser, his spiritual counsellor. She had noticed that not all counsel was welcome, but it was her duty nevertheless. She bent her head back over the letter.

> *As your sister in Christ, I beg you to be directed by God in all that*
> *tends towards peace and tranquillity, and to undertake such acts*
> *in defence of the kingdom as may be necessitated with justice.*
> *We grieve to learn of the destruction of certain monasteries and*
> *churches during the Irish campaign undertaken by your general,*

and earnestly counsel you to recall the counsel of blessed Theodore,
who taught us to prefer reconciliation to bloodshed.

Aelfled sat back and re-read her words, then signed it:

Aelfled, Abbess of Whitby.

A month later she was in York for the consecration of Aylwin's chapel, sitting with her sister-in-law in the gallery of the great hall.

"If only Edith could be with us!" sighed Ermina, pushing her needle sharply down into her embroidery frame and out again. She and Aelfled sat a little apart from Ermina's women who were laughing over some piece of gossip. Ermina loved to gossip too, but for just now her sister-in-law was more interesting.

"How it must grieve her not to be here! Her own brother!"

Ermina's eyes filled with sympathetic tears, and she had to pause for a moment to take out a handkerchief to wipe her face. Turning back to her work, she exclaimed with annoyance.

"O look at that! I have put the stitch backwards."

There was silence for a moment as she pulled the thread out, re-threaded her needle and started again. Aelfled watched her, amazed. Ermina never appeared to give any attention to her stitching, constantly talking and looking up to see who might be entering the hall or taking another gulp of wine. She was always restless and distracted. Yet her needlework was exquisite. She could create flawless interlocking patterns across a piece of linen, or conjure a bright-eyed creature peering out from a tree. It seemed to have been created by a different person altogether. Perhaps one day she would get to see more of that other Ermina.

"She's all on her own!" Ermina resumed. "They say Athelred hardly goes near her. She hasn't even a babe to comfort her."

"She has a convent now, at Bardney, where she can go."

"A convent, Edith? Oh no! A baby is what she wants."

Ermina leaned across, bringing her wine-flushed face close to Aelfled's. "It's what I want, sister. Why does God not grant me a child?"

"We all pray for it, Ermina."

"I've seen so many physicians. Do you know what a midwife said to me? She said, 'You need a miracle.'" Ermina's needle darted swiftly through the linen again. "A miracle! That's what I need. So do you know what I plan to do?"

"Tell me."

"I shall go and see the holy man who lives on the island. Everyone says he can work miracles."

Aelfled was silent. Ermina stared at her.

"Don't you think that's a good idea?"

"Father Cuthbert is a hermit, Ermina. Women aren't allowed to visit the island."

"Oh." She paused, dashed for a moment. Then she brightened again.

"Well, he won't be a hermit much longer. I just remembered! Edfrith wants him to be a bishop! He's going to get rid of Bishop Trumbert, because he's one of Wilfrid's. And he said it would have to be Cuthbert! I'm sure he did! I WILL be able to see him!"

Delighted by her conclusion, she turned back to her stitching. Aelfled dropped her head and concentrated all her attention on her distaff, pulling the thread finer and finer.

The palace at York had been built by Wilfrid before his downfall with all the splendour due to his expected archbishopric. As well as a fine galleried hall, it had several adjoining rooms, and a small hall where Wilfrid had held his councils. Edfrith had made this into his private apartment. The Frankish hangings imported by Wilfrid still adorned the walls, and Edfrith sat on Wilfrid's ornate throne, draped with purple, his arms regally spread out and a ring of gold around his neck. He had taken Wilfrid's power and made it his own, Aelfled thought. He looked like a Roman emperor sitting in majesty. There was a smaller seat for Ermina, but guests were expected to stand before him, or sit on the benches at the side of the hall. She stood before him, uncertain.

He patted the chair beside him. "Come and sit beside me till Ermina comes," he said. She sat down, feeling the cushions and soft furs yielding beneath her. She thought of Cuthbert in his hermitage sitting on a stone. She wanted to ask Edfrith about his bishops, but she knew he would speak first.

"We hear good news of Whitby. All the clerics tell me you are a worthy successor to Hild."

She bowed politely.

"And learned too, I hear! As learned as any woman in Europe, so they say! I have a wise counsellor to advise me!"

"No great wisdom in political matters, I'm afraid."

"But you're not afraid to counsel me on my commander's campaign in Ireland!"

Yes. Her letter. She had felt bound to remonstrate. Surely his authority extended to protecting churches from looting. But he didn't wait for her to respond.

"No—I understand. But warriors are hungry for gold and glory. Why else would they fight? It's regrettable, but you have to see the bigger picture." He turned to her.

"It was a successful campaign. Laying the ground. There'll be no more interference from the Irish when I go to war in the north."

Fear coiled up Aelfled's back, all the way to her throat and gripped it so tightly she could hardly make words. She looked at Edfrith, and for the first time was reminded of her father. There was a new ruthlessness in his manner. How little she really knew him, she thought. She tried to speak.

"But the kingdom is at peace, brother."

"It won't last. I've been biding my time. We suffered at Athelred's hands at the Trent, and his warriors killed Aylwin. That's why we're here. To remember Aylwin's death at their hands. But they will never humiliate us again. I'm going to make Northumbria the greatest of the kingdoms. It will stretch from the Humber to the farthest tip of the north. I shall subdue the Picts and make them my vassals . . . "

As he talked on she was aware of another voice in her head, speaking so clearly that she no longer heard Edfrith.

> *God said to him, "You foolish one, tonight your soul is required of*
> *you. The things which you have prepared—whose will they be?"*

She looked round. Edfrith was still speaking, absorbed in his plans. Her fear grew. Why had the words come to her? What did they foretell?

"That's where you come in, Aelfled," Edfrith was saying. She struggled to pay attention to what he was saying.

"You can help me settle things down in the Church. There's trouble over in the west with the British. Theodore appointed a bishop called Trumbert. He's still trying to impose Wilfrid's line, and the British hate him. He'll have to go. I can't risk a rebellion out there when I'm dealing with the Picts. So I'm going to give them a bishop they'll love."

He paused, watching her. "Cuthbert. The holy man."

In a moment she forgot everything else. Thank God she had had some warning from Ermina. She felt furious with him. How could he do this? How could he use a man of God for his own ends? As an instrument in his war-mongering?

"I want you to help me, Aelfled. You've known Father Cuthbert a long time. I want you to go and sound him out. Use your woman's wiles."

"Father Cuthbert has given up the world."

"He's a good son of the Church. If the Church needs him, he might have to change his mind."

"Inner Farne is a monastic cell. Women are not allowed to visit."

"Well, visit him somewhere else then. There are ships." There was a long silence between them. Edfrith spoke again.

"I want you to do this, Aelfled."

She understood it was an order.

The next morning Edfrith's chaplain came into the hall and sent a servant up to the gallery to fetch her. Ermina peered over to have a look at him.

"Isn't he good-looking? What does he want to talk to you about?"

"Church matters. Nothing interesting."

But Aelfled could feel Ermina's eyes following her down to the hall. When she had greeted the chaplain, she suggested they might talk in one of the apartments at the back of the hall.

Once polite enquiries after her mother and the community at Whitby were concluded, he turned to business.

"As you know, it is the king's wish that you talk on his behalf with Father Cuthbert. If it seems suitable to you, I will send messengers to propose to the holy father that he might meet you on Coquet Island. It's not a long voyage. He would be able to stay in the small monastery on the island without breaking his retreat. You can stay with your attendants at the guest-house in Alnmouth and join him on Coquet Island during the day."

Clearly, it had already been decided. All the arrangements would be made for her, the chaplain assured her. She felt the iron beneath his pleasant manner. She was to be Edfrith's spy, whether she would or no. But who would be there but her and Cuthbert? Who would know what passed between them? After all these years, to speak with him again! Her heart was light in spite of herself. She had not thought to see him in this world, but God had arranged it otherwise.

A gusty drizzle drove sideways across the ship, showering her face with a fine salty spray and sending a trickle of water down her neck. She pulled up the hood of the cloak and wrapped it more tightly around her. It had been calm when they left Whitby yesterday, but since clearing the heads at Tynemouth this morning, a boisterous swell had got up, tossing the ship from side to side. A tall wave would lift the ship high for a few giddy seconds before letting it drop with a sudden slap into a trough between the waves. She clutched the edge of the bench with both hands and concentrated on watching the oarsmen bend and pull. It was reassuring. They kept a steady rhythm in spite of the leaping sea, driving the ship forward through showers of spray. How strong and fearless they were! She was shaking, half with the cold and wet, half with fear of the great blue waves rolling towards them. She glanced at the two sisters who were accompanying her. One had made her way to the aft rail and was leaning over, vomiting. Cuthbert! she implored him inwardly. Make it easy for us to come and see you!

A few minutes later she saw the distant outline of the island. It was very small, a flat lozenge of brown and green hardly higher than the waves surrounding it. But there it was, and soon it grew closer. She could see the low huts of the monastery. She clutched her belly. If she could hold out for half an hour, they would be there.

The ship beached on a narrow stretch of sand on the landward side of the island. Terns flew up screeching from their scrapes. She stood unsteadily and let two of the sailors help her over the side of the ship, gathering up her skirts to step down onto the wet sand. A sudden wave took her by surprise and sent her stumbling up the beach, half falling. Someone caught her, and when she looked up, it was Cuthbert; tall, spare, smiling as he steadied her. All at once she was a child again, and Father Cuthbert was catching her as she stumbled down the hill at Whitby. She laughed, and the fears of the voyage were forgotten as she greeted him. She saw at once that he had changed. His face was worn and weathered like a piece of sea wood, half covered with a white beard. His eyebrows had turned white too and grown bushy. Only the eyes were the same; bluer than ever against his white hair and full of laughter. He took her arm and helped her up the beach. She turned for a moment to wave farewell to her seasick sisters.

"Only a little further!" she called to them.

The ship would sail over to the mainland, to the monastery's mother house at Alnmouth. Her people would stay there, but she would stay a night or two on Coquet Island, in the monks' tiny guest-house.

When she had recovered from the voyage, she sat with Cuthbert at the rough slab table in the hut where the brothers took their meals together. The doors stood open; the wind blew in the pungent island smell of nesting gulls and seaweed. Father Cuthbert would drink only water, but she took the wine brought for her by the brothers. Still unsteady from the voyage, it made her light-headed. She didn't care. At last she was here. At last she was with him. They sat side by side at the table like a king and queen looking out at their kingdom. His habit was stiff with salt, she noticed; it was stained and the sleeves were frayed over his wrists. His hands were swollen at the knuckles and blistered. She laid her own hand on his.

"You take little care of yourself, Father."

"Maybe so."

She looked up at his rough cheeks and chapped lips. The rigour of his life on Farne had aged him. He was like an old man.

"Why must you stay there?"

"Is that what you have come here to ask me?"

"No. But it grieves me—that is . . . "

Her words fell away. She wouldn't speak of bishoprics and politics. Not yet. Let it take as long as it would. Already the world was slipping away beyond the edges of the island.

As she settled, she noticed more. He was slower. It caused her no impatience though. It calmed her. The smallest things he did—sitting down on the bench, lowering the hood of his habit down from his head— occupied his full unhurried attention. When the monks brought food for them, he said a grace over the broiled fish and bread and ate in silence, using his knife to slip the dense flesh of the mackerel off the bone. He ate each mouthful as if it were a special feast prepared for them, and eating with him, she felt indeed, it was. When a brother came to serve them, Cuthbert spoke to him with the same attention, the same interest. She felt herself apprehended by him within the same immediacy. It was true that his body was older, but she saw his spirit was more vividly alive than before. She was used to running from one task to another at the minster, but here, with him, she felt herself enter a different order of time. He had no concern with tomorrow. No anxiety about tasks to be accomplished, as she did.

After they had eaten, they walked together to look at the brothers' garden, three broad beds of herbs and vegetables. She scanned the herbs; mugwort, plantain, rosemary, chamomile. She rubbed the soft fronds of fennel between her fingers.

"I'm surprised fennel will grow here. You'd think the salt winds would scorch it."

"The beans too—see these."

The field beans were sturdy, with black and white curved flowers opening out to the sun. He bent over them. "Better than mine. They've got them mulched all around with seaweed to keep the wind off them."

She imagined him on Inner Farne, alone, working his vegetable beds.

"What else do you have there?"

"Barley. They haven't room for it here. I have half a hide of land that gives the best barley in Northumbria. If the rooks will leave it alone."

She laughed. Two black pigs rooting in a pen behind the garden lumbered over to the fence. He went over to the pen to greet them and scratch their bristly foreheads.

"Do you remember the pigs?" she asked. "At Whitby, when I was little?"

He nodded.

The brothers placed a bench for them at the north end of the island, so that they could talk privately. She told him about Whitby, about her new life as abbess since Hild's passing, about her mother. She knew she would have to tell him Edfrith's wishes, but she had her own questions first.

"Do you remember what you told me, before my vows? About being a link between the earthly powers and the spiritual?"

"Yes."

"Then advise me, Father. Edfrith means to go to war. He wants to bring all the kingdoms of the Picts under his rule. He is misguided, I am certain, but . . . "

"Against the Picts? He is going to war against the Picts?"

His voice had changed, and she glanced at him. She had meant to continue, to tell him of the voice she had heard, of her fear at Edfrith's pride and ambition. But she saw he was abstracted. His face was still as stone, his eyes staring at nothing. She waited. In the silence she could hear only the sound of the sea breaking on the rocks beyond. She was suddenly frightened. A question broke out of her.

"How long will he live, Father?"

A shudder shook his body. He straightened himself and looked at her. "I can't say."

"But you can! What did you see? Tell me!"

He shook his head.

"How long, Father? In God's name, I beg you tell me."

He was still, head bowed. At last he spoke.

"Even if a man's life were long, wouldn't it seem short if only a year remained to him?"

It took her a moment to understand him. "A year? He will die in a year?"

His face answered her. Tears sprang to her eyes. All her fears broke out within her and she burst into tears. Edfrith! How could she stop him?

"What will happen?" she wept. "He has no son or brother, no heir! What will happen to our people?"

He sat silent till all her tears were exhausted. He took her hand.

"You say he has no brother."

"Aylwin is dead, Father." Did he not know? He nodded.

"An heir will be found." He pressed her hand. "He will be as dear a brother to you as Edfrith."

His words were like a riddle. A brother as dear as Edfrith? Did he mean a spiritual brother? What could he mean?

"Where is he? Where is this brother?"

He hesitated. At last he said, "There are many islands in the sea. Would it be hard for God to find a brother for you in one of them?"

It was a prophecy, she understood. He was telling her what had been revealed to him. It was like a dream that she must interpret. Many islands in the sea. What could it mean?

Suddenly, it dawned on her. Iona. An island of the sea. Her father's illegitimate son. He lived there, or on some other Scottish island. No-one ever talked about him, though she knew his name. Aldfrid. He was born out of wedlock, to a concubine, when her father was a young exile with no future. No-one had ever supposed he might be an heir.

"Aldfrid?"

"Yes." She saw that it was possible. Surely it was. Hadn't God revealed it to Father Cuthbert? She wanted to ask more questions, but he shook his head.

"Don't speak to anyone about this. It's for you alone." He got up, and she saw he was exhausted. They walked together back to the monastery.

On the last morning they sat for an hour or more in silence, gazing out at the light shifting on the sea, stretching away endlessly to the horizon.

"Do you stand like this on Farne? Just looking at the sea?"

"Sometimes."

"I never do. There's so much to do. I never stand still."

"It's good to work. Benedict says work keeps us humble."

"I must be very humble then!"

She knew she wasn't. She was used to being in charge, to giving orders. But she would have given it all away in a moment to stay here.

"Do you remember Hild's tales, of the Isles of the Blessed?" she said.

"I do."

"I can believe them. Look, you can see, for all the sea is so vast, it touches the sky at the horizon. It touches heaven. Surely you would find the Isles there, with gardens and fruit trees like Paradise."

He said nothing.

"How long a journey would it be?"

"There are blessed isles closer to home, without the trouble of such a journey."

She stared at him. "Do you mean Inner Farne? But it is full of demons."

"And angels."

"Do you truly want to remain there?"

"Why would I not?"

"But it's . . . that is, it's the king's wish . . . ."

"What's his wish?"

And she told him everything at last, about the troubles over Bishop Trumbert and the British Church, about Edfrith sending her to persuade him to leave the island and become bishop in Trumbert's place. When it was all told, she looked at him. His face was grave and still. Had he known it already? Had it been prophesied to him?

"It is wrong of Edfrith," she hurried on. "But might not God's will be in it too? Your presence would be a light to so many." She found her words drying up in the face of his stillness and sat at last helpless, waiting for what he might respond. Would he be angry with her for pleading Edfrith's cause?

But when he spoke his manner was unchanged.

"It's in God's hands. I swore a vow in Christ's name to end my days on Inner Farne, and I believe He will make it possible for me. If the king should press me to take office, I may be forced to accept, for a time. But it won't be for long. You're a physician. You know there's no remedy for old age."

"Old age or neglect?"

He smiled his old smile, but she saw suddenly his fatigue. She understood that it was true. Sorrow stabbed her heart.

"I am waiting for the other life, if God will bring me close."

Tears rose in her again, but different now, for a loss that had no remedy. She felt death at her shoulder. She took his arm, made him turn and look at her.

"Promise me one thing."

"What is it?"

"That you will send for me. When you know it is close—that you are dying—you will send for me. So that I can care for you. Care for you properly. Promise me."

He looked down at her, his eyes meeting hers. At last he nodded. Smiled, half-laughing at her. "I promise."

"Swear that you will. Swear that you won't forget."

"I swear."

CHAPTER 34

PARADISE LOST

684 AD

*King Ecgfrith gave him the land which is called
Cartmel and all the Britons with it.*

Anonymous Life of Saint Cuthbert

After the visit to Coquet Island he put all he had spoken of with Aelfled from his mind and gave himself up to his vocation. He resumed his daily rhythm of work and prayer and thought no more about it.

It was months later when they came. When he was taking a walk about the island, he noticed a pair of ships to the south. Heading for Bamburgh, he thought. He stood for a moment, watching their red sails billowing out in the sharp south-easterly wind. He turned away, down the path to his cell. He went into the oratory and closed the door behind him. Although he was not troubled by the cold, he slid the casement shut as well.

The longer he lived on the island, the more his reputation grew as a healer and counsellor. To endure such hardship must be pleasing to God, people believed. Such a holy man would surely have God's ear. The voyage to the island became a pilgrimage for visitors. On a fine day with favourable tides there might be two or three small craft beached below the guest-house. It was hard to explain to his visitors that their presence destroyed the very thing they sought from him, intimate silent communion with God.

The walls around his cell were his enclosure, like any other monastic enclosure. Lay people were not allowed to enter, so he had placed a bench outside the wall and spoke with his visitors through the open casement of the oratory. He sat within, listening to the suffering and turmoil they brought with them, doing his best to counsel and console them. But he found that each one drew strength from him. If he was to intercede for all his people, he needed to be sustained by solitude. At last he would close the casement.

If his brothers from the monastery came to see him and found the casement shut, they understood it was a sign that he did not wish to be disturbed. They would go back down to the guest-house and prepare themselves a meal, making enough for themselves and to last him for a few days. Other visitors still came, still sat outside his cell. It was enough for them to be close to him. He felt their presence, felt the opening of Christ's love within himself towards them.

Today his visitors were more persistent. He was aware of several voices outside the cell, speaking loudly and without restraint. A few moments later someone entered his enclosure and started knocking at the door of the oratory. He got up from his knees. When he opened the door he found a man dressed in a long clerical robe standing outside, with two attendants at his side. A priest of some sort. The man spoke to him.

"God be with you, Father."

Cuthbert looked at him again. He knew him. He recognised his voice. What was his name? Trumwin. That was it. He was bishop to the Picts, up at Abercorn. But what was he doing here? And why should he be knocking at his door?

He responded to his greeting. "And with you, my lord bishop. May I wait upon you at my guest-house?"

Trumwin shook his head. "No, Father. It is an urgent matter. We have come from Synod at the king's command to speak with you."

A Synod. One of the brothers had mentioned a Synod was taking place somewhere. And there had been messengers lately, trying to speak to him or leaving documents in the guest-house which he didn't bother to read. They were like the first wisps of smoke rising from the fire. Now, it seemed, the flames were growing stronger.

"I am honoured by your visit, Trumwin, but sorry that you should have had the trouble of this journey. God knows it is beyond me to offer any advice to the Synod."

"The king requires your presence, Father. He waits on you at the guest-house with a company of our brothers."

The king? In his guest-house? He stared at Trumwin, disbelieving. Trumwin persisted. "It is the Synod's wish to appoint you bishop, Father. The king himself has come to urge you to accept."

Trumwin's words struck him like a blow. Finally, his destiny had found him out. He felt his breath coming fast and the blood rushing through his veins. Boisil had foretold it, and Aelfled had warned him, but he had thought himself too old. Too far beyond the world. Suddenly it was here. The king in his guest-house.

"No. That's impossible."

"Please come and speak with him." Trumwin took his arm.

As he walked from his cell with Trumwin, he felt the island around him with sudden intensity; the spongey turf beneath his feet, the tide beyond the rocks running dark and fast, all of it so alive, so beautiful. It was as close to him as his breath.

He stooped to enter the guest-house, and there, in the low hut where the thatch was coming through the rafters, the king sat on a bench, resplendent with rings and a fur-lined purple cloak. Cuthbert's eyes fell to his boots, long leather boots with a silver tracery . . . But he would not wash the king's feet. The king was not here as a guest.

The hut was full of people; the king's attendants, priests in robes, monks. For a moment he thought, they are phantoms, come to torment me. But they remained stubbornly flesh and blood. He felt their gaze on him, on his stained habit and his tangled beard. Surely, seeing him, they would realise their mistake.

"Father Cuthbert!" said the king. "We have need of you." His tone was jovial, but his face was stony. Cuthbert looked at him directly, but the king avoided his gaze.

"My lord the king, it is my duty to serve you. But my first duty is to God, and to the oath of solitude I have taken."

Edfrith stared at him in surprise. One might have thought he would rejoice to be released from this wilderness. A holy man, he supposed, but stubborn. He shrugged.

"Let your brothers convince you." He waved to the churchmen standing around.

One after another they stood forward and pleaded with him. They told him of the distrust and bitterness that still troubled the Church after Bishop Wilfrid's war on heresy; how the British churches wanted to break away, how arguments persisted over endowment, over governance of the Church. Trumbert had made things worse, trying to enforce Wilfrid's decisions.

"Everyone knows that you are a man of God, Father. They trust you. You're the only person they'll accept," they told him.

Some of them he knew, knew to be good and holy men. They were his brothers in God; he had a duty to listen to them. His heart grew heavier with every speaker. When all of them had spoken, the king leant forward.

"You've heard the voices of your brothers, and I add my voice to theirs. Give us your answer."

He gave himself up to God's mercy. "I accept," he said, and almost at once was shaken with a storm of weeping before them all. They came and embraced him, kissed him, called out congratulations and blessings. The king's attendants started to hustle him out of the door, down to the beach to the ships, to carry him away to Alnmouth and the Synod.

As the ship turned into the wide mouth of the Aln, a fresh westerly headwind made the sailors lean hard into the oars and brought a tang of wood smoke to Cuthbert's nostrils. Camp fires, he thought. The monastery couldn't house everyone. There would be an encampment. Even for the king. He glanced up. Edfrith was standing at the prow, his attendants pressed close about him, eager to alight now he had got what he wanted. Cuthbert felt a terrible oppression of his spirits.

When the ship was tied up and he finally stepped ashore, a crowd of people pressed forward to greet him. They all wanted to take his hand and embrace him, to question him. They had to insist that he warm himself, that he eat, that fresh clothes be brought for him. The uproar dazed him. He turned away, and found Eata behind him, waiting. His presence was like a cool draught of water in a desert.

"Will you stay in our camp?" Eata inquired. Cuthbert nodded. Eata took his arm, and they made their way together through the crowd.

There was so much noise, he found. The island was seldom still; there was always the sound of the sea, of the wind, of the birds. When a storm blew up it could be deafening. But this noise, the noise of the world, was different and distracting. There was so much talking; a constant hubbub of chatter and laughter, to and fro between the camps. Men shouting orders to servants, horses whinnying and pulling at their tethers, the cooks clattering and scraping at cooking pots. He felt assailed by the constant uproar.

In the great hall it was worse. It was crowded, men pushed onto the benches, clergy and lay together, with the king and his household at the top table. Servants bellowed to each other as they ran between the tables carrying great platters of food and pitchers of ale, the guests shouted to make themselves heard above the din, everyone drank and ate freely, the noise growing as the ale cups were filled and refilled. He had no stomach for the rich food in front of him.

There was silence of a kind later, for the deliberations of the Synod, but he found it hard to interest himself in the speeches and discussion. He heard himself being proposed for the vacant bishopric of Hexham and being elected unanimously; heard the arrangements for his consecration being made and learned that it would be at York. It was too late in the year now for the consecration; it would be done at Easter. He felt a flicker of relief. He would have a few months more on the island.

His diocese would include the British churches to the west, and the king gifted him the British lands at Cartmel and the royal estate at Carlisle. He acquiesced in all of it. Afterwards, priests and monks came to him full of exclamation and congratulation all over again, begging him to tell them of his life as a hermit. He smiled and thanked them and said nothing.

When it was done at last and all the men spilled away out of the hall, Eata found him. He took his arm and walked with him, away from the furore of the encampments down to the river. The light was fading and the air had a dank autumnal stillness. Pale leaves dropped from the trees into the dark water of the Aln and floated down the current towards the sea.

"Now this is all over, I'll talk to Theodore privately and arrange an exchange between us," Eata said. "Between the dioceses of Lindisfarne and Hexham. I'll go to Hexham. I have held office there before, and I know the people. It doesn't matter to the king whether you're there or at Lindisfarne."

"Is that possible?"

"I don't think there'll be any objection. Further to travel, to Carlisle and the British centres. But better for you to be at Lindisfarne."

"Yes."

He felt great relief. How good, how kind of Eata. At least, at Lindisfarne, he could still smell the sea. Still travel sometimes to the island. He turned to his friend and embraced him. They stood still together for a few moments, and Cuthbert remembered the first time he had stood before Eata, at Melrose, all those years ago. Eata had never failed him.

They walked on together along the river bank, sending coots scuttling into the rushes. "I'll go back to Inner Farne once this is finished," said Cuthbert. "Till Easter."

"Go back now if you wish, but you should come to Lindisfarne for Christmas. Then stay. While I'm still there. You must prepare yourself. You don't know how to live with people any longer."

It was true. He nodded.

He stayed overnight in Eata's encampment, sleeping on the floor of his tent and saying the night offices with him. He saw that although Eata was a bishop, he still lived as simply as he had in the monastery. He wore a plain habit, as Aidan had done. When it was time to breakfast, they stayed away from the hall. They sat together on a bench by the tent, eating bread together in silence. As they ate, they heard a distant commotion in the camp. A little party of women were making their way among the tents, calling out and bursting out into little screams and giggles. Eata stood up and peered down the encampment. Cuthbert heard the voices getting closer. A woman peeped round the side of the tent flap and caught sight of him.

"Look, my lady! He's here!" she called out, giggling and pointing.

The women fluttered towards them, like a little flock of bright birds among the tents. What could this mean? Cuthbert wondered. One of the women came forward from the group towards him. She was quite small, but very richly dressed. Her veil band glittered with amethysts, and the veil fell about her face in soft folds of royal blue. Her gown was trimmed with fur around her neck, which was hung with silver. Her small face was flushed with excitement, her red-lipped mouth wide.

"Father Cuthbert!" she cried. He stood up.

"Edfrith said I mustn't bother you, but I had to see you! Before you go back to your island again."

For all her finery, she was like a child, eager and impulsive. He smiled at her.

"You'll talk to me, won't you? Please, Father."

She has some trouble, he thought. Someone has told her to come and see me. He looked at her again, carefully. Under the excitement and folly, he saw she was distraught.

"Yes," he said. "I'll talk to you but let us clear somewhere for you to sit." Eata beckoned to his servant to fetch another bench. The little group of women pressed forward, but Ermina waved them away.

"Go away! I don't want any of you! Leave us alone!" She sat down on the bench. "Sit down, Father. Please."

He sat down, not too close. He could smell her perfume. He saw that for all her girlish manner, she was no longer young. Her skin had lost its first bloom and freshness, and there were lines between her eyes.

"Do you know who I am, Father? I am Ermina, Queen of Northumbria."

"My lady," he responded, bowing. He watched as she struggled between her self-importance and her need to talk to him. She twisted the rings on her fingers and looked at him. He held her gaze and waited to see what she would reveal to him. She looked down, and back up again, suddenly struggling with words.

"I want you to . . . . That is, I need . . . ." She stopped. He waited patiently, watching her face change as her vulnerability edged outwards. She looked up at him again, and her face turned haggard. Tears started to well up in her eyes. Words suddenly burst from her.

"I'm so unhappy! Oh Father, I'm so unhappy!"

The tears spilled over, and she wept loudly, noisily, wiping her eyes and running nose on a linen handkerchief. He saw that she was utterly lost and confused. The pangs of his own loss brought tears to his eyes in a kindred pity. When her weeping was done and she sat sniffing and gulping, he leaned forward to her.

"Trust in God," he said. "Certainly He loves you."

She bowed her head and fumbled for his hand. He let her hold it till she was calm.

"Why doesn't He give me a son?" He lifted her hand gently back into her own lap. "I will teach you a prayer," he said. "For you to say each night before you sleep."

She was too spent with weeping to object. He said the prayer for her, then got her to repeat with him, mumbling and snuffling. He said it for her again, and again, till she had it by heart. "Each night," he reminded her. She gave a little nod. He stood up, looking round for her women, and beckoned to them.

"The queen needs to rest quietly for a while," he said. "Warm a little wine for her to drink."

The women gathered round the queen, inquisitive but hushed, and helped her up. She turned back to Cuthbert as she left.

"When can I see you again, Father?"

"When I am made bishop at Easter."

"But before then!" He saw her imperiousness returning and sighed.

"I will be at Lindisfarne after Christmas."

Then the bright company moved away, disappeared between the tents and was gone.

THE INVESTITURE

685 AD

St Peter's Church at York. Wilfrid's great church, built on the foundations of the first Roman church, so that no-one could mistake the inheritance. As he waited for the monks to come and clothe him in his bishop's vestments, Cuthbert felt Wilfrid all around him; felt his breath still fresh on the air, his footprint on the wide stone flags of the floor, the echo of his voice from the pulpit. His vision had brought this place into being, with its mortared stone walls and lofty pillars, its windows filled with glowing glass saints and angels. Even the vestry where he waited now was twice the size of his cell and oratory on Inner Farne.

"He hath put down the mighty from his seat and exalted them of low degree," he thought. Where was Wilfrid now? In prison? On some dusty road to Rome? He wished with all his soul that Wilfrid were sitting here instead of him, in all his state and glory, that Wilfrid could have made his peace with all God's people. He prayed that one day it might be so.

But since God had placed him here, it must be His will. He would submit to all the magnificence and ceremony that seemed now to attend on him. Once it might have been a temptation for him, to pride, to self-aggrandisement. Now he knew himself to be indifferent. He had seen that Eata held his office after the spirit of Aidan. He meant to do the same.

The Roman ways had not disappeared with Wilfrid. The king still wanted his alliances with the Catholic kingdoms of the South and in Frankia. He had given estates to found new monasteries after the Roman style at Wearmouth and Jarrow and made them centres of learning to equal anything in Kent or Frankia. Eata had taken him to visit the new monasteries. He saw that the monks lived all together in stone buildings, in dormitories, not in the separate cells of his own tradition. There was a great kitchen and bakehouse, a refectory, and a library full of books brought from the Continent. A dozen or more monks were kept busy copying in the scriptorium. The brothers sang all the offices according to the Gregorian fashion, and their Rule was pure Benedict. None of the Celtic practices remained. Cuthbert was certain that at heart there was no difference between them; in His house are many mansions. Nevertheless he had felt as if he were in another country.

Three monks entered with his vestments. He rose, bowing to them, took off his woollen habit and stood in his undergarments. They brought the alb first, the long white linen robe that symbolised his purity before God. It slid over his head in a smooth cool rush. They handed him the cincture, made of rope, signifying his monastic vocation. He tightened it round his waist. He was very thin, and the alb gathered in loose folds. A slight sigh escaped him. Next, they brought the stole, a richly embroidered length of cloth that would go round his neck and drop forward over the alb on either side. One of the monks leaned forward and spoke confidentially.

"The queen and her women embroidered it for you," he said.

Cuthbert gestured to them to hold it before him. At each end of the stole an embroidered tree sprang up, sending green branches coiling upwards through a golden sky. Blue and red birds spread their wings between the branches, and silver stars glowed against the gold. He stared, astonished and transported by the vivid life of it.

"How beautiful it is! Please offer the queen my gratitude and tell her I give thanks to God for what she and her companions have created."

It was laid around his neck and tucked carefully beneath the cincture to hold it close to the body. Then it was time for the chasuble, heavy with cloth of gold and panels of purple silk alternating with white. All three monks lifted it carefully, and he ducked so that they could lift it over his head. He felt the weight settle onto his shoulders. Then they fetched a matching cape.

"I don't need the cape."

"It is usual, my lord bishop." He submitted. Finally it would be the mitre, the weighty headpiece of gold and white, but first they must hang his pectoral cross around his neck. It was beautifully wrought, with equal arms of gold set with garnets to symbolise the blood of Christ. Then the mitre. The episcopal ring and the crozier would be bestowed during the consecration. He stood firm and let his body grow used to the unfamiliar weight of the vestments. He muttered a final prayer, then nodded to the monks. He was ready.

Would the procession ever end, Aelfled wondered, shifting her weight from foot to foot. First the boys, singing as they moved slowly up the aisle and took up their positions on either side of the altar. There were twenty of them at least, and the sound of their high clear voices filled the church. It was entrancing, enthralling, but she was impatient for Cuthbert to arrive. Then the deacons and all the clergy of the church. Then the six bishops, from all the Christian kingdoms, one after another, each with his own attendants and each one taking his place in front of her. Tall men she couldn't see over. She would see nothing of the consecration. She glanced at one of the sisters accompanying her, and they exchanged a sigh. At last Archbishop Theodore himself entered the church, with Cuthbert behind him. For a moment she was shocked to see Cuthbert dressed in the magnificence of a bishop's vestments. He looked unlike himself; she would hardly have known it was him. He had become distant, absorbed into bishop-hood. Even his face was half covered by the mitre, but as he passed her, she glimpsed his expression for a moment. He looked tranquil. Calm. He might have been walking across the island to scan the sea. Involuntarily she thought of Coquet Island, how they had sat together like the king and queen of their tiny domain. Since then, she had waited so eagerly for this moment of his return. Yet now it was here she felt separated from him by a wider gulf than the ocean. Everyone wanted to be near him, to have his special attention. Even the queen had suddenly become a fervent Christian, she had noticed. Ermina, who had so hated Wilfrid and had worked so hard for his downfall. Now she seemed to be constantly at Cuthbert's side and had insisted she would sit next to him at the feast after the consecration. Aelfled felt a stab of jealousy.

She glanced across the aisle at the royal party, at Ermina in her finery. Aelfled had hardly settled into her apartments at the royal hall before her sister-in-law was there to see her, full of her news.

"Father Cuthbert is a holy man," Ermina had informed her confidentially. "He's a very holy man. He's not like the other priests." She leaned close to Aelfled.

"Do you know what I mean to do? Edfrith is going up north with the army after the consecration to fight the Picts. I shall be on my own for weeks while he is on campaign. I am going to Carlisle with my sister. She wants to be a nun, and Father Cuthbert says he will give land there for a convent. Father Cuthbert will come and see us."

Aelfled had been astonished. Cuthbert going to Carlisle to see the queen? It would be his first opportunity to visit the British churches and to see the estate Edfrith had given him. Why did Ermina have to be involved?

Now, as she glanced across the aisle to the royal party, a glimmer of understanding dawned in her mind. Edfrith stood with legs wide, broad-chested and magnificent in royal blue and scarlet. It was easy to see that the consecration was a moment of triumph for her brother. He was assured, confident. Complacent, even. The factions within the Church were reconciled, he had appointed a bishop everyone was pleased with, including his wife, and he had been generous in his endowments. God would be well pleased with him. He would stretch forth His right arm and subdue the Picts beneath His foot, and he, Edfrith, would be ruler of a mighty kingdom.

No-one could doubt it. The Picts were warriors, but the armies they could command were scarcely more than raiding parties. A Northumbrian victory was certain. To everyone except Aelfled. Cuthbert's prophecy was constantly in her mind. A year, he had said. It wasn't yet a year. It might not be yet. Or Cuthbert might be wrong. Or God would hear her prayers for Edfrith's safety. Looking at him now, in the flower of his kingship, it seemed impossible to believe he could be mortal.

But that was why Cuthbert was going to visit Carlisle, she understood. He wanted the queen under his protection if the worst happened on the campaign. Suddenly, in the midst of the celebration and glory, she was gripped with fear so sharp that she could scarcely breathe. The prayers and hymns washed over her, till at last the moment of consecration was reached. Theodore was an old man, but his voice was strong and his Latin was fluent. The phrases echoed through the church. As he bent over Cuthbert to slide the episcopal ring onto his finger, she felt her fears subside. Cuthbert was made bishop. Whatever happened, he would be there. She bowed her head and prayed with all her heart to God to be a shield to them all—Cuthbert, her family, the people of her kingdom.

BATTLE OF NECHTANSMERE

20 May 685

Soon King Edfrith was rashly leading his army against the Picts and devastating their kingdom with ferocious cruelty.

Cuthbert knew that what he had predicted was soon to happen, that is, the king was soon to die. So he went to the city of Carlisle to speak to the queen, who was there waiting for news of the war, living in her sister's convent.

Next day, as some of the inhabitants were showing him the walls of the city, and also a marvellous fountain left behind by the Romans, Cuthbert suddenly became troubled in spirit, leaned on his staff and looked down to the ground. Then he stood up straight, lifted his eyes to heaven, groaned deeply and softly muttered, "Perhaps at this very moment the battle has ended." A priest who was nearby understood what he was talking about and blurted out, "How do you know that?" But Cuthbert didn't want to say any more than he had said, and he asked, "Don't you see how amazingly changed and disturbed the air is? And who among mortals can understand the judgements of God?"

Nevertheless, the saint went straight to the queen and spoke to her in secret (this happened on Saturday). He said to her, "See that you mount your chariot at dawn on Monday (because you can't ride it on a Sunday) and go as quickly as possible to the royal city of Bamburgh, in case the king has been killed. I'm dedicating the church of a nearby monastery, but I will follow you straight after that."

Next day the truth was learned when a survivor of the battle arrived. It turned out that King Edfrith and his entire bodyguard had been killed at the precise moment when Cuthbert, standing by the fountain, had sensed that this had happened.

Bede, Life of Cuthbert, *Ch.27*

King Edfrith, ignoring the advice of his friends and in particular of Cuthbert of blessed memory, who had recently been made bishop, rashly led an army to ravage the province of the Picts. The enemy pretended to retreat, and lured the king into narrow mountain passes, where he was killed with the greater part of his forces in his fortieth year and the fifteenth of his reign. Henceforward the hopes and strength of the English realm began "to waver and slip backward ever lower." The Picts recovered their own lands that had been occupied by the English, while the Irish living in Britain and a proportion of the British themselves, regained their freedom, which they have now preserved for about 46 years. Many of the English at this time were killed, enslaved or forced to flee from Pictish territory.

Bede, Ecclesiastical History, *IV, 26*

CHAPTER 36

A House Accursed

685 AD

Enfleda sent them all away, even Aelfled. She couldn't endure their calmness and their patience. Her heart was breaking and they tried to give her milk and herbs. She tugged again at the covers they had laid on her, but her strength had all drained away. She was too feeble now to do more than lie there, tossed helplessly to and fro in the dark troughs and swells of her grief.

She couldn't tell how long she had lain there. Her old life had stopped the day they told her. She knew—she could dimly remember—how she had once lived; how she had risen in the morning and had gowns brought to her, how she had busied herself with some folly or another, had walked and eaten and laughed at stories. All that seemed like a dream now. A delusion. They had deceived her. True, they had told her that Edfrith was taking a campaign against the Picts. But there had always been campaigns against the Picts. Skirmishes across the border, a few men killed. If it had been the Mercians, she would have prayed, made offerings. But she had done nothing. Edfrith had not even been to bid farewell to her. She had been blithe. How could she have known?

As if her grief were not suffering enough, since this morning a new torment had possessed her. A dreadful realisation had come to her. She saw that it had been her doing, at the very beginning. She had sown the seed that had led to Edfrith's death. His, and Aylwin's too. Guilt burned her like the fires of hell. She could confess it to no-one. Aelfled would think it fanciful. But she knew it to be true. They had died because of Wilfrid. Wilfrid had cursed them. And it was she who had chosen Wilfrid, seduced by his youth, by his beauty. She had thought him an angel and wanted him for her own. It was she who had arranged for his passage to Rome, so that he could enter the Roman Church and return to be her priest. Her intimate companion. Her beloved. It wasn't holiness that had made her send him. It was desire. She had wanted to possess him. To have him as hers.

And now God had punished her. He had punished her by means of the very cause of her sin. Wilfrid himself. It was like a dark light breaking upon her. After Edfrith had banished him, Wilfrid must have taken revenge. Of course he had. He had laid God's curse on the house of Iding. Wasn't Aylwin killed on the anniversary of the banishment? And now, her first-born, Edfrith, her king and first-born, was food for ravens on some Pictish field. Oswy's royal line, his noble sons, were no more, and God had granted none to succeed him. It was the cause of Ermina's barrenness too, she saw. Wilfrid must have cursed them all.

When Aelfled came back to see her, she clamped her mouth shut and said nothing. She felt her sit on the bed beside her. Her robe was cold, and she smelled of outdoors. She must have hurried over, for her breath was coming fast. Her daughter leaned over and kissed her.

"Dearest mother!"

She felt Aelfled's cool young hand, first on her forehead, then stroking her hair. In spite of her torments she felt soothed. Aelfled sang a song to her—not a hymn or a psalm. It was a lullaby she must have learned from Nurse, and Enfleda longed suddenly for those far-off happy days. Tears started to run down her face. Aelfled wiped them with a soft cloth and sang some more. Suddenly Enfleda felt she must tell her. She struggled to sit up.

"Will you drink this, mother? Just a sip or two. It will help you."

"I must tell you something."

Aelfled put the drink down and took her hand.

"Tell me."

So she told Aelfled of her own wickedness and of the curse that Wilfrid had brought upon them. It was difficult to tell it because words no longer came to her in their proper order, and sometimes tears stopped her altogether. But Aelfled sat and listened and waited. When she was done Enfleda fell back on the pillows, exhausted. Aelfled squeezed her hand.

"I don't think it was so very wicked," she said. "Don't blame yourself. Destiny is spun of many threads."

"But his curse."

"Yes. Whether it's a curse from Wilfrid or not, it's certain that God has struck sorely at our house. I fear it too." Aelfled leaned close to her.

"But there is someone to succeed him, mother. You remember what is happening? Bishop Cuthbert and the council will send to Iona for Aldfrid to come and take the throne. Do you remember? Father's first son."

Aelfled held her hand. Enfleda struggled to remember. A first son. Yes. But it was his concubine's child. How could they make him a king?

Aelfled was talking again. She tried to pay attention.

"I will speak to him, mother. To Aldfrid, once he is king. I will ask him to allow Wilfrid to return. Wilfrid was consecrated before God, and Edfrith set that aside. If there was a sin, mother, it was Edfrith's. Not yours."

Not her sin. She should have been comforted, but the mention of Edfrith's name made her weep again. She felt Aelfled's arms around her, and she knew that Aelfled was weeping too. She let herself be held, rocking to and fro. A small glimmer of light shone in the darkness. At least she still had her daughter. God must have some pity for her. The daughter she had thought lost to her was restored and was her only comfort.

CHAPTER 37

RITES OF PASSAGE

686 AD

Unnoticed amidst the turmoil in the aftermath of the defeat at Nechtansmere, Cuthbert suffered a loss of his own. When the messenger who had brought him the news left, he got up and went outside to look at the sky. Slate grey clouds were blowing from the west, and the sky behind them was black. An offshore wind, already fresh and strengthening. Too strong to think of putting a ship out. It could be a storm blowing up; he might have to wait days for sailing weather. He would have to take the road.

His heart sank at the thought of the long miles on horseback. At once he was reminded of that first ride with Eata, after his return to Lindisfarne. It must have been soon after the Christmas feast. Eata took him on a diocesan visit, riding over the mudflats from Lindisfarne onto the mainland and deep into the countryside. It was the first time he had been on a horse in eight years. The next morning his thighs were so stiff he could scarcely stand. Eata had watched him staggering out of the hut and started laughing. Cuthbert caught hold of him to steady himself, and in spite of the pain he had laughed too, till they were both swaying about and gasping with mirth. The alderman who had been their host stared at them. Two old monks, clutching each other and roaring with laughter. Unseemly, he must have thought.

In spite of his grief at leaving Inner Farne, it had been a joyful time, those first weeks and months he'd spent with Eata on Lindisfarne. And necessary. It wasn't only his thighs that were unused to exercise. He had to accustom himself to all the talking, to the small upsets and squabbles of communal life, to the constant presence of others. To feast days and the endless hours of eating. He shared Eata's rooms and saw the constant flow of visitors, messengers, plaintiffs that a bishop had to deal with. Would he ever be able to manage it as Eata did? Always kind, always ready to receive, however fatigued he was, and always just in his response. He was often away, visiting, attending council at Bamburgh when the king was there, preaching and baptising in the diocese, consecrating a new monastery or convent.

But sometimes on a fast day Eata would shut the door of his apartment and give orders that he was to be undisturbed. They would spend a day of silence together, celebrating Mass and sitting in contemplation. In the silence their communion was complete. Eata's insight reached Cuthbert's heart without words, and he knew the same occurred for his companion. After so many years together, first as novice and master, then prior and abbot, they were soul companions. Both knew their contemplation would sustain them in what was to come; the different destinies that would carry them apart after Cuthbert's consecration.

And now Eata was gone. Cuthbert was alone. It was hardly three months since they had said their farewells. He had planned to make a visit before the winter. Now he would go to Hexham to perform the funeral rites. His last act of brotherhood. He would make sure that his brother was sent to his eternal joy with all proper observances. He knew what he must do, but as yet it wasn't real to him. He had had no intimation, no sense of his passing. He felt his friend still present, so strongly that it was impossible to feel sorrow. He had not asked the messenger what had caused his death. Why should he? Eata was an old man, worn down with work. He was ready for death. I will be with you soon, he thought. But even as he thought it he knew; not yet. He had to finish the task that had been laid upon him.

After Edfrith's death, Cuthbert had sent a group of monks from Lindisfarne to Iona on behalf of the dead king's council, to negotiate with Aldfrid. Although Wilfrid had stirred up enmity with the Irish, Cuthbert was trusted. The Lindisfarne monks were acceptable to Iona as emissaries. For the decision was not Aldfrid's alone. It was essential that his kingship had the support of the Irish. The kingdom needed allies.

Cuthbert had no sooner travelled back from Eata's burial at Hexham than two of the emissary monks returned to Lindisfarne. Aldfrid had accompanied them from Ireland. He was at Ad Gefrin and Bishop Cuthbert was summoned to attend the council there.

Cuthbert saw that he was not to be allowed time to mourn his friend, to say masses for his soul in tranquillity as he had planned. He reminded himself of Eata's constant fortitude and rallied himself. He summoned new horses, new attendants, and sent word ahead to Bamburgh for the widowed queen to accompany him to Ad Gefrin.

But when he rode through the gatehouse into the courtyard there were no signs of preparation. He sent servants to report their arrival, but Ermina did not appear. At last he hauled himself down from the saddle and made his way to the bower house.

Since Edfrith's death she seemed to have grown smaller. Her gowns hung loosely from her, and she took no trouble with her appearance, brushing away her maidservants.

"What's the point?" she would cry. "Who cares what I look like?"

She stood before him, dishevelled, half defiant. "I shan't come, Father. Why should I come?"

"He is your brother-in-law. He needs your welcome."

"How can he be my brother-in-law? I have no husband. And besides no-one knows if his birth is true."

"You might find he is a comfort to you. He shares your grief."

"No-one can share my grief. No-one's grief is like mine!" She burst into tears and turned away, petulant as a child.

"Tell your servants to make ready," he persisted. "We will wait for you."

She must have her travelling litter, she declared. She was too weak to ride. Then when it was brought, she changed her mind and had the servants bring up her favourite mare. Then she decided she would have her second cloak, the wind was so sharp. At last she was ready, and their little party clattered away down the causeway and through the village.

After a while she brought up her mare beside him, so his attendants had to give way to her. He saw the air had brought some colour to her face and dried the tears.

"Is Aldfrid certain to be king?" she asked.

"The council will decide upon it when they have met with him. But he is the only heir of Iding blood."

"Is he a monk?"

"No. He is a man of God, but not a monk. He is a scholar."

"A scholar! For a king! Dear God!"

Cuthbert was silent. She twisted on the saddle.

"It's so far! I should have had them bring my litter. I won't be fit to meet anyone by the time we get there." She fidgeted this way and that. "Do you think he will marry, Father?"

"Yes."

"Where will I go? If he has a wife, she will take the bower hall. I couldn't bear it, Father! If she had children. I couldn't bear it!"

"Princess Aelfled would welcome you to Whitby. Or you could join your sister at her convent."

"You think I should go to Carlisle. That's what everyone wants, to shut me away in a convent."

"You should ask God if He wants it. Does He want you for himself?"

She stared at him, taken aback. She let the mare fall back in step with her attendants and said no more.

✛

The council were ranged around the side of the hall; king's thegns, aldermen, senior churchmen like himself. There were few younger men. So many had died at Nechtansmere. There was hardly a noble family in the land that had not lost a son. The council might not relish the idea of a scholar king, but there was little sign of dissension. The longer the kingdom was without a ruler, the greater its peril. For the moment, Mercia was distracted by conflicts of its own, but they would soon smell blood. While the Picts were flushed for the moment with victory and might try for further conquests, Aldfrid's connections with their allies in Ireland would open the door to peace.

Cuthbert had gone to meet with Aldfrid as soon as they reached Ad Gefrin. He found a man of medium height, stoop-shouldered from hours in the scriptorium. There was nothing of Oswy's swagger and cunning about him; nothing of Edfrith's ambition. His face was angular, like a half-cut block of stone waiting for the mason to finish it, with the pale skin and red hair of the Irish. He wore a royal cloak around his shoulders with an awkward air, as if he felt it didn't fit him. Two thegns were urging some matter to him in loud emphatic voices. He was clearly relieved to turn away and speak to Cuthbert. They spoke of Iona and of Aldfrid's interest in the teachings of the early Fathers of the Irish Church, and his face became animated. At the end of the conversation Aldfrid took Cuthbert's hand.

"I am obliged to you for your support, my Lord Bishop. I hope to enjoy further conversations with you, and to visit the monastery at Lindisfarne."

Now Aldfrid sat on the king's chair at the head of the council, with Aelfled beside him, to give her support to his claim. He was dressed with the full dignity of an atheling, with a royal blue and purple cloak over a padded tunic embossed with silver, and silver bands around his arms and neck. He looked as uncomfortable as the day Cuthbert had met him. Aelfled wore only her abbess' robes, but with a circlet of gold around her veil to denote her royal lineage. The last of the Idings, save for Edith in Mercia. Aelfled was all warmth and affection towards her half-brother, but Cuthbert saw that he was ill at ease with her. He was not used to the company of women. A seat had been set for Ermina, as dowager queen, but it was empty. How she would have courted attention in the past, with her silks and jewels! But for now, she could not bear the world to witness her loss.

He felt his loss too. There was no Eata beside him on the bishop's bench. The see of Hexham was vacant again. Trumwin was at the council, but he was not a bishop anymore. He and his monks had been driven out of his bishopric at Abercorn by the Picts. Cuthbert would have to think of something for him to do. And the Bishop of York, Bosa, was not well enough to travel. Cuthbert, Bishop of Lindisfarne, stiff and straight in his alb and cope, with Ermina's embroidered stole around his neck and his pectoral cross on his breast, was the sole representative of God to His kingdom of Northumbria. In a moment the king's senior councillor would ask him to open the council. He felt the gaze of the council upon him. For many of the thegns, he knew, he was still an object of curiosity; the hermit plucked back from the wilderness to become a lord of the Church.

As he sat, waiting, Eata's advice came back to him. "Don't think you know what should happen or try and do things. A bishop's job is not the same as worldly power. Your work is to help bring God's will into being."

The senior councillor nodded to him. He stood up and started to speak.

"Let us pray to Almighty God to bring healing to our kingdom. May He defend us from the malice of our enemies, and comfort those who grieve."

There was a commotion outside the hall. A few minutes later Ermina came through the doors with her attendants, a long veil over her head. There was a stir and a murmur through the hall. She made her way very slowly to her seat, leaning on her attendants. At last she was seated. Aelfled leaned towards her and took her hand. Bishop Cuthbert started again. Aldfrid bowed his head. The council had begun.

The council elected Aldfrid, son of Oswy, as King of Northumbria. They agreed he would send envoys to the Picts and British to recognise the new bounds of their territories and to discuss terms for peace. They proposed to the new king the possibility of a marriage with the sister of King Ine of Wessex to strengthen the kingdom's southern alliances. Little by little, they started to fit back together the shattered fragments of the kingdom.

Cuthbert watched Aldfrid. There was something pedantic about him. He would become preoccupied with some minor issue and ask question after question about it till his councillors grew impatient. More important matters slipped by without him seeming to grasp what was at stake. Cuthbert thought of Oswy's shrewdness. Aldfrid had none of it. He would need good advisers.

When the first day's council was done, Cuthbert returned to the guest-house and had his servant take off the vestments, piece after piece.

"Pack them away," he said. "Bring my habit for me."

"Won't you wear the vestments for council tomorrow, Father?"

"No. Pack them away."

That was enough. He might be a bishop, but he was a monk by vocation and he meant to live as one. They would get used to it.

As the man leaned over the chest, carefully folding away the heavy fabric, an idea occurred to Cuthbert.

"Will you give that to me?" he asked the man. "No—that piece. The embroidered one."

"The stole, Father?"

He took it, and gazed again at the coiling tree, the glowing stars of the embroidery. It was so alive. Such exquisite work. He stood holding it, thinking, till the man said, "Shall I take it now, Father?" But he shook his head and laid it down on the table.

The next day he sent his servant to ask if the queen and Abbess Aelfled would honour him with a visit. He heard Ermina's voice as they approached the guest-house. She didn't trouble to lower her voice.

"I can't go back to Bamburgh! Not once he is living there. He hates me."

"He's not used to women, sister. That's all."

"They want him to marry! How I pity his wife!"

Cuthbert met them at the door and brought them inside. He had laid the stole out on the table and beckoned them over to look at it.

"Look!" he said to Aelfled. "This is the stole the queen and her women embroidered. I've never seen work so fine. Every time I look at it I'm filled with wonder." He turned to Ermina. "It is a gift from God, to create such a thing. You must have learned these skills from a Frankish seamstress. There's not a convent in Northumbria that could do work like this." He paused for a moment and looked at her directly.

"I have a request for you. I hope you'll consider it."

She stared at him, eyes wide and curious, cheeks flushed at his praise.

"I would like to set up a workshop at the new convent in Carlisle where the sisters could learn your skills. I want you to teach them. So that they could produce such work to the glory of God."

"Oh yes!" said Aelfled. "How wonderful that would be!"

Ermina looked at them both, half-pleased, half-startled. Cuthbert pressed on.

"You know that Edfrith gifted me the royal estate at Carlisle. There is a bower hall that could serve for your household."

"But where would the workshop be?"

"In the convent, for the sake of the sisters. You know, I believe that in time visitors would come from far and wide to learn there."

"It would be a memorial to Edfrith," said Aelfled. "Part of his legacy with you."

Ermina's face crumpled. Tears started to run down her face. Aelfled put her arm round her.

"It is a gift from God," Cuthbert said again. "I pray that you'll consider it. We'll talk again when you're ready."

CHAPTER 38

THE BISHOP'S COMPANY

686–87 AD

The first moves were made. Aldfrid was installed at Bamburgh with experienced councillors to guide him. Ermina had agreed to visit Carlisle, at least for the present. Cuthbert returned to Lindisfarne. He knew that his next task was to go out into his diocese.

When it was a travelling day, Cuthbert would go to the stables and visit his horse, Feran. He liked to stand with his face close to Feran's smooth dark-brown neck, warm and horse-smelling, listening to his breath. The horse would toss his head a little, or put one ear back, and Cuthbert would reach up and rub his forehead. Or Feran would turn and push at Cuthbert's body for the apple he knew was in his pocket. Cuthbert would offer it to him on the palm of his hand, and the horse would gently mouth it up, his soft muzzle brushing against the skin. When the servant came to saddle him up, Feran stood still, alert, waiting. He knew they would be on the road again.

It was not like the journeys of his youth, when he had ridden out from Melrose into the hills for weeks on end, alone and unannounced. Now he was a bishop, he had a chaplain and a small household of servants and monks. His chaplain, Ethelwold, made the arrangements; the bishop would come on such and such a day, he would consecrate a church, there may be a priest to ordain, he would lay hands on the newly baptised, or whatever the task of the expedition was. Messengers were sent out in advance so that preparations could be made to receive the bishop and his household.

Ethelwold was a good planner. He liked to have everything in order, Cuthbert knew. He had a timetable and knew when they should arrive, when they should leave. But sometimes villagers would plead with Cuthbert to stay another night, or the nuns would want another teaching, and he would agree, trying not to look at Ethelwold. "My Lord!" Ethelwold would remonstrate, "you are fatigued. You must have time to rest!" And indeed, there would be weariness in every joint and sinew of his body, in his brain, in his very eye sockets where his eyes willed themselves shut, but he would not. Ethelwold would sigh, send out messengers and give new orders to the servants.

They were constantly on the road. Feran, Ethelwold and his household people were his comrades now, and though there were sometimes grumbles and arguments, they were loyal. They rode together through all weathers, hunched up on days of teeming rain and wind or high-spirited in sunshine. They sang psalms and hymns, and Cuthbert prayed the offices for them. They stayed in monasteries and convents, great halls and village houses; ate feasts at high table or hard cheese and bread at the roadside. They rode on Roman roads and ancient trackways, up into the hills, along the coast. The diocese was wide and long, from the border with the Pictish kingdoms in the north to Carlisle in the west. Cuthbert insisted on travelling to the remotest of hamlets in the hills, and when they arrived at the meeting place in some distant valley, they would find a makeshift village suddenly grown up of shelters made of branches and turves where the people camped to hear the bishop's preaching. Cuthbert's servants put up a tent for him, and he would stay for two or three days, preaching and baptising.

He found he didn't need to trouble himself about what he would preach. Once he stood before the people and sensed their presence, the words arrived.

Wherever they went in the year of the king's death, there was talk of war; would the Picts come down from the north? What of the Mercians? Was it a punishment from God?

"It's over," Cuthbert would tell them. "God has given us a new king. Pray for him and for peace."

They asked him for healing, and he would have water brought to him. He blessed it so they could use it as holy water, for the sick to drink and to drive out devils. Sometimes the suffering he saw struck his heart, so that a stronger impulse was born in him. On a visit to a convent a nun was brought to him who had suffered unbearable pain in her head and side for more than a year. When her sisters helped the woman into his presence, he saw the terrible anguish in her eyes. He sent one of the servants for the small phial of consecrated oil he kept for the last rites. When it was brought, he had her sit before him while he anointed her head. He beseeched Christ to heal her, and as he prayed, he was certain she would be relieved. The next day she was brought to him, still weak but free of pain. She fell to her knees at his feet, kissing them.

There was an awed stillness then, even in his household people. "Don't speak of it," he told them. How could he explain? If such things occurred, it was God's will, not his. He couldn't bring it about like a magician.

When winter brought foul weather and the roads were thick with mud, Cuthbert called a halt to the journeys. They returned to Lindisfarne for the Christmas feast.

It had been a year since he'd left Inner Farne, and his yearning for solitude intensified. The constant round of activity wore at his spirit. With the burden of the day ahead, he no longer rose for the first of the night offices. Instead, he attended Lauds and spent the next hours till Prime in contemplation. It was his sole time of private prayer. Then the day started. He sat with Ethelwold and planned diocesan meetings; he held church courts for disputes and offenders; he met with visitors. He went to the court at Bamburgh and spent long hours in council with the king. He received messengers from Carlisle; the dowager queen needed more money for her workshop; the dowager queen wished to see him; the dowager queen was unwell. He sent word, I will visit in the spring.

But with spring came a pestilence that brought devastation worse than war. Terrible stories started to arrive of villages all but wiped out, of towns left half empty in the wake of the disease, of children left orphaned. Cuthbert knew he must be a witness to Christ's love in their suffering. He summoned Ethelwold and told him to prepare for travel. They would visit every town, every settlement; he would see every family who had suffered and pray with them. As he gave the order, he saw that Ethelwold was afraid. Everyone stayed away from places where there was pestilence. Why would you risk your own life?

"Ethelwold," said Cuthbert. "I don't ask you to accompany me. Nor the servants. Make the arrangements, but only those who are willing should come. No-one is under an obligation."

Ethelwold struggled with himself. "I will ask the servants, my Lord."

The next day Cuthbert called his household together. "It is not difficult for me," he told them. "I have suffered the plague, and in His Mercy God let me live. I will not take it again. But if we have love and faith in our hearts, Christ will protect us." He looked at them, staring at him, torn between fear and willingness. How much he loved them. "I will pray to Christ for each of you," he added, "that He shield you."

Two days later they rode out. They were all there; the servants, two brothers and Ethelwold, his face grey with fear. The servants led packhorses, carrying tents and provisions. The journey had begun.

When they came to a village, they set up camp outside. Sometimes they could hear the keening of mourners as soon as they drew near. The servants went into the village, and called at each hut, asking if anyone suffered from the plague. When they had visited them all, they returned to the camp and told Cuthbert which huts he should call at. Then he and Ethelwold started the round of visits. Ethelwold talked to the bereaved, saying words of comfort, asking after their needs, praying with them. Cuthbert sat with the sick, consoling and praying for them. If necessary, the servants helped to dig graves for the dead.

They were all afraid at first, sickened by the suffering they saw. But Cuthbert saw they were changing as the visits continued. The need was so great, and the gratitude they received from people so overwhelming that they became dedicated to the task. He felt Christ's presence close among them. They couldn't halt the plague, but they brought comfort. They shared the grief and desperation. As word spread of the visitation, people would come out to greet them, to beg for blessings and prayers, for holy water to sprinkle on the dying.

In one village, when they had finished their rounds, he turned to Ethelwold and asked, "Is there anyone else? Should we continue?" Ethelwold pointed to a woman some way off, standing outside her hut with a tiny child in her arms. "The woman has already lost one child," he said. "That one will soon follow it."

Cuthbert moved towards the woman. Her body was shaken with sobbing, and tears poured down her face. "It is too late!" she said. "He's dying." Cuthbert felt an intense pity for her suffering; prayers sprang to his lips. In an instant he knew they had been answered. He put his hand on the woman's head and blessed her, then leaned down and kissed the child. "Don't be afraid," he said, "don't be sad. This child will recover and live. Nobody else in your house will die of the plague."

She stared at Cuthbert in astonishment, and then at her baby. Her tears stopped. The infant lay quietly in her arms. Cuthbert blessed her again, then returned to Ethelwold.

After they had been travelling for many weeks, one of the servants took the sickness. They stayed in their camp and Cuthbert sat with the man day and night watching the fever. It was bad, for sure, but less strong. He had witnessed this before. When there was an outbreak of the plague, it would rage fiercely at first, carrying off nearly all its victims. As time went on, it seemed to lose strength. The fever was less prolonged, the boils fewer. He was certain Sibba would survive.

When he was well enough to travel, Cuthbert gave the order to return to Lindisfarne. They were all exhausted. He believed too that the outbreak was coming to an end. In His mercy, God would spare his people further suffering.

CHAPTER 39

ABSENCE

687 AD

Aelfled thanked God every day for sending Trumwin. And Father Cuthbert too, since it had been his idea. It had been a year or more since he arrived, but it had only taken a few weeks for her to feel she couldn't do without him.

Cuthbert had seen she was struggling to manage, with her mother feeble-minded and all the affairs of the minster to deal with. Its estates kept growing, with daughter houses being established further afield, and they all needed management and guidance. It was too much for her on her own. When Trumwin had been forced to flee Abercorn, Cuthbert had arranged for him to be transferred to Whitby, with a few of his brothers as his attendants. With another man the arrangement might have caused difficulties, jealousies with the abbot of the monks' house, but Trumwin was so generous, so good-natured, it was impossible for the abbot to feel resentment.

As she always did when there was a crisis, she turned to Trumwin. Distraught as she was, he was the first person she thought of. She had hurried over to knock on his door, and soon she was knocking again in her agitation. What if he were not there? But one of his monks opened the door and nodded politely towards the good father writing at his desk.

"Oh!" she said, "Father Trumwin! I'm disturbing you. But I must tell you right away."

Trumwin got up and came over to her.

"Bishop Cuthbert has arrived, but he is not well! He could scarcely stand when he got off the ship, and his attendants had to half carry him up the hill. I had them take him to the infirmary. We must postpone the sisters' consecration."

"What ails him?"

"He has pain in his stomach. I don't know yet what it is."

"I'll send a messenger to the convent now. I'll ride over myself in the morning when we can see how the bishop is. Don't worry. You take care of the bishop."

How good he was! She felt relieved at once. She turned and hurried back towards the infirmary.

She kept Cuthbert in the infirmary for a week, in spite of his protests. He was exhausted, she saw, and she made him rest in bed without stirring. She gave him chamomile to soothe his innards and fed him with warm milk and broth. The pain started to ease.

"It is my old trouble, since I took the plague," he told her. "Nothing makes any difference to it."

"But it does, Father! See how it has eased since you took rest and proper food."

He smiled at her. "I can't lie abed for ever."

"You must be patient. It WILL heal, I swear it."

"There'll be time enough. My work is nearly done."

She stared at him.

"My work as bishop. I am making the last of my visits now."

"What do you mean? Won't you make visits anymore?" Then she looked at him, at his weakness, and changed her mind. "Perhaps it is better if you don't. We can come and visit you."

"I will go back to Inner Farne after the Christmas feast."

To Inner Farne? She couldn't believe she had heard him correctly. "For a retreat? In the winter?" She was baffled, incredulous.

"I want to go back to the place where I have been closest to God. To find that closeness again before I die."

"It will kill you! To go there, in the depths of winter, with no-one to care for you . . . " Tears started from her eyes.

"I have done the worldly tasks that were laid on me. The kingdom and the Church are at peace, with God's help. It's done. I can fulfil the vow of my retreat."

She felt the sudden tightness of her heart. It was the old anguish, the anguish of losing him, when she had thought never to feel that again. Or at least not till God took him.

"And Wilfrid," he said. "The king told me that he has written to Wilfrid telling him that his position as Bishop of York will be restored to him, to atone for the wrong that was done him. Bosa, in his goodness and humility, has agreed to resign the see."

She should be glad, should rejoice that Edfrith's sin was atoned for. But she could think of nothing but that bleak and windswept island with the deeps of the ocean all about it.

"Don't go!" she begged him, taking his hands. "Stay here with us at Whitby. All you need is proper care. God will give you many more years of life."

He smiled at her and shook his head.

"When we were on Coquet Island—you promised! You promised you would let me care for you when you were close to death!"

"I haven't forgotten. But it may not be as you expect."

CHAPTER 40

JUBILATE

688 AD

Light. There was nothing but light. The low winter sunshine lit up the waves lapping round the harbour in a dazzling shimmer. On the pasture below the crag the short grass was stiff with gleaming frost; the rock above soared upwards like a dark pillar of smoke. Sheep nibbled at the frozen grass, and a flock of curlews rose suddenly into the air, their mournful calls echoing through the still air. He saw it all to be perfect, complete, Christ's being in creation. The wet stones gleaming in the sunlight, the dark tangle of swollen bladderwrack; it was all alive with His glory. He saw his brothers, busy loading the ship and bothering him with their questions, in their essential nature as sons of God, unaware though they were. His heart was filled with joy. He gazed at the curving bow of the ship that would carry him to the island, at the slender oars resting in the hull, the sail neatly folded beneath the mast. It seemed to have been made for this moment, to have appeared ready-crafted as if by a miracle.

It was bitingly cold, and the brothers wore thick jackets and cloaks, rubbing their hands together and blowing on cold fingers too clumsy to tie a knot. They were filling the hold with supplies; firewood, bags of onions and apples and dried fish, blankets, cloaks. It was their love for him, and he submitted to it. True, there had been no crops on the island these past two years, and he would need to eat a little. But he had no interest in the preparations.

When all was ready, he made his farewells. He embraced his brothers in turn, his heart filled with love for each of them. When it was Abbot Herefrith's turn, the abbot asked him,

"When should we look for your return, my Lord Bishop?"

Did he still not understand?

"When you bring back my body," he replied.

Herefrith said no more. Two of the brothers took his arms, one on either side, and helped him into the ship. Sharp pains stabbed his body as they moved him but he managed to give no sign. He wanted no more remonstrance. At last he was settled and the ship moved out into the bay. He felt the lovely rock of the sea, the swell lifting him in its embrace. A fresh wind blew across his cheeks as the ship entered the open water. The tide was running strongly now, and the oars moved up and through the water without resistance. Like a horse slipping the reins the ship leapt forward across the waves. The waters of the earth were bearing him home.

Epilogue

Eleven years after the Saint's interment, God put it into the minds
of the brethren to dig up his bones. They were going to put them in a
casket in some fitting place above ground to give them due veneration.
On opening the coffin they found the body completely intact, looking
as if still alive, and the joints of the limbs still flexible. It seemed
not dead but sleeping. The vestments, all of them, were not merely
unfaded but crisp and fresh like new and wonderfully bright.
Bede: Life of Cuthbert 24, 720 AD

Item: a linen cloth of double texture which had enveloped the body of St
Cuthbert in his coffin; Aelfled the Abbess had wrapped him up in it.
From the Inventory of the Church at Durham, 1104 AD

CHAPTER 41

The Promise

699 AD

They were at the door again, like dark shadows. Let them learn patience. Chervil, now, that made one long for life, and it was true, she did. The garden about her was blue with sage and lavender, bees in every bloom; such loveliness! They took no notice of such things. They were bobbing and beckoning till she had to leave off and speak to them.

"This woman is sick, Brother Bertred. I must finish the preparation. Please wait in the hall."

After they had visited her in the morning, she had burned juniper in her room to get rid of the smell. Surely they could find other ways to mortify the flesh. She told the almoner to lay out fresh undergarments in the guest-house.

The sick woman in the infirmary had griping pains. Her belly was swollen out, although she had eaten nothing for three days. No, she was not with child; she swore she had not been with a man in years. It must be a blockage in the intestines. Or a bad case of worms. Aelfled took wormwood, garlic, fennel, chervil and pounded them together. The pungency of the wormwood caught her breath like a purge. And ginger— she had forgotten the ginger. She steeped the herbs in ale to macerate. A cupful three times daily. And the prayer, to be repeated three times daily also—but the ink was not there. She called to a novice to fetch it.

When the abbess had seen the woman settled, she took the apron from her waist and hung it on the peg by the door of the infirmary. She walked slowly past the herb beds. There was a pain in her hip in spite of the mild air, a malicious sting of rheumatism from the illness long ago. In any case she was in no hurry. She liked to look about her at the June afternoon, sniff the salt breeze from the sea, inspect the infirmary washing tugging on the line. As she left the garden, she pulled the gate shut behind her and turned along the dusty path between the huts. The sisters slept three or four to a hut now and used the smaller ones as workshops for weaving or copying. As the minster continued to grow, the headland had become honeycombed with holy cells.

Outside the kitchen there were two novices by the bread oven, their heads close together as they leant over the dough trough, so she couldn't tell who they were. They were too absorbed with their chatter to notice her. When she finally entered her own rooms, the visitors were already arranging themselves on the bench in the hall, laying out parchment on the table and mixing ink.

Herefrith had sent them. It was a thousand pities he hadn't come himself. He was with Cuthbert at the end. Why had he left it to these two unknown men? The incident in the church, she supposed. He hadn't forgiven her, but he needed her nonetheless. Needed her memories. She called for her chair and a cushion, so that she could sit at a distance from the brothers.

"I am willing to help you, but you must write down only what I say." She surveyed them both, and added, "And afterwards I will read it."

The older man, Bertred, glared at her. He would have liked to tell her to hold her tongue, she observed. But she was a princess of the royal blood, the king's only living relative, and might speak as she pleased. The younger monk leant forward politely. He was pale from long hours in the scriptorium; his chest was sunken, so that his breath came in shallow gasps. Plantain, she thought. Pine oil.

"Brother Bertred and I are only scribes, Mother Abbess. We are here to record whatever you would like to tell us of holy Saint Cuthbert that we may include in the abbot's book about his life—teachings you have had from him, or miracles you have witnessed."

Yes. They wanted miracles. There were events that could be thought of in that way, and they should be shared, to bring the people to faith.

"You knew him from childhood. Longer than anyone else still alive," continued Brother Cedd.

It was true, and she should speak of what she knew. But not yet. There were some things she would tell, and some things she would not. It would be folly to blurt out the first thing that came into her head. She wouldn't start today.

She rose abruptly, startling the two men.

"Dear brothers, I must take time to reflect on what is most suitable to tell you. You must be wearied from your voyage, you must have time to rest. Let us meet in the morning."

When they were gone, she stood for a while, thinking. Then she turned to the back of the room, to her press; pushed up the heavy oak lid and propped it against the wall. There was little light from the casement, but her hand felt out what she was seeking. It was a narrow length of plain linen; a girdle to cinch in the waist of a gown or a habit. The linen was worn thin and frayed at the ends. She gathered it up, bringing it up to her face and breathing in the musty odour. It was warm against her cheek. She closed her eyes and gave herself up to memories.

The next morning she was ready for the brothers and welcomed them affably into the hall. When they were settled, she announced, "I will tell you of a miraculous healing that I myself had at the hands of the holy father and of how he knew what was happening in places far distant from himself."

The brothers brightened. They leant forward and took ink onto their pens, smoothing down the vellum. The abbess spoke slowly, choosing her words carefully.

"It happened after Father Cuthbert had withdrawn to solitary contemplation on Inner Farne. Not long after he left, I was afflicted with a fever. It spread to all my joints with a terrible burning pain. The anguish was so great that I thought I should die. However, by God's grace I was delivered from the fever—but I could no longer stand or walk. For weeks, I had to crawl and drag myself across the floor. In my suffering the thought came to me with great longing, if only my beloved Cuthbert could be with me!"

The pens paused. The monks glanced up at her uneasily. She continued with her story; how her plea was heard, how Cuthbert had sent the girdle to her, how it had cured her. Soon the pens were scratching away again. When she was done Bertred looked up.

"Were there any further healings with the miraculous girdle?"

"I lent it to one of the sisters who suffered headaches. Afterwards it disappeared."

She sat back in her chair while they wrote. They would write it in English first and then the younger monk, Cedd, would translate it into Latin. She considered the two men. The older, Bertred, was liverish, she decided. There were long vertical furrows between his eyes. Intolerant, as such men tended to be. It was clear he didn't approve of the Whitby minster. He could hardly bring himself to worship in their church. Where Cuthbert worshipped whenever he visited them, she felt like pointing out to him. The minster was still a double house, and she, Princess Aelfled, had charge over both monastery and convent, as Hild had before her. Men and women gave praise to God with one tongue in the church at Whitby.

When the two monks looked up after completing the first translation, they saw that the abbess had fallen asleep. Or perhaps a contemplation had taken her, for she sat quite upright in her chair. Bertred moved his ink pot noisily across the table, but she didn't stir. He let his breath out sharply with irritation. Cedd, though, breathed more easily when her appraising eye was not upon him. He leant back on the bench and let the cool air from the casement relieve the stricture in his lungs. He glanced at the abbess.

In repose, the princess was just another old woman, with wrinkled cheeks and a fold of skin beneath the chin. Was she beautiful once, as they said? He looked away. At the back of her room stood the chest of black oak, a great chest full of secrets that she would never tell them. She had made the holy father leave his hermitage and meet with her. Everyone had heard that story. Eight years of solitude on Farne, and the holy father must leave at her behest. Who knew what was revealed to her?

But Bertred would ask her, for he shrank from nothing. As soon as she stirred he said,

"Mother Abbess, it is said that you requested a meeting with Father Cuthbert on Coquet Island during his time of solitude—and that he prophesied to you."

Coquet Island. She felt a pang still at the name. But her expression didn't change.

"Yes," she said. "But you must understand. God's secrets were open to him, but he would not betray His confidences. A hint—a clue—he would give nothing more. You had to see it for yourself."

"So what exactly did he tell you?"

"He told me there were many islands in the sea."

Bertred reddened with irritation. How could they make sense of that? She took pity on him.

"I will recount what he told me. But I have other duties now that I must attend to. We will continue again tomorrow."

She waited for the brothers, watching them as they made ready at the bench. The previous day she had bidden Cedd come to the infirmary. She had made him a remedy for his chest, and she could see that already his breathing was easier. She smiled at him and turned to Bertred.

"Have you thought about the islands, Bertred?"

He scowled at her.

"I didn't understand either, not at first. Then it came to me that he was referring to Iona, where the king was then living."

Bertred was mortified. How could he be expected to understand that? He felt she was mocking him.

"Cuthbert told me Aldfrid would become a true brother to me, that I would embrace him with real affection. It has all turned out as he foretold."

She settled into her chair and began the story of Coquet Island, how she had begged and pleaded with him to reveal what he knew, how he had given way at last to her entreaties. It took half the morning, and the two quills were busy on the vellum. Bertred was satisfied. He had suspected her of subterfuge, of concealment. But his firmness had borne fruit and he believed they had learned much that was unknown before. It was, truly, a miraculous tale that showed the saint's prophetic power.

Later in the day, Cedd waited for her alone in her workroom. He saw that she had already checked the manuscript over and left it for him. It was corrected here and there in her elegant hand, with additions and amendments. Her Latin was fluent, and Cedd had started to admire her scholarship. And she had given him healing for his chest. Truly, he thought, she was a mother to her people. He would venture to ask her one more question, he decided, since Bertred was not yet here. About that evening last year on Lindisfarne. It would not leave his mind.

He had entered the church with his brothers for Compline as usual. Suddenly, in the fading evening light, they caught sight of a woman in the church. It was the abbess, although he did not know that then. She was kneeling by the altar, leaning over the saint's coffin with her hand under his head. A bitter aromatic odour wafted towards them. She was singing. None of them knew what to do. At last Abbot Herefrith went forward, took her arm and helped her to her feet. He closed the coffin and walked back beside her, down the aisle and out of the door into the evening. The brothers took their customary places, and the office began.

Herefrith, he knew, had not mentioned the incident to the bishop, telling him only that Abbess Aelfled had provided the new shroud in which the saint was wrapped. The bishop had duly recorded it in his inventory of the shrine. He did not enquire: how had she known?

When the abbess entered the room, she greeted him kindly, and they looked over the manuscript together.

"Is there anything else, Brother Cedd?"

"Just one thing ... I hope it may not be impertinent." She nodded him on. "Last year, Mother. When you came to Lindisfarne."

"Yes."

"How had you . . . how was the opening of the saint's grave made known to you, when no-one else knew of it?"

She looked at him, surprised. Of course. He must have seen her in the church at Lindisfarne last year, and probably Bertred too. He would have his own judgements no doubt. But here was Cedd, his face guileless, open. A sweet boy, she had decided.

"Have you known loss, Brother Cedd?"

He didn't know how to answer.

"It is not always as you think."

Cedd's quill hovered over the manuscript, uncertain.

"I'll tell you what happened, Cedd, but you can put your pen down. It is for you, not the book."

He lowered the quill, staring.

"I was not able to be with Father Cuthbert at his death, and it grieved me very much."

He hadn't sent for her. His last illness came about in March, when the spring storms were raging and no-one could reach him. Herefrith told her he had endured terrible suffering, alone on the island. Of course Herefrith thought it glorious, a martyr's death.

"For all those years, I thought he had forgotten me. I felt nothing but his absence. But then, the very same day they opened his grave, the saint appeared to me in a dream. He put it into my mind to go to Lindisfarne. I knew I should take linen with me for a shroud, and precious oils, though I did not know for whom. It was not till I arrived that I learned the news. I understood then it was for him."

It was the last of his riddles, and the most wonderful. In spite of Herefrith's protests, that women were forbidden from the monks' church, she had entered, alone. It was only three days since the brothers had opened the saint's coffin. The news had not been made public. No-one knew how she could have learned of it.

When she lifted the lid of the coffin, she had stood quite still, trying to take in what she was seeing. It was true. His body was incorrupt. His face was tranquil, eyes closed as if sleeping. She saw at once that his skin was bloodless and shrunken, but it was still his face. She bent down and kissed his forehead.

The brothers had removed his burial garments to show the bishop their freshness, and his body was naked save for a loin-cloth, waiting for new grave clothes. She laid the linen cloth beside the coffin and took the phial of oils. She would anoint him first. She leaned into the coffin and lifted his head and shoulders, holding him in the crook of her elbow. She tipped the oil from the phial onto his leathery forehead, letting the oil run down over his tonsure, into the half circle of white hair. The air filled with the odour of the bitter aromatics. She lowered him again, then took his hands. Even his finger nails remained, crescents of pale horn. The skin on his palms and fingers felt parchment dry. She held them for a moment in hers before smoothing the oil over them. Then she moved down to the end of the coffin to anoint his feet.

When she was finished, she put away the phial in the box and took up the linen cloth. Unfolding it carefully she laid it to one side of the coffin. Then, lifting Cuthbert's feet, Aelfled started to wind him in it, taking the cloth first round his calves and thighs, then his buttocks and back. She worked with the practised intimacy of a physician. It was true, his body was incorrupt and yet, how strange it was. She knew death and was used to the sullen weight of mortality, the hard struggle of shrouding heavy limbs. His bloodless flesh was light as an empty nest in a hedgerow. "Why?" she asked him. "Why have you chosen this?" She paused. She half expected to see his eyes open, his lips smile as usual at her questions. But he did not stir. She continued, lifting and winding the soft cloth loosely about him till she reached his shoulders.

There was enough linen left to cover his head, leaving his face open. She took the phial again, tipped the last of the oil onto her fingers and smoothed his brows. Taking a small cloth from her box she laid it on his face for a moment, wiped her fingers carefully and folded it away.

She sat back on her heels. A trace of bitter aloes lingered in her nostrils; the oils had made her giddy. His face swam beneath her eyes. He was there, and yet not there. As it had always been.

Cedd was looking at her, his pale face open, intent upon her words.

"Yes," she said. "It was the fulfilment of a promise he made me long ago."

The next day, Bertred was eager to be gone with his little crop of manuscripts. He was down at the jetty at first light, having the men make ready, so that he and Cedd could leave on the morning tide. As the ship slipped out between the heads into the wide bay, his good humour was plain to see. No more old women and their unpredictable ways. But Cedd stood in the stern, looking back towards Whitby. He would have liked to have stayed; to have talked longer with the abbess. They were carrying away her stories, but for sure she had many secrets left to tell. Who knew the saint better than she? He stared up at the minster on the headland, the huddle of huts and tall church. He fancied he could see her still, brown robe caught back in the wind, gazing out across the bay.

Afterword

Wilfrid was restored to the bishopric of York in 687, shortly before Cuthbert returned to Inner Farne for the last time. After Cuthbert's death, the administration of the See of Lindisfarne was placed in Wilfrid's hand. Bede relates what happened immediately after Cuthbert died, and the troubles that ensued:

> *Abbot Herebert (who was with Cuthbert on Inner Farne as his death approached) immediately went out and announced his death to the monks, who had also passed the night in wakefulness and prayer. At that moment they were chanting the fifty-ninth Psalm, which begins, "Oh God, you have cast us off and destroyed us; you have been angry and had mercy upon us."*
>
> *One of the monks ran and lit two torches, and holding one in each hand, he went up to a higher place on the Island, to show to the monks who remained at the monastery of Lindisfarne, that the soul of Cuthbert had now departed to the Lord (this was the signal agreed).*
>
> *When the monk who was keeping watch on the Lindisfarne watch-tower saw this, he ran quickly to the church, where all the brothers were assembled to sing the night-psalms. It so happened that they were singing the same psalm as the monks had been singing on Cuthbert's island. Given what happened later, we must take this as a sign, because after Cuthbert was buried, a violent storm of temptation shook that church, and several monks chose to leave, rather than face such dangers.*

> *The year after Eadbert was made bishop, and because he was a*
> *man noted for great goodness and deep learning in the scriptures,*
> *and above all given to charity, he stopped the storm that had arisen.*

Bede is too discreet to explain the details of the "violent storm" that shook the Lindisfarne community, so we can only guess at Wilfrid's actions!

King Aldfrid also found Wilfrid a troublesome prelate. Wilfrid had been restored to the bishopric of York, by then one of three bishoprics in Northumbria (the others being Hexham and Lindisfarne). However, Wilfrid continued to press the king to restore his bishopric to its original boundaries, comprising the whole of Northumbria. Aldfrid refused, leading to constant arguments between the king and his bishop. Three years after his return to Northumbria, he was again expelled.

Once more, he set off to Rome to enlist papal assistance in restoring his bishopric. The pope ordered the English clergy to hold a council to make the decision. The Council of Austerfield in 702 stripped Wilfrid of all his monasteries except Ripon and took away all his episcopal powers.

Wilfrid set off for Rome for a third and final appeal against this decision. When he finally returned to Northumbria, having nearly died of a seizure on the way home, King Aldfrid was dead, and his boy son, Osred, was king. Advised by Abbess Aelfled, Osred was reconciled with Wilfrid and allowed him to return to Ripon, where he ended his days at the ripe age of 75.

GLOSSARY

Atheling   The heir apparent or a prince of the royal family.

Alderman   Member of a village or district council.

Bower   Private living quarters, separate from the communal great hall.

Fyrd   A local militia in which all freemen had to serve. It could be summoned for local raids or to form part of a king's campaign.

Haugh   A low-lying water meadow.

Minster   Although a minster is now understood as a large or important church, in Anglo-Saxon times it denoted any settlement of clergy living a communal life and maintaining the daily office of prayer. Because Whitby was a double house and can't be described as either a monastery or a convent, I have used "minster" to refer to it.

Nithing   A vile or despicable person.

Reeve   Official supervising a land-owner's estate, or acting as a local magistrate.

Thegn   Nobleman holding land from the king in return for services.

Acknowledgements

Bede's *Life of Cuthbert* (trans. J. E. Webb and D. H. Farmer, London: Penguin Classics, 1988) and the earlier *Anonymous Life* by a monk of Lindisfarne (in *Two Lives of Saint Cuthbert*, trans. Bertram Colgrave, Cambridge: Cambridge University Press, 1939) are the foundation of this novel.

I owe a large debt to Nick Higham's recent history of the period, *Ecgfrith: King of the Northumbrians, High-King of Britain* (London: Paul Watkins Publishing, 2015). Higham correlates all available sources for the history of the period and assesses differing interpretations of the often-scanty evidence. I have chosen to preference certain of his conclusions, for which the responsibility is mine.

Finally, huge thanks are due to Michael Tiernan, who was reader-in-chief, editor and ever-patient support.

Lightning Source UK Ltd.
Milton Keynes UK
UKHW041611140222
398666UK00008B/155

9 781789 590098